"Nicole!"
Aaron shouted desperately.

The only response was the chilling, bansheelike scream of the wind.

"Nicole!"

Nothing.

Everywhere he looked, he could see nothing but gray—the dull gray of rolling waves, the pale gray of bubbling foam, the slate gray of rain-filled sky.

Then he saw it: a muted orange speck bobbing in a trough about ten feet out. The twelve-foot wave hovering over the trough broke, taking her under. He saw her break through again, flailing her arms to keep above water.

He jerked the life buoy from its hook and threw it toward her. The wind caught the white ring and threw it back at him. He tried again, bracing himself against the tilted rail for leverage. This time the life buoy landed within a few feet of her.

"To your right!" he yelled, defying the wind to outscream him. "There's a buoy to your right!"

She either couldn't hear over the wind and waves or was too panic-stricken to comprehend. Within an instant, the ring was beyond her reach—and she was going under again.

There was only one thing to do. Removing his safety line, he slid over the side.

Dear Reader,

Welcome to the Silhouette **Special Edition** experience! With your search for consistently satisfying reading in mind, every month the authors and editors of Silhouette **Special Edition** aim to offer you a stimulating blend of deep emotions and high romance.

The name Silhouette **Special Edition** and the distinctive arch on the cover represent a commitment—a commitment to bring you six sensitive, substantial novels each month. In the pages of a Silhouette **Special Edition**, compelling true-to-life characters face riveting emotional issues—and come out winners. All the authors in the series strive for depth, vividness and warmth in writing these stories of living and loving in today's world.

The result, we hope, is romance you can believe in. Deeply emotional, richly romantic, infinitely rewarding—that's the Silhouette **Special Edition** experience. Come share it with us—six times a month!

From all the authors and editors of Silhouette **Special Edition**,

Best wishes,

Leslie Kazanjian,
Senior Editor

CHRISTINE FLYNN
Walk upon the Wind

Silhouette Special Edition

Published by Silhouette Books New York

America's Publisher of Contemporary Romance

SILHOUETTE BOOKS
300 East 42nd St., New York, N.Y. 10017

ISBN: 0-373-09612-7

First Silhouette Books printing July 1990

Printed in the U.S.A.

Books by Christine Flynn

Silhouette Romance

Stolen Promise #435
Courtney's Conspiracy #623

Silhouette Special Edition

Remember the Dreams #254
Silence the Shadows #465
Renegade #566
Walk upon the Wind #612

Silhouette Desire

When Snow Meets Fire #254
The Myth and the Magic #296
A Place to Belong #352
Meet Me at Midnight #377

CHRISTINE FLYNN

is formerly from Oregon and currently resides in the Southwest with her husband, teenaged daughter and two very spoiled dogs.

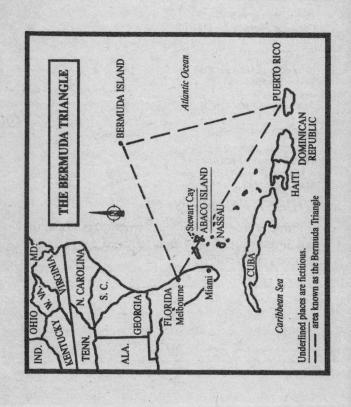

THE BERMUDA TRIANGLE

BERMUDA ISLAND

Atlantic Ocean

PUERTO RICO

DOMINICAN REPUBLIC

HAITI

Stewart Cay
ABACO ISLAND
NASSAU

CUBA

Caribbean Sea

IND.
OHIO
W. VA.
MD.
VIRGINIA
KENTUCKY
TENN.
N. CAROLINA
S. C.
ALA.
GEORGIA
FLORIDA
Melbourne
Miami

N

Underlined places are fictitious.
— — — area known as the Bermuda Triangle

Nor God alone in the still calm we find,
He mounts the storm, and walks upon the wind.

—*Alexander Pope*

Prologue

I'll bet he won't even recognize me." Nicole Stewart fidgeted before the antique cheval mirror in her room, obviously delighted at such a prospect. She tipped her head to one side, then to the other, enthralled with how much older and more sophisticated her new, daringly short hairstyle made her look. "What do you think, Selina? Will he?"

The genteel English-born woman smiled. "Half of the people at your party won't recognize you. Most of them are accustomed to seeing you dressed in jodhpurs, pulling around a horse and with your hair flying in your eyes."

"I don't look like a tomboy now, do I?"

"No, Miss Nicole. You most definitely do not look like a tomboy. Stand still now so I can get this zip without catching you in it."

Nicole took a deep breath and made herself stand as still as a statue while her beloved Selina zipped her into the strapless dress. She hadn't realized that she'd had a figure, at least not a womanly one, until her friend from Holyoke Day School for Young Ladies dared her to try on the beautiful creation. The minute she had, she'd felt different in it. Softer. Prettier. And after she'd told Selina about it, she'd gone back and bought it—even though it had taken her entire month's allowance and the money she was supposed to save for visiting her cousin in Italy. Selina's philosophy about clothes was that if a garment made you feel good, then it was meant for you and you should wear it. Nicole figured, too, that her governess of the past five years was secretly pleased to see her showing an interest in something other than pants.

Seeing her reflection in the mirror, Nicole felt pleased herself.

The pale blue satin faithfully hugged her torso, accenting the bloom of her small breasts and neat waist. It skimmed her hips, molding them just enough to show their feminine flare before falling in gathers to her calves. At her throat was a single diamond, the only possession she owned that had belonged to her mother. She touched it absently, scarcely able to remember the woman who had left so long ago.

"Do you think he's here yet?"

"Unless his plane was delayed, I imagine that he is." The gentle-woman turned her young charge by the shoulders and touched the tip of Nicole's nose. "He'll be here. Don't worry."

Nicole wasn't worried. Not really. Today was her sixteenth birthday and her father had said he had the very best surprise for her. That he would be home for her birthday was present enough. But she loved surprises, especially if he would let her first try to guess what they were. This time she had a surprise for him, too. It seemed that whenever she saw him he told her to quiet down—though she wasn't sure what that meant since she never raised her voice—and to act like a "proper lady."

Well, she thought, smiling at the lovely and rather regal young woman in her mirror, she definitely looked like a proper lady now.

Five minutes later, word came by way of the housekeeper that Mr. Stewart had arrived. He was waiting for his daughter in the foyer.

Nicole hurried to the top of the stairs, doing her best not to grin when she reached them. After adjusting the folds of her skirt, she stood a little straighter. Her posture was already near perfect, thanks to the years she'd spent riding and taking the ballet lessons she detested, but she wanted to do this right. She wanted to make a dignified entrance to show her father that she was a young lady now. She wanted him to be proud of her.

From the top of the long and curving mahogany staircase, she saw him turn. Tall, distinguished and staid as always, he hadn't yet had a chance to smile when he noticed her. He did, however, go stock still.

Pleased that she seemed to be getting the correct reaction, she placed one high-heeled slipper on the carpeted step below and began her descent. She was a little over halfway down when she realized that most of the color had drained from his face.

"What is this?" he asked, his question a disbelieving whisper.

Confused, Nicole glanced to Selina waiting by the banister. Just as concerned by Harrington Stewart's reaction, Selina hurried past Nicole, stopping on the last step. "She meant to surprise you, sir. Don't you think she looks lovely?"

The bright sparkle in Nicole's eyes had disappeared, her delicate features turning pale. The lack of expression clearly betrayed her hurt and something about that haunted look seemed to goad him even more. "She looks like a damn...debutante," he snapped apparently sensing that whatever word he'd wanted to use would only make an already horrid situation worse. "What happened to her hair? And where did she get that dress? Did you approve of this?"

Selina clearly did not understand the problem. Nicole was dressed quite appropriately for a young lady attending a formal evening party given in her honor. "I did, sir," she replied, watching helplessly as Nicole made a blind grab for the railing and backed up the steps. "I thought it suitable for the occasion."

"Well, I don't. She looks ridiculous. Go put on something that covers you, Nicole. Then get back down here before the guests arrive. Selina, go help her. You and I will talk later."

Nicole's father came to her room later that night. He sat with her for a while, trying to make amends with small-talk about the evening—about some of the people who'd attended the party, and about how boring it was to have to laugh at the same stale jokes. He never mentioned the incident that had occurred a few hours earlier. Nicole was grateful that he didn't. She knew she had displeased him and there was nothing else to be said. It never crossed her mind that he might apologize or explain what had been so wrong with how she'd looked. Harrington Stewart explained himself to no one, and he most certainly never apologized. And Nicole, as she did with anything unpleasant or distressing, wanted only to forget that it had happened.

and owned a private island in the Bahamas where Aaron was to deliver it.

Assuming he was to sign for the items Stewart had ordered, Aaron reached for the clipboard.

A small, decidedly feminine hand beat him to it. "I'll take that."

Aaron jerked around. Intercepting the clipboard was a small, nondescript woman whose face was overwhelmed by a pair of large, tortoiseshell glasses. With a flash of gold pen, she placed her neat and very tiny signature at the bottom of the bill.

"Thank you, Michael. I really appreciate your taking care of this for me on such short notice. Were you able to get the beluga?"

"I was, ma'am. Twelve tins."

"And the pâté listed here is foie gras?"

"Of course."

"Splendid." She handed the clipboard back to the steward with a smile, tucking the pen into her enormous shoulder bag at the same time. "I made it worth your while."

It was with some effort that the man kept a grin from cracking his austere expression when he saw the percentage she'd added as a gratuity. After thanking her with a formal nod, he asked that she give his regards to Mr. Stewart, then summoned his underlings with a flick of his wrist.

Watching the performance, Aaron felt vaguely disappointed that the steward had failed to salute before heading up the dock.

"We can get under way now," the woman said, her voice so quiet he barely heard her. "Thank you for waiting."

He turned from the departing trio to see her step from the pier to the sloop. Before he could ask what she was doing, she slipped below decks, lugging a briefcase with her.

For a moment, Aaron stared at the doorway through which she'd disappeared. His agreement with Jake Wilton was to deliver this sloop to a place called Stewart Cay in the Bahamas. Not one word had been mentioned about a passenger.

That thought compelled him to move. The sloop bobbed gently with the tide, and a quick glance at his watch indicated that he didn't have much longer if he was going to sail with it. The soft squeak of his soles on the deck was barely audible over the lap of water against pilings.

He reached the stern in half a dozen strides. Shoving his hands into the pockets of his white cotton slacks, he planted a sockless sneaker-clad foot on the sidewall and leaned against the aft rail to wait for the woman to come out. He wasn't going anywhere until he discovered what was going on. He'd give her two minutes to do whatever it was she was doing down there and then he was going in after her.

He didn't have to wait long. Scarcely sixty seconds passed before she ascended the five short steps leading topside.

Apparently, she didn't understand his failure to comply with her instructions. Tucking a strand of hair back into her severe and very tidy bun, she looked to the dock, then back to him. "Is there a problem, Mr. Wilde?"

She had the advantage. She knew his name. He didn't have a clue as to who she might be. When she'd first appeared, he'd thought she might be a member of the yacht club staff. Maintaining his casual stance, he slowly shook his head. "Not that I'm aware of."

"Then why aren't we moving?"

"We aren't moving because I don't know what you're doing here."

The explanation sounded perfectly reasonable to him. From the incomprehension in her expression, it was apparent that she thought otherwise. She seemed a bit puzzled at having to explain her presence, yet it was clear that she expected him to be doing something other than leaning against the rail.

When no answer was immediately forthcoming, Aaron decided to help her out.

"You are going to tell me who you are, aren't you?"

Straightening her slender shoulders, she laced her fingers together and tipped her head back. The tone of her voice, cool and mildly reproachful, was clearly designed to establish her position. Once established, however, he found it interesting that she had trouble holding his glance.

"My name is Nicole Stewart, Mr. Wilde. This is my father's boat. Mr. Wilton called yesterday to advise that it was being taken to our island and since I was on my way there myself, I decided to sail with it. I'd asked Mr. Wilton to tell you of my plans."

"Which Mr. Wilton?"

"Junior," she promptly replied.

That explained it. Jake Wilton, whom Aaron had known since their days on the rowing team at Harvard, was one of the best refitters on the East coast. Jake also had a lousy memory regarding anything that didn't float. "It must have slipped his mind."

She waved off the oversight. "Surely my presence doesn't pose a problem."

A hint of challenge shaded her words, almost daring him to suggest that she would be in his way. Aaron scarcely noticed. He was too busy marveling at her incongruities.

Nicole Stewart's demeanor spoke of finishing schools and privilege. She carried herself with a refined bearing and exhibited the poise of a person who knows she is either very rich or very beautiful. The beauty eluded her. And though her daddy obviously had money, she didn't *look* at all like the daughter of a rich man. At least none of those Aaron had known. If pressed, he'd be more inclined to think her the daughter of a jungle missionary.

She wore sensible brown loafers and a straight brown skirt, the hem of which hit her mid-calf and effectively hid what hinted to be long and shapely legs. Her prim beige blouse was tucked in at the waist, buttoned at her throat and tied with a thin brown bow. The large glasses she wore shielded her long-lashed dark-brown eyes. The only luxurious thing about her was her rich, sable-colored hair and that she had tamed in a tight, fat bun.

She looked like a sparrow or a mouse, and that impression might have remained if Aaron's scrutiny hadn't settled on her mouth. Sensuous and full, it softened all that severity and somehow invited a person to take a closer look at the woman beneath the drab propriety.

A natural glow suffused her cheeks, her fine-boned features remarkable in the delicacy. No makeup marred the silken perfection of her honey-colored skin. He knew women who would kill for her cheekbones, and a couple of others who'd paid for such a pert little nose. Yet, unlike most women, she seemed to do everything in her power to play down her assets.

"Is there something else, Mr. Wilde? Or may we go now?"

Nudged from his scrutiny by her polite tone, he abandoned his post and stepped forward. "Can you swim?"

"I beg your pardon?"

"Do you swim?" he repeated with patience. "You know. Sidestroke. Breaststroke," he added, deliberately dropping his glance to the row of buttons on her blouse.

Despite the blush of color that moved into her cheeks, she held his gaze with admirable aplomb. "Yes, I swim. Are you planning to throw me overboard?"

The thought was enormously tempting. "I just wanted to know if you should be wearing a life jacket. You weren't part of the deal, but as long as you're on board, I'm responsible for you."

"Thank you," she said, to note his concern. "But I'll take care of myself."

"Fine. Then just stay out of my way."

"I assure you," she stated in quiet resolution, "I will."

With that, she smoothed the side of her tightly restrained hair, gave him a nod that was as much dismissal as anything else and returned to the cabin. She'd almost managed to hide the flash of anxiety he'd caught in her expression just before she'd turned away.

With their positions established, Aaron made short work of the moorings. He had no idea what to make of Miss Nicole Stewart. On one hand, her appearance demanded deference, the kind of respect a person would show a maiden aunt—or a stodgy old schoolmarm. That Boston Brahmin manner of hers, however, cancelled his more gentlemanly leanings. It goaded him. Not because he was intimidated by it, which was surely her intention even though she really didn't carry off the disdain very well, but because he'd spent most of his life living with those same elitist attitudes—and the last eighteen months escaping their effects. He didn't particularly appreciate her presence reminding him of that. But he could put up with just about anything for a day.

Nicole stopped at the foot of the steps, just inside the galley. Her hands were shaking. She was shaking inside, too.

The faint trembling might have been blamed on the fact that she'd had only tea for breakfast. Or it could have been passed off as a consequence of all the rushing she'd had to do in the past twenty hours. These sudden whims of her father's could be terribly taxing. Invariably, they were ill-timed. She couldn't blame her slightly discomposed state on her present duties, however. The fault there lay largely with the man she could hear moving about the deck.

She had every right to be here. This was her father's boat and this Aaron Wilde, whom the refitting company had hired, was simply being paid to pilot it. She had no doubt that he was competent. The Wilton Company had taken care of her father's boats for years and the senior Mr. Wilton would never place such an expensive craft into the hands of someone he didn't trust. Even without the assurance of a long-standing and respected acquaintance, Nicole wouldn't have questioned the man's sailing ability. Something about Aaron Wilde spoke of an intimate familiarity with the sea. It was his insolence that unsettled her. Somehow, he had made her feel as if she were imposing on him.

The refined hum of the docking engine changed pitch, momentum gathering as the sloop slid from its berth. Through the long narrow windows that ran at eye level the length of the small salon, she saw the dock slip by. For a split second, she thought about getting off. Immediately, she canceled the thought. She wanted to sail rather than fly to Stewart Cay because she needed this uninterrupted time. Time all to herself. Her father wouldn't understand that need, which is why she'd left advice of her plans with his secretary rather than telling him herself. It shouldn't matter how she got to the island anyway, as long as she arrived in time to prepare the villa and greet his guests.

Swallowing what tasted suspiciously like rebellion, she pulled a heavy textbook from her briefcase and then stowed her shoulder bag in the storage bin in the small forward cabin. She normally didn't carry such a large purse, but this one had enough room in it for the petit point she was working on and for her favorite herbal soap and shampoo. Both were difficult to get in the islands.

Book in hand, she returned to the main salon. The interior of the newly refitted sloop was in the dark woods and grays and navys her father preferred and the smell of teak oil and brass polish was everywhere. In the confines of the luxuriously appointed space, the aromas were a bit overpowering. Opening the windows to air the room out, she decided that she might as well return to the deck. That was where she wanted to be anyway—out in the fresh air and sunshine. It was only thoughts of the enigmatic man guiding them out of the harbor that had made her consider hibernating down here.

He didn't notice her slight hesitation when she saw him. For that matter he didn't pay any attention to her at all as she settled herself on a built-in side bench and resecured a pin in her hair. Nicole took no offense at his failure to acknowledge her. She was accustomed to being treated as if she were invisible. Especially by men. Most especially by *attractive* men.

Aaron Wilde was definitely that, she conceded, studying him as she would any intriguing piece of art. He stood at the steering console, his back to her as the sloop idled slowly toward the breakwater. She couldn't see his eyes, but she knew they were green. The silvery gray sort of green the sea turned after a storm. His hair varied in shades from pale gold to bleached wheat and it ruffled about his head in the steady breeze. He wore it longer than the more conservative men she knew and it curled against the collar of his white cotton-knit shirt. He was brawny in the way of men accustomed to physical work: broad through the shoulders, lean in the hips, and his arms, tanned and beautifully muscled, would undoubtedly make a woman feel very secure.

Nicole blinked at his back, then darted a furtive glance to either side as if to see who'd caught her thinking such a thought. Stretching her legs out in front of her, she pulled her skirt down to cover as much of them as possible, positioned the large cumbersome volume on her lap and opened to the marked chapter. The words *Erotic Subjects in Detail* jumped back at her.

She immediately stifled a groan. Perhaps this trip wasn't such a good idea after all.

Unable to avoid it, her glance moved back to Aaron. He seemed quite occupied, his thoughts obviously on his work as he set the wheel and uncoiled a line from its brass cleat on the deck. The jib and genoa lay unfurled and limp along their booms, waiting to be raised so the wind could breathe them to life. On the bow railing, a gray gull perched, catching a free ride to the end of the pier. When they reached the upright, rope-lashed logs, the bird flew off to circle with his mates. Nicole saw Aaron shield his eyes against the glare of the sun to watch it go, then slowly drop his hand when he caught her staring at the broad expanse of his chest.

Guiltily, she lowered her eyes and stared down at the book in her lap. Always before she'd been able to lose herself in the printed word. She therefore expected no difficulty in her mental escape now. She would simply ignore the man moving about her father's sloop. She had to. She didn't have time to let her mind wander. Aside from the pile of paperwork on her desk at the Stewart Foundation and all that needed to be done at the villa when she arrived there, she had four weeks to digest this volume and two others like it on Peruvian art. Specifically, that of the pre-Columbian era. An internationally acclaimed exhibit presently on tour in England was due at the Boston Cultural Museum next month. As a museum volunteer, one of her jobs was to conduct tours. It would help enormously if she knew what she was talking about. The curator, in fact, insisted upon it.

"Hang on," she heard Aaron call and a second later the sloop lurched forward when the sails filled.

Catching her book before it could slide from her lap, Nicole allowed herself the thrill she always felt at the sight of gleaming white sails stretched taut by the wind. Although her father owned several boats, she rarely had the opportunity to sail. But when she did, she always felt this same exhilaration. It was a very primitive feeling actually, one she would never admit to because to describe it would sound so uncivilized. It had nothing to do with the romanticism of clipper ships or men of the sea. Nicole was too pragmatic to be drawn by such notions. Or maybe, as she had admitted to herself in her more honest moments, she didn't know how to be anything other than her very practical self.

Not that either mattered. What she felt was much baser, and too private to share. The feeling she experienced at the snap of the sails had more to do with the raw power of nature: the might, the energy. The force of the wind was invisible, yet it could be so strong, almost overwhelming. Or so gentle, so calm. A mere whisper of air against skin. And unpredictable, like the man who again had caught her watching him.

He smiled this time, and having nothing to do for the moment but steer, he sat down behind the large, six-spoked wheel and propped his foot on the opposite bench. Her glance slid to his bare ankle. She'd never known a man who didn't wear socks with his shoes.

The skepticism in his eyes indicated that he found her something of an enigma, too. "Are you comfortable there?"

She sat with her back in the curve of the side bench, unprotected from the wind. The slight pitch of the sloop, now under full sail, tipped her toward the deck.

She shifted a bit to accommodate the awkward angle, and told him she was fine.

Stubborn, thought Aaron. She would have been a lot more comfortable on the opposite bench. There, she would be supported by the side of the boat rather than tilting away from it. But if she wanted to sit with all her muscles tensed to keep her balance, he wasn't going to question her. He also wasn't going to ask why she didn't change out of that god-awful skirt and blouse and put some shorts on. Running around on a sail-boat in such attire—especially that straight skirt—was far from practical. If she happened to be standing when the boat pitched, she'd never be able to spread her legs enough to maintain her balance. She'd land right on her nicely rounded rump.

The thought of her sprawled in an ignominious heap on the deck made Aaron smile to himself. All that propriety could stand a little loosening up.

"Why don't you pull your skirt up?"

Stunned silence met his question. Her head snapped up, her brown eyes huge behind the clear lenses of her glasses.

"So you can get some sun on your legs," he explained when he realized how truly shocked she was by his suggestion. "You look like you could use a little color."

She'd have thought there was more than enough color in her cheeks at the moment, but he wasn't looking at her face. His glance moved from her hips to her ankles, his scrutiny thorough as he studied the shape of her legs beneath the brown fabric.

Oddly, his expression seemed to soften, then grow more curious. It was almost as if he liked what he saw. Or, possibly, was disturbed by it.

Nicole dismissed that thought the instant she saw him grin. She doubted that anything disturbed Aaron Wilde. Especially where she was concerned. On the other hand, he definitely had an unsettling effect on her. Rather than feeling flustered by his suggestion, she should be chafing at his audacity.

Smoothing her skirt as if it somehow protected her from him, she managed to meet that smile with a polite one of her own. "I'm fine as I am," she assured him and returned her attention to her book. Even as she did, she thought she saw a faint trace of disappointment in his features. She was sure it had to be a trick of the bright morning light.

"I didn't know I'd have company," he said, ignoring her attempt to ignore him. "So I didn't bring many supplies on board. If you want breakfast, there are a couple of rolls in the galley."

The tiny print of her text stared up at her. With absolute determination, she stared right back at it.

"Thank you, but I brought a few things with me." Her yogurt, a fresh pear and two bottles of springwater were in the refrigerator—next to his incredibly huge meat-and-cheese sandwich and some packaged chocolate cupcakes with white icing loops on them.

"I thought maybe you were planning on having that stuff you had delivered. What's it all for, anyway?"

Nicole stifled a sigh of exasperation. Some efforts were doomed from the beginning. The whole reason she'd taken the boat was for the peace and quiet. She truly needed to get this reading done. " 'That stuff' is for my father's guests. He's having some people in for a regatta next weekend. That's why he wants this boat there," she added, hoping to cover all his questions so he'd leave her alone. "He's going to race it."

She doggedly concentrated on the page.

Not a single word registered. That little detail was made all the more frustrating by the fact that her inability to concentrate was no longer Aaron's fault. Not directly, anyway.

Taking the hint, he'd disappeared into the galley and returned with a bottle of orange juice and two large muffins. The food was consumed while in silence he stood at the steering console, frowning at a printout he'd obtained from the sloop's weatherfax when he'd gone below. The weatherfax was new, one of the latest electronic toys her father had had The Wilton Company install. Ships' crews no longer had to radio for weather reports. Reports were now available by satellite and printed out on a chart that made it possible to "see" favorable weather or troublesome fronts.

Nicole knew little about electronic gadgets, though she understood that some people were fascinated with them. Her father's companies all seemed to be run by microchips and programs. Even the Stewart Foundation, the philanthropic institution she oversaw for him, was on computer. Its installation was the only thing Nicole had ever openly disagreed about with her father. She'd thought the old filing systems worked just fine. Her father's opinion had, of course, prevailed.

Though her thoughts had wandered, her glance still rested on Aaron. He was doing his job. She should be doing the same. And she would, she promised herself. Just as soon as she got situated.

Fighting the breeze for control of her hair, she gathered the loosened strands and tried pushing them back with their pin. The scarf packed in her purse would serve her purpose better. She was about to go and get it when Aaron started to bring the sloop about. Now was not the time to stand up.

The sails flapped wildly as the wind left them, then snapped stiff when the boom slammed from port to starboard and caught the breeze again.

Even when the turn was complete and she could maneuver the deck without threat of landing on it, she remained seated, transfixed as Aaron trimmed the sail and secured the rigging. Ignoring him was impossible. The best she could do was try not to be too obvious as her eyes followed his every move.

No motion was wasted, each movement performed with the calm efficiency of a man who knows exactly what he has to do. There was purpose about him. And strength. The hard muscles in his arms flexed and relaxed with leashed power and once again she was struck with the thought of how it might feel to be held by a man like him.

It was unlikely that she would ever know. Men like Aaron Wilde weren't attracted to women like her—women who desperately wished they could be something else.

That realization brought her to her feet. It was ridiculous to wish for the impossible. If she had learned anything in her twenty-eight years, it was that people only made fools of themselves when they tried to be anything other than what they were. Heaven knew she'd made the attempt and fallen flat on her face in the process. She would never allow herself to be so humiliated again. Therefore, she didn't want to want anything else.

Even if she did, she wouldn't know how to handle the yearning.

Had she not been so busy quieting her agitated thoughts, she might have noticed that Aaron was turning the *Valiant* farther into the wind. The waves were a little higher now, the running less smooth than when they'd left Biscayne. The deck, already slightly angled, tilted sharply. The next thing she knew she was grabbing for air.

She hit something solid. And warm.

Aaron had seen her start to go down. Catching her back to his chest, his left arm clamped around her waist as his right reached back to snag the wheel.

"I *knew* that was going to happen," he muttered, the feel of his breath on her ear as disconcerting as his iron grip at her waist. She could feel the entire length of him; his rock-hard chest pressing to her, the bite of his belt buckle in the small of her back. Most especially, she could feel his granite-hard thighs against her bottom and the back of her legs as his knees flexed to balance them. Heat seemed to gather in her stomach, turning her insides liquid.

His voice grew harsher. He seemed to know she'd been headed below. "Get out of that damn skirt while you're down there and put on some shorts. I'm not going to be responsible for you breaking your neck."

She'd had a bad fever once, when she'd been about twelve. Her throat had been so dry she could barely speak. It felt like that now. "I don't have any shorts."

He didn't know why he wasn't surprised. He did know, however, that he could let her go now. That he'd *better* let her go. The feel of her small soft body carried an unexpected jolt of pure sensuality and the clean, exotic scent that clung to her skin carried a message she had no idea she was delivering. A woman like her shouldn't wear a perfume that smelled like jasmine on a hot night. And she shouldn't feel as if she'd been custom-made for him.

"Pants then." His hand splayed over her stomach. Easing himself back slowly so she wouldn't lose her balance again, he stepped away.

Nicole didn't turn around. Nor did she say a word before she darted down the steps. For several seconds after she'd closed the narrow door behind her, she leaned against it, as if doing so would prevent the crazy confusion she felt from following her. She didn't know what to think of Aaron's irritation, or of the odd and intriguing sensations he'd caused her to feel. Making sense of what had just happened wasn't possible at the moment. Her only thought was that he'd had his arms around her and that they'd felt even more wonderful than she'd imagined.

The fact that she'd been imagining such a thing at all already had her bewildered. It wasn't like her to fantasize, she thought, wondering if her mental wanderings qualified as such. Whatever she labeled her preoccupation, the last couple of minutes had shown her that she was in even less command of herself and the situation than she'd pretended to be. Normally, she was a little better at keeping her insecurities to herself around strangers. The way she'd hurried away from him had clearly announced how intimidating she found him to be.

Reminding herself that a Stewart was always in command, she straightened her shoulders and prepared to disabuse Aaron of any such notion. She also whispered a silent prayer that Aaron not be upset with her when he saw that she hadn't changed her skirt.

She'd forgotten all about the scarf she'd originally set out for.

"I don't have anything else," she said the minute she returned and found Aaron's glare fixed on her skirt. Her glance flitted toward his face, never quite reaching his eyes.

"You didn't bring any other clothes?"

Her simple "No" seemed to confuse him.

"Why not?"

"Because I keep clothes at the villa and I didn't think it necessary to bring more." Certain he wasn't interested in the extent of the wardrobe she maintained there, she saw no further reason to discuss it. Instead, she sought to reestablish the ground rules. "Tell me, Mr. Wilde, how long have you worked for The Wilton Company?"

She was trying very hard to maintain her composure. An admirable effort and one that might have been convincing if not for the skittish way she avoided his eyes. Their little encounter a few minutes ago had obviously shaken her. What bothered Aaron was that it had shaken him, too.

He leaned against the wheel, his stance as casual as his inquiry. "Are we changing the subject?"

"Yes. Please."

"I see."

Those glasses were all wrong for her. They overwhelmed her delicate features and made her look owlish. The lenses were so thin that he wondered if she really needed them or if she just used them to hide behind. People used all manner of devices to protect themselves. Maybe, instead of using the glasses to see, she used them to prevent others from seeing her.

Intrigued by that thought, he then wondered why he was bothering to think about it at all. In another few hours, he'd plop her and this boat in her father's hands and be on his way.

"I don't work for the company," he said, loosening his grip on the wheel to straighten the rudder. His movements were automatic, his mind so attuned to the nuances of sailing that, in fair weather, he was barely conscious of his actions. "I owed Jake a favor. He's replacing the shaft of my docking engine while I make this delivery for him. We're trading services, so to speak."

It was difficult to tell what her sudden silence meant. The trouble with women raised on her end of society was that they were trained to guard their expressions. The emotion, or lack of it, on the outside didn't necessarily coincide with what was going on inside. That talent came in handy for the games women played. Yet, while this one seemed even more guarded than most, he doubted she had a clue as to exactly what those games were.

"Is that a fair trade?" he heard her ask.

"What do you mean?"

"Is the shaft for your boat worth this much of your time?"

"That depends on what you think my time is worth. I didn't have anything else to do and with *Salvation* in dry dock I needed somewhere else to stay. Between this and a motel room on Abaco, it's all covered."

Salvation was obviously his vessel. But that was all she understood of his comments. "What is all covered?"

"My accommodations." The expression in his eyes was watchful. "*Salvation* is my home."

"You live on your boat?"

"She's a sloop actually. Pretty similar to this."

All she could think to say was, "Oh," which seemed remarkably unintelligent considering all the other possibilities. *How interesting*, would have been more polite. *How bohemian* more apt. But all she'd managed was "Oh," because there were too many questions forming in her mind for her to decide which she wanted to ask first.

By the time she returned to her place on the bench and picked up her book, she'd decided not to ask him anything. He confused her. Quite thoroughly. And she didn't like the way that made her feel; off-balance and a little edgy. Aside from that, personal conversations were for people who'd had some acquaintance and this man was a virtual stranger.

It occurred to her that everyone was a stranger until you learned about them, but that logic wasn't enough to overcome her basic sense of decorum. Absolutely determined to accomplish what she'd set out to do, she deliberately concentrated on her reading. Considering the subject matter in Aaron's presence wasn't an easy task.

Though the text was presented in a most scholarly fashion, the descriptions beneath photographs of the artifacts were quite...explicit. So were the pictures. The Moche, who had lived in the Andes during the first millenium A.D., had an affinity for stirrup-spout pots. Round, with an arched hollow handle that formed a drinking spout, their shape invited decoration. Many depicted foods or hunting scenes. But the particular pots on these pages were decorated with all manner of eroticism. Nothing was left to the imagination. And based on the size of some of the figures' body parts, their artists had had quite an imagination indeed.

A gray shadow fell across Nicole, blocking the late-morning sun. "What are you reading?"

Oh, dear heaven, she thought when she saw Aaron's hand come down to take the book from her lap.

Chapter Two

Aaron looked from the book to Nicole, then back to the book again. He was more than a little surprised to discover what Nicole was studying. His grin, however, removed any indication that he suffered any discomfort with the subject.

"This is most interesting, Miss Stewart. I'd never have guessed you to have an interest in pornographic pottery. I prefer drawings myself. Etchings, actually."

The man was incorrigible. Nicole reached for the book. He took a step back.

"That's *not* what it is," she protested. Not sure whether to be embarrassed or insulted, she settled for a muddled combination of each. To be fair, she had to admit that what he'd seen was probably unexpected. There was no reason, however, for him to call it such a name.

Pornographic pottery, indeed. Enormous historic value lay in the clay renderings and she couldn't allow a cultural Neanderthal to slander important pieces of the past—even if she, herself, wasn't as comfortable with the subject as she wanted him to believe.

Striving for the calm that had slipped moments ago, she managed a commendably tolerant expression. The effort was wasted. Aaron wasn't looking at her. He was staring at the photographs, a wicked light dancing in his eyes.

"Sure looks like it to me. What else would you call a pot that has a spout shaped like an engorged—"

"Art," she choked, seeing no need for specific identification of that particular part of the male anatomy. She knew the picture to which he was referring.

Despite the devilish gleam in Aaron's eyes, he appeared to give new consideration to the object in the photograph. There was no mistaking what that spout was shaped as. "What did they do with this thing? Drink from it or pour?"

She was of half a mind to tell him they used it for a flower vase, but a comment like that was beyond her ability. That she'd even *thought* it was startling enough.

"I haven't read that far," she lied. She wasn't about to tell him it was believed that the little pots were drinking vessels—and there was only one way to drink from them. The obvious one. Heaven only knew what he'd do with that response.

"Well, one thing's for certain," he commented dryly. "The guys who made them didn't know much about creating to scale. This picture of the crouching woman and the man with the huge—"

"Exaggeration seems to be part of the art form."

"Exaggeration might be an understatement," he muttered, mercifully allowing her interruption. He tipped the page sideways. "The guys who made these seemed to be suffering from delusions of grandeur."

She wasn't going to touch that one. Nor was she going to correct his assumption. He seemed to think that men had created the objects in the photographs. Actually, it was believed that women were the potters in Moche society. Loyalty to her sisterhood wanted to give credit where it was due. Self-preservation held her tongue. He was having enough fun as it was.

"Do you collect this stuff?"

The quick shake of her head indicated that, despite her appreciation of it, to own and display such objects took more sangfroid than she had. "If I collected anything, it would be Picasso."

The arch of his eyebrow indicated Aaron's surprise at her choice. He would have thought a nice Impressionist piece, such as a Monet or Renoir more suited to her than the bold cubism of the artist she'd chosen.

"I do volunteer work at a local museum," she went on, nodding toward the book. "Moche art is something I'm studying for an exhibit. The tours I lead have a preset format, but I also answer questions. If I'm not prepared," she added, not at all sure why she felt compelled to explain herself to him, "I won't be able to do that."

"Is the whole exhibit of this stuff?"

She quickly explained that most of it consisted of musical instruments, utensils and jewelry. To her amazement, he actually appeared interested. At least that was what she thought until she realized that what he was really doing was suppressing a tolerant smile.

"I doubt you'll have any difficulty answering questions about that," he told her. "But I am wondering about the other. How do you plan to answer questions about these little pots if you couldn't answer mine without blushing."

"I wasn't blushing."

"Yes, you were. You're doing it now."

Even as she'd denied the charge, her hand moved to her face. Her skin felt quite warm to her touch. His smile, re-

strained before, grew broader. That made her feel even
warmer. He wasn't making fun of her. He was teasing her.
There was a difference, she knew, though no man had ever
engaged in this kind of verbal taunting with her before.

"I believe what you see," she hastened to assure him, "is
only the effect of the sun."

"What I see," he countered, "is the effect of your discussing a subject you aren't comfortable with."

"I'm perfectly comfortable talking about art, Mr.
Wilde."

"Aaron. My name is Aaron. And we're talking about sex.
Take it from someone who as a teenager used to sneak
National Geographic magazines into his bedroom so he
could look at the pictures of the naked natives. I can guar-
antee you that some precocious high school kid is going to
take one look at you, another look at this 'art' and let sail
with a question designed to uncoil your bun. Trust me," he
said with a glance toward the book. "The possibilities with
this stuff are endless."

It was apparent that he thought her something less than
sophisticated in such matters. Even if he hadn't been correct, it was not a point she would argue. She knew she fell
short in actual experience, but she did read a lot. That, she
believed, ought to count for something.

"I'm sure they are," she replied, refusing to imagine what
those possibilities might be. This wasn't the time to ponder
them—or the unsettling effect this man's boldness had on
her. He was obviously waiting for something. "I take it you
have a suggestion?"

He handed the book back to her, his hands immediately
settling on his hips. Standing that way, with his legs planted
apart to keep his balance, he looked decidedly predatory.
"Maybe you should practice with me."

The slam of her heart against her rib cage caused her breath to catch. He was talking about practicing questions and answers. She knew that. She also knew that he was well aware of how his suggestion had sounded and was waiting to see what she'd do with that loaded line.

The one thing she would not do was give him the satisfaction of letting him know how thoroughly he unsettled her. It was obvious that he already had some idea of his power to do so. That he enjoyed rattling her was something he didn't even have the decency to hide.

Years of living in a privileged and protected environment hadn't prepared her for the verbal liberties this man took. No one she knew would speak with such inuendo to a stranger. For that matter, no one she knew would engage in such conversation at all. Certainly not the more civilized men dominating her life. Yet, some ingrained sense—self-preservation, perhaps—told her that to gain this man's respect, she'd have to give as good as she got.

Why she wanted to do that, she had no idea. All she knew for certain was that she had to hold her own with him. Or, at least, try. "I'll manage quite well without your help, Mr. Wilde. Thank you, anyway."

"Aaron," he corrected.

"Aaron," she repeated, hoping the rush of the wind made it impossible for him to hear the strain in her voice.

For three seconds that felt more like thirty, he kept his eyes steady on hers. A smile moved into them and a moment later he accepted her declination with a shrug. "Let me know if you change your mind" was all he said and looked up at the sky.

The feathery white clouds that had accompanied them this far were thickening and starting to turn gray. The wind had picked up, too, pushing the sloop along at a nice, steady clip. Aaron headed forward, his attention on the jib.

Recognizing a reprieve when she saw one, Nicole grabbed her book. Careful to gauge the surge of the sloop, she made her way to the steps. She'd noticed when she'd been down before that the cabin wasn't quite as stuffy as when she'd first boarded. The fresh sea air had softened the smells of teak oil and polish, leaving only a lingering scent of newness.

She moved past the galley with its sink and refrigerator and three-burner propane stove. Just beyond, across from the table, a narrow band of sunlight poured over the navy-and-gray striped settee that formed an L on the port wall.

Angling herself into the corner cushions, she tossed her book aside and sighed in resignation. She couldn't concentrate, so there was no sense in pretending to read. Even if she had been able to concentrate, reading would probably only invite a case of mal de mer. The ocean was getting choppy, its up-and-down motion seeming more magnified in the cabin's confines. She wasn't going back up on deck, though. She had the constitution of an ox, so she wasn't worried about seasickness. Even if she had been prone to that sort of thing, the discomfort seemed preferable to remaining in Aaron's provocative presence. Something about him caused the most alarming thoughts to skitter through her brain.

His suggestion that she "practice" with him had elicited a brief but quite vivid mental picture of him stripped to the waist. The image hadn't taken much imagination to conjure up, especially since the casual white shirt he wore was unbuttoned enough to reveal a glimpse of a very solid and tanned chest. It had been no trouble at all to fill in the remainder of what the shirt had concealed. She'd never seen a real naked man before, so she'd simply used the most perfect model of raw masculinity she knew—Michelangelo's *David*. The image had fit perfectly. All she'd had to do was picture that exquisite sculpture as warm flesh and blood as she'd glanced up at Aaron's face.

Recalling the amusement she'd seen there, she stood right back up. The man, she decided, was no gentleman. Even worse, she was actually intrigued by that circumstance.

With that thought fueling a burst of activity, she gathered a notepad and pen from her purse and pulled her father's guest list from her briefcase. With more than twenty people scheduled to descend on the villa in three days, many of them to remain for the week, she had meals to plan, entertainment to line up, and seating arrangements to work out. In addition to working for her father, she also ran his household and handled his social affairs. Each responsibility carried its own set of frustrations. At the moment, she was grateful for the demands her duties placed on her. Trying to figure out if she dare seat Archibald Rutlidge, her father's dearest friend and a financial libertarian next to Congressman Holt, her father's closest political ally and a raging conservative, was at least keeping her mind off of Aaron.

She wanted everything for this week at Stewart Cay to be perfect. Harrington Stewart had a reputation for entertaining with style, though few people knew that it was his daughter's efforts behind the lavish, sedately elegant soirees. That oversight didn't matter to Nicole. All that did matter to her was that she please her father.

He worked far too hard, she thought, for a man who should be thinking of slowing down. Yet he insisted that if he retired, he'd be dead of boredom the next day. Knowing him as she did, how fiercely competitive and driven he was, she figured that could very well be true.

She sometimes wondered if he would have been so obsessed with his work if her mother hadn't walked out on them. He would never talk about her mother, though, and

Nicole had long ago stopped mentioning her. The woman had abandoned them and in Nicole's mind, she had ceased to exist long before they'd learned that she'd passed away some time ago. Nicole didn't hate her mother. She just didn't think about her. It hurt too much when she did. Besides, she felt there was no point bemoaning something that had happened over twenty years ago and if she could make her father's life easier for him now, then she would. It was a point of pride with her that he relied on her for so many things.

Pleasing him, however, seemed to be something she never quite managed to do.

Not wanting to dwell on that inadequacy, she determined that *this* time, she would make him proud of her. This time she would do everything so well, so spectacularly, that he would have to notice her efforts.

As if to lend approval to her decision, the lean of the sloop became more acute, telling her that they were picking up speed. The boost from mother nature was more than welcome. A good stiff wind would get them to Stewart Cay faster. The sooner she arrived, the sooner she could get to work. She hated having time on her hands. Right now, she felt that she had wasted several good hours. Unable to accomplish her reading, she now knew she should have flown to the island. Her father was forever telling her that she failed to think far enough ahead.

As usual, she admitted with the same disheartened feeling that accompanied all of her failings, it appeared that he was right.

The next two hours were put to practical use. She tackled the menus, and in the process compiled a four-page grocery list which she'd give to Luisa as soon as they arrived on the island. Luisa and her husband Jerome lived in the small caretakers' house below the villa. Jerome tended the grounds and Luisa tended to Jerome and everything else. Nicole was sure that the efficient, perpetually cheerful woman had started airing out rooms and putting out fresh linens within minutes of her phone call yesterday.

Nicole saw Aaron twice during the afternoon. The first time he entered the cabin, he went straight to the chart desk beside the galley where the ship-to-shore radio and the weatherfax were secured. From the corner of her eye, she saw him do whatever it was he did to get the information he was after, then watched him frown at that information while he went back on top. The second trip down, he did the same thing, complete with frown—only this time he stopped at the refrigerator before leaving. Reaching inside, he grabbed a can of soda.

"You want anything?" he asked, the door hanging open behind him.

"No, thank you," she replied, and he bumped the door shut before leaving with a shrug.

Apparently, not being able to get a rise out of her, he'd become bored with trying.

By midafternoon Nicole was fighting boredom herself, along with a nagging fatigue. She'd had little sleep last night and the lack had finally caught up with her. Crossing her arms over her notepad on the table, she lay her head on her forearms, thinking she'd rest for just a few minutes. Lulled by the gentle roll of the sea, she promptly fell asleep on her lists.

It seemed that she awoke just as abruptly as she'd drifted off. Only when she opened her eyes, it took her a moment to realize where she was—and what seemed so different about her surroundings.

Bright sunlight had poured through the narrow windows earlier. Now, the light was the dull gray of evening. Unsure of how long she'd slept and wondering if they were within sight of the Abaco Islands, she got up to look out the window. The sun hadn't gone down. It was obscured by heavy clouds.

Even as she noticed the patter of raindrops above her, Nicole became aware of a slight queasy sensation in the pit of her stomach. Sitting back down, she gripped the edge of the table to keep from sliding sideways. It wasn't lack of food making her queasy, though she'd had only her pear for lunch. It was the interminable motion of the sea.

The swells had become higher, the troughs lower and the overall effect was not terribly pleasant. The rise and fall, she knew, wouldn't be nearly as bothersome outside.

A sharp "Hey, Nicki!" was called from the top of the stairs when the door swung open. It hadn't been closed before, so Aaron must have latched it. Now, cool air rushed into the cabin along with Aaron's terse command. "Wake up and come here."

It was one of those inescapable aphorisms that it is always irritating to have someone tell you to do something just as you are about to do it. That Aaron *had* deigned to tell rather than request irritated her even more. What really got Nicole's petticoat in a knot was his use of the nickname she hated. No one called her Nicki. At least, no one had in the past twenty years.

Prepared to advise Aaron of that, she smoothed her bun, straightened her glasses and marched up the steps.

All her indignation died when Aaron met her at the top. He shoved a life jacket toward her. "Put that on."

A misty rain was falling, pushed at an angle by the wind that whipped at her hair. Aaron had put on a yellow slicker. He hadn't bothered with a hat. Damp tendrils of hair the color of wet wheat stuck to his forehead.

Nicole glanced down at the orange flotation vest, trying to assimilate what was going on.

Braced against the wheel to hold it in position, Aaron reached over and took the life jacket from her. She started to tell him she could put it on herself, but when he held it out for her to put her arms in, she decided it wasn't worth the trouble. Turning her back to him she slipped it on and felt a quick scrambling of her pulse when he took her by the shoulders and turned her to face him.

"Looks like we've run into some weather," he muttered unnecessarily, fastening the clips on the bulky jacket. When he fixed the last one at her waist, he stuck his hand beneath it, pushing his fingers up between her breasts. At the contact, she sucked in a startled breath. "Too loose," he muttered and removing his hand, he tightened the tabs on the sides. The whole ordeal, which is what it was in Nicole's befuddled mind, took mere seconds.

Aaron obviously thought nothing of it. "Either put on a slicker or go back below. You'll get drenched if you stay here."

She didn't question the terse order. Reaching into the compartment where the foul-weather gear was stored, she pulled out a yellow oilcloth coat like the one Aaron wore. It was too big. Rather than dig around for a smaller one, she put it around her shoulders and gripped the front closed. In just a few seconds, her blouse had already become wet.

A low, rolling rumble sounded off in the distance.

Nicole wadded the slicker a little tighter in her fist. She wasn't particularly fond of thunder. It didn't seem to bother Aaron. His attention remained fixed on the gray-green waves breaking over the bow.

Sea spray joined raindrops on his face. He wiped the moisture from his brow so it wouldn't run into his eyes. "I hope this doesn't last too long," she heard him mumble.

The temperature had dropped considerably, the once-balmy air now turning chilly. Hunched back into the semi-protection afforded by the sides of the stairway leading below, she hugged her arms over the bulky life jacket. Aaron stood three feet away, his hands tight on the wheel.

"I didn't realize we were heading into anything like this."

"I didn't either." His mouth twisted wryly. "According to the weatherfax, this isn't even happening. The only thing showing up on it is a mild tropical disturbance fifty miles south of here. This stretch is supposed to be a nice, steady easterly blowing at around 10 knots. We're getting gusts of 25 and 30 and this is coming out of the south." He looked toward the sky, frowning at the low gray ceiling. "Near as I can figure, the computer can't pick up weather satellite signals because of the cloud cover."

"You're not going to go back are you?"

A note of urgency carried in her voice. It was echoed in her expression, only there it took on a faintly frantic quality. He wasn't surprised to see her barely concealed fear, but he was a little surprised at why it was there. He'd have thought that turning back would be exactly what she'd want to do. Rough seas were difficult at best; downright deadly at worst. But the weather clearly wasn't the cause of her panic. She seemed stoically determined to ignore the squall, despite the fact that she flinched at every clap of the encroaching thunder. Her concern lay with getting to that island.

"I have to get to Stewart Cay tonight," she explained. "I mean, I really *need* to be there. Can't we go around this?"

Her desperation intrigued him. It removed the air of haughtiness she was so lousy at anyway and allowed him a glimpse of her determination. "If I knew how big it was, I'd be happy to. The information I'm getting on the fax obviously isn't reliable and all I'm getting on the radio is static." His grip on the wheel was momentarily threatened by a stronger gust of wind. The sloop jerked sharply, testing his footing, but he maintained his hold. Within seconds, he turned his attention back to Nicole. "Why do you have to get there tonight?"

Her worried glance moved from the blackened sky to the puddle of water collecting by the closed cabin door. Her reasons would sound petty to him, she was sure. Oh, why had she hoped for more wind? "I just do."

"Not good enough. If I'm going to risk my neck getting you somewhere, I'm going to need to know why I'm doing it."

Nicole realized that she knew next to nothing about Aaron Wilde. One thing she did know for certain. He was a man who did only what he pleased and only on his terms. You either played his way or you didn't play at all.

She deeply resented the position he'd put her in. A man like him couldn't possibly understand the sense of obligation she felt. He was a vagabond, after all. "My father needs me to get our villa ready for his guests. If we head back now, I'll lose an entire day."

"Guests? You need to be there to greet guests?" Beseeching the rolling black clouds, he muttered something unintelligible and undoubtedly profane. "I could see being worried about not getting there on time if you were donating a kidney or something. But you'd risk your neck for that damn party?"

It wasn't the party. It was the responsibility. She didn't get a chance to make him understand that, not that she thought she could. Another ominous rumble sounded off in the distance, carrying over the water until it cracked overhead like a bullwhip. As if a giant tap had been turned, water poured from the sky. A split second later, what felt like a solid wall of air slammed into them.

Nicole knew she opened her mouth, but she never got the chance to scream. The wind sucked her breath from her as it pushed the sails nearly parallel to the curling claws of water. Only the keel projecting from the bottom of the sloop kept them from going right on over.

She was thrown flat against the side of the stairwell. An instant later, as the sloop righted, she slid back to her feet and kept right on going to her knees. Her irritation with Aaron no longer mattered. Startled, scared and aware of all the horrible possibilities of what could happen next, she scrambled toward where she'd last seen him.

He wasn't there.

"Nicole!"

At the sound of her name, she jerked toward the bow. Aaron was on his stomach, trying to right himself as he reached for a winch. He was trying to get rid of some sail.

"I'm right here," she yelled, gasping for air as she reached for the wheel. It was spinning crazily, indicating that the rudder was going every which way.

The roar of the wind threw his voice at her. "Get the safety lines!"

"What about the wheel?"

"Get the lines first! Put yours on, then bring me one."

The lines would keep them from being washed overboard by the waves leaping on deck. If one of them went over, there was no way the other could help. They'd be blown away and sucked under that foaming green soup within seconds.

She had to ask him where the lines were kept. Then she had to get there. Crossing from one side to the other was no problem when the deck was level. Even a slight tilt wasn't too bad. When it kept dipping in a near forty-five degree angle, traction was impossible.

Still, she managed to reach the storage bin by the time Aaron reefed the genoa sail enough to give the wind a smaller area to push. With the boat riding a more even keel, Nicole made faster progress. She could have done even better if her slim skirt, now soaking wet, hadn't clung so tenaciously. It was like trying to move with her legs bound together.

Crouched by the bin, she gripped the side of her skirt and pulled on the seam. The fabric was too wet to tear. She glanced back into the bin. She had no idea what she was looking for until she saw it. A conch knife. With the tip of the thin blade she sliced down the side seam from her knees to the hem. An instant later, having clipped one end of a line by its belt to her waist and the other end to the base of the wheel, she scrambled over the slick boards toward Aaron. A vertical pipe that vented air from the cabin provided something to grab on to when she reached him.

He was on his knees, one arm looped around the mainmast. Rain drenched them from above. The sea attacked them from the sides. With his free hand he attempted to push the water from his face. She couldn't believe it when she saw him smile. "Nice day for a cruise, huh?"

It took a moment for his incongruous question to register. When it did, she merely looked at him in disbelief—and gasped when the sudden pitch of the sloop loosened her hold and she slid into the mainmast herself. *How can he joke at a time like this?* she wondered, looping her arm above his. She was scared to death.

Death was not something she wanted to think about. Especially, when it was an imminent possibility. "Splendid," she replied to his question, and held out the belt to him. As with her own, she'd clipped the other end to the bulky stem of the wheel.

There was too much to do in the next several minutes to give in to her fear. As long as Aaron kept barking orders, she kept following them, even when some of what he had her do wasn't strictly necessary—such as coiling ropes in the more protected area by the wheel. She suspected the chore was designed to distract her from what was happening. Though it didn't work, she was grateful for the attempt.

The question of whether to continue on or turn back had never been resolved. They were over halfway to their destination so Aaron hadn't really considered it anyway. He'd just let Nicole think he might to find out why she didn't want to go back. It didn't matter now. Choosing their own direction was no longer an option. They were being blown off-course, but that was the least of their concerns. Keeping the craft upright was all that mattered, and the sloop was pretty much on its own there. Once he'd locked the wheel to give it a straight rudder and they'd battened down by closing the vents and windows in the cabin and securing the door to keep the water out, there was nothing to do but ride out the storm.

That had to be done on the outside. If the keel snapped off and the boat overturned, they would at least be thrown clear and might be able to get back to the sloop and hang on. Inside, they'd be trapped.

Given the choice, Aaron would rather drown out in the open. He'd spent enough of his life in traps. Glancing over at the woman hunched an arm's length away, he had the feeling that he wasn't the only one that had happened to.

He didn't know why, but he could suddenly picture the uncut opal his mother kept on her writing table. The exterior of the gem was an ordinary pale brown, much like any other rock. But inside, where no one could see it, were hidden brilliant flashes of color. His father had wanted to polish the stone and have it made into a pin or a ring. His mother had said absolutely not. She wanted it left as it was to remind her that not all beauty is visible to the naked eye. She kept that reminder in a little crystal box where she could see it every day.

Pulling his glance back, he couldn't help but wonder if Nicole wasn't a little like an uncut opal in a glass cage.

He also couldn't help speculating on how much longer she could take the pitch and roll of the sloop.

They sat in the well formed by the benches on the aft end, their backs to the stern and their safety lines trailing out ahead of them to the wheel a few feet away. Since they had to be outside, it was the most protected place to be. But the motion was definitely getting to her.

"How are you doing?" he asked as much to distract her as anything else.

"Okay," she whispered.

"Good." Picking up the end of his line, he ran it through his fingers. "Listen, Nicole. I owe you an apology."

A frown flitted over her pallor. "What for?"

"For giving you such a bad time about your pottery. I'm sorry if I embarrassed you."

Oddly, she didn't want him to apologize for that. "It's all right. What you said was probably as close as I'm likely to get to having a man make suggestive comments to me."

She tried to smile, and that made Aaron wonder at her courage. The brunt of the storm had hit so fast that he'd barely had time to think, let alone react. Once he'd noted that she was all right, he'd simply started barking orders. He didn't know what he would have done had she panicked. Stuffed her inside the cabin, he guessed, though he didn't know how he'd have done that and drop that sail at the same time. Thank God, he hadn't been faced with hysterics.

"I doubt that."

"You don't have to be kind. I know that I'm not very appealing," she concluded with a shiver.

A slight frown touched his forehead. "Who told you that?"

"I don't have to be told." Her tone was gently chiding, as if he was the one failing to grasp the point. She seemed to accept herself as she was and made no apology for seeing less that he did. "All I have to do is look in my mirror."

"You should look closer."

The rain sluiced over her high cheekbones and moistened the fullness of her mouth. She'd lost her glasses when the wind had first tried to tip the sloop. Now he could see how lovely her eyes were and how long were the dark, wet lashes that swept down in confusion.

He was struck by the way his words had affected her. Most of the women he knew took compliments for granted. Nicole appeared to have never heard one.

The sloop rose abruptly, seeming to hang midair, then crashed back into the water. The jolt was tremendous, the stress on the hull evident in the groan of metal and wood. If they didn't get washed overboard or the sloop didn't capsize, there was always the possibility that it could break up under the beating it was taking.

There was always the possibility, too, Aaron thought, that Nicole wouldn't care if it did. The first couple of times he'd become seasick he'd have considered a deal with the devil himself for relief from the debilitating nausea. After almost a year and a half on the water, he'd become fairly accustomed to constant motion. Not always this constant, of course, but he figured he could probably take a little more than the next guy. Nicole, however, didn't seem to be faring too well. The constant up-and-down motion was taking its toll on her, her skin taking on a greener hue in the process.

When he saw her eyes widen, he realized that this last surge had been all she could take. She lurched forward, obviously intent on the privacy of the cabin's head.

Hoping she'd understand, he caught her safety line as she scrambled forward. "No, Nicki."

Eyes frantic, she clamped her hand over her mouth and tried to pull away.

"You have to stay up here," he explained, reaching for her. "It's not safe in the cabin."

He couldn't let her go. And she clearly didn't want to be sick on the deck. Catching her around the waist, he pulled her up to the bench, pushing her head toward the side. No doubt she'd have preferred her privacy, but this was the best he could do.

He slipped his palm across her forehead, supporting it as he felt her retch. The poor kid had actually held out longer than he'd expected.

Nicole sank back against Aaron. The awful rolling in her stomach had subsided. Seconds later she slid to the deck. She wouldn't look at him. She couldn't. Clutching his handkerchief, which not surprisingly had been sopping wet when he'd handed it to her, she crouched back against the stern and tried to disappear.

She heard him jokingly tell her that no matter how badly she wanted to, she wasn't going to die and after he made sure she was tucked back into her corner, he resumed his position as the roller-coaster ride continued. She assumed that this was what a carnival ride would feel like, anyway. She'd never been on one.

It occurred to her as she sat there hugging her knees that there were a lot of things she'd never done.

An hour passed.

"The lines seem to be holding," Aaron told her after he'd come back from checking them. "How about you? How are you doing?"

"I'm okay." There was no way she could manage a smile, though she knew it would have been a nice way to answer his concern. "Can I ask you something?"

"Sure."

She hesitated, focusing on the darkening sky before returning her glance to him. "Are you scared?"

There had been a time in Aaron's life when he would have scoffed at the idea of such a weakness. A real man—one other men respected—didn't admit his fears. But after jumping off the treadmill, it no longer mattered if he was perceived as ruthless or invincible; all the things he'd needed to be to survive and rule in the world he'd left behind. He'd found that things like honesty, especially with himself, eventually brought more peace of mind.

"Yeah," he muttered, wishing there were something he could do to ease her anxiety. He'd been in storms before. Nasty ones. But not a hurricane. He was very much afraid that was what had them caught in its grip. The instruments were showing sustained winds of seventy-five miles an hour. Once they hit and held seventy-six, the hurricane would be official. "I'm scared."

"Me, too."

She needed comfort. And assurance. He couldn't give her the latter. God knew, he wanted to. But how could he say everything was going to be all right when they were experiencing a reenactment of the day God created the earth? Every time the sloop plunged, his heart went with it. And that happened every thirty seconds or so.

He couldn't give her assurance, but he could give her a shoulder if it would make her feel better. He put his hand on the space beside him. "You want to scoot over here?"

Her eyes were large and frightened and her bottom lip was caught between her teeth. Half-swallowed by the orange life jacket, there was an almost waif-like quality about her.

She nodded.

He held up his arm, making room for her under it and settled her next to his side. She was shaking, or shivering. Probably, he thought, it was both. "That better?"

Again, a nod. "Thank you."

"My pleasure."

She saw the ghost of a smile play over his lips before he nudged her head to his shoulder. He tightened his hold, seeming to find a certain comfort in the contact himself. They stayed that way until the gray light faded to the deeper grays of evening. The approach of night made the raging storm even more ominous.

Nicole was trying not to think of how awful it would be not to be able to see anything with all this turbulence when, suddenly, everything stopped. There was no wind. No rain. The sea still surged around them, raising the waves like foaming pyramids and pushing them down the steeply angled sides. But the sky above them was calmer—and much lighter than the strange column of swirling clouds surrounding them.

"Oh, my God," Nicole heard Aaron whisper, the words spoken half in awe, half in prayer.

She hadn't known how furiously her heart had been pounding until the peculiar near-silence allowed it to be heard in her ears. "What is it? Is it blowing over?"

A giddy sense of relief teased her, just waiting for his affirmation to be felt. One look at his face and her hope vanished.

"I don't think so." The tension of the past few hours had worn deep lines of fatigue into his brow. Even in the dull gray light, she could see the toll the storm had taken on him. "The eye. I think we're in the eye of a hurricane."

For several seconds, Nicole said nothing. She simply met his eyes, searching there for the strength she didn't think she had herself. How horribly cruel to anticipate relief then discover that nature was only taking a breather before starting round two. Dear heaven, she didn't know if she could stand any more.

"Aaron, I don't think I can do this again."

The brush of his finger to her cheek was gentle. The abrasive note in his voice was not. "You can do anything you have to do. It's not like you've got a whole lot of choice."

His touch warmed her, giving her the courage she'd begun to doubt. "I've never had to be brave before."

"Then we're even. I've never had to be brave for anyone before, either."

He withdrew his hand as he stood up, the loss of contact leaving her to feel alone and colder than she'd realized.

"You can go below, if you hurry," he told her. "Grab another slicker to cover yourself with and turn on the lights." The running lights were already lit. Aaron had turned them on as soon as they'd hit the bad weather. The interior lights would throw enough illumination out for them to see once night fell. "I'm going forward to check the lines."

The thought of going into the cabin nearly made her stomach rebel again. With the constant pitch and roll, being down there would be like stuffing herself in a spin dryer.

"Bring back something to drink, too, would you?"

"How about some scotch?" she asked, thinking of the bottle she'd tucked into her bag in case Luisa hadn't been able to get the brand her father preferred. She'd never tasted

the stuff, but anesthetizing herself sounded like a marvel-
ous idea.

"I was thinking more along the lines of water or soda.
Bring the scotch, too, if you want. I imagine sharks like their
meat marinated." When she failed to match his droll smile,
he wiped the sea spray from his face and headed toward the
bow. Scowling at the taste on his lips, he added, "I'll take
anything without salt in it."

Nicole scooted along the deck on her bottom until she
reached the stairs. Her progress halted there. Her safety line
had somehow wrapped itself around one of the winches and
she couldn't go any farther. Aaron had said to hurry. Not
wanting to waste time untangling the line, she unclipped it,
and slid on down the steps. The water puddled at the door's
threshold entered the cabin with her.

She felt like a ping-pong ball bouncing from wall to wall
inside the cabin. It was with no little effort that she got the
bottle of sparkling springwater from the refrigerator and got
it back to Aaron without breaking it or a leg. He took a
long, healthy swallow, then handed it back to her.

In the back of her mind was the niggling thought that
there was something terribly intimate about drinking from
the same bottle. She ignored it. Propriety didn't seem to
matter much when basic survival was at stake.

That thought had barely occurred to her when she was
slammed backward by a curtain of wind-driven rain. They
had passed the edge of the eye. Reentering the eyewall, they
met again the violence of the storm.

They had won the first round. It seemed that nature
would win the match.

Nicole hadn't replaced her safety line.

Chapter Three

Aaron saw Nicole lurch backward as the sloop angled sharply. As if in slow motion, she twisted with an eerie grace to face where she was going. All that lay below her was water.

An instant later, time sped up. He lunged for her, the bite of his safety belt jerking him back even as his own momentum pushed him forward. He fell against the rail, still grabbing for her. But she was beyond his reach, her scream cut off as the boiling sea swallowed her.

Before he could see where she had gone, the sloop jerked again, leveling enough to throw him to the deck. His shoulder connected with the unyielding handle of a winch. The jolt of pain was breathtaking; the impact not unlike a car hitting a brick wall.

An eternity seemed to pass in the seconds it took him to find footing and pull himself to the side of the badly listing sloop. Straining to see through the sheeting rain and the waves that rose to slap him back, he shouted out a desperate, "Nicole!"

The only response was the chilling, banshee-like scream of the wind.

He tried again, swiping at the water that kept blurring his vision. "Nicole!"

Nothing.

Everywhere he looked, he could see nothing but the churning shades of gray that turned sky and sea into an apocalyptic nightmare. The dull gray of the roiling waves, the pale gray of the bubbling foam, the slate gray of the rain-filled sky.

Then he saw it; a muted orange speck bobbing in a trough about twenty feet out. The twelve-foot wave hovering over the trough broke, taking her under. Aaron saw Nicole break through again, her arms flailing to keep above water. He could only imagine how much of the sea she had swallowed by now.

Having sighted her, he now had a channel for the charge of adrenaline that made him mindless of the pain in his shoulder. But when he jerked the life buoy from its hook and threw it toward her pain sliced from bicep to collarbone, radiating to his chest. He'd obviously bruised or broken something, but he had no time to indulge the discomfort.

The ache was forgotten as the wind caught the white life ring and threw it back at him. He tried again, bracing himself against the tilted rail for better leverage. This time, it landed within a few feet of Nicole.

He shouted for her to grab it. "To your right!" he yelled, defying the wind to outscream him. "There's a life buoy to your right!"

She either couldn't hear over the cacophony of wind and waves, or she was too panic-stricken to comprehend. Within an instant, the ring was beyond her reach—and she was going under again.

There was only one thing Aaron could do. He pulled the lifesaving device back by its rope. Knowing better than to ponder the consequences, he removed his safety line and, taking the life buoy with him, slid over the side.

As wet as he already was, he scarcely noticed the cool temperature of the water. What he did notice was that the current was taking him straight toward Nicole. Unfortunately, that same current also carried her farther away from him.

He made it to her anyway.

She gasped and struggled, though the cold had sucked the heat from her muscles making her movements sluggish and ineffective. He didn't know if she realized he was there or not.

"I've got you," he tried to say, but a faceful of water cut him off. Another wave caught them both, lifting them with it, then dropping them again even farther from the sloop. Aaron kept hold of the strap of Nicole's jacket and when they popped to the surface again, she was sputtering.

Aaron came up coughing, too. But when he caught his breath, he went right back under. On purpose.

He'd felt something with his foot. Going back down, he felt it again.

Sand.

Another wave picked them up, again propelling them away from the sloop. When they surfaced this time and Aaron began to tread water, his feet hit bottom.

It was too dark to see much of anything now. Not that there was much to see beyond the crashing waves. Aaron wasn't going to let that technicality stand in his way. Fighting the forward surges and the backlash of water returning to sea, Aaron literally hauled Nicole with him. Like so much driftwood, it seemed that they had been washed ashore.

Sunlight.

Nicole felt it on her face and snuggled deeper into the warm cocoon surrounding her. On the periphery of her consciousness, the gentle lap of water met the peaceful sigh of a breeze rustling palm fronds. The light teased the backs of her eyelids, and heated the breeze as it caressed her body. Warm. She'd never thought she'd feel warm again.

The reason for that thought nudged her toward wakefulness. A sense of unquestioning security teased her back toward sleep. Stirring against something very solid, she opened her eyes just enough to focus on a torn and dingy white shirtsleeve, and a very broad, very male, chest.

Aaron. She was wrapped in his arms, her head tucked to his chest, and her right leg imprisoned between his legs.

She closed her eyes, reluctant to release the dream. Even as she did, bits of memory forced the haze of sleep to lift a little more.

She remembered the sea, and not being able to breathe. She remembered floating and struggling. Then, finally, stumbling from the water with Aaron before they had both collapsed on the beach. All she'd cared about was getting a decent breath of air—a full, deep, unobstructed lungful of air—and getting warm. No matter how hard she'd tried, she hadn't been able to stop shivering. Aaron had told her to hold on to him, and she had. She'd practically crawled inside him seeking his body heat.

It occurred to her, vaguely, that she should be distressed by such behavior. She should be embarrassed by the way she was clinging to him now. Needing his strength to fight the remembered panic, she couldn't bring herself to let go. As long as she held on, she'd be safe.

"Are you all right?"

His question was gentle, as was the pressure of his knuckles under her jaw. Nudging her chin up, he searched her face, his eyes kind and questioning. His concern touched her. But it was the feel of his hand pushing her hair back from her forehead and the way he drew her closer after she nodded that added to the unreality of all that had happened. All that still seemed to be happening.

She hadn't meant to start shaking again. The faint trembling began deep inside, working its way out even though she tried to stop it. She knew it was just reaction. She had been terrified when she'd been washed overboard, but what she remembered most beyond the fear and awful helplessness was an overwhelming sense of disbelief. She could recall with absolute clarity the frozen instant when the sea was rolling her like a ball beneath its stormy surface and her only thought was that this couldn't be happening.

People told of having their lives flash before their eyes when faced with death. Nicole had experienced nothing so dramatic. She recalled only that numbing disbelief—and a profound sense of disappointment.

Aaron gathered her closer to him, whispering assurances to calm her trembling. "It's all right," he told her, tucking her head back to his shoulder. His lips were at her temple. Every time he spoke, she could feel their faint vibration. "We're safe now."

She tried to nod. All she seemed able to do was hold on tighter.

"It's okay," he murmured, stroking her back, her hair. "I've got you. Don't be afraid."

She started to tell him that she wasn't afraid anymore. In his arms she felt safe. Protected.

His breath whispered from her temple to her ear. "Don't be afraid," he repeated, but in her mind the words no longer had anything to do with the storm. His mouth touched her earlobe, then grazed the hollow of her cheek. Whispering her name, his lips moved over hers and the words were forgotten.

Only moments ago, she'd known a feeling of security unlike any she'd felt since she was a child. There was nothing the least bit childlike about what she felt now. For a few mind-numbing seconds, she didn't know how to identify the feeling knotting her insides. She knew only that she refused to question what he was doing. There was no thought of pulling back, only of drawing closer.

A low moan reverberated in her chest as her breathing altered. She held on tighter, as if seeking sustenance in his kiss. The illusion of safety she'd experienced had vanished in the space of a few frantic heartbeats. What she felt now was very much like... hunger.

Aaron's body was hard against hers, his solid strength making her more aware than she'd ever been of her own softness. His hand shaped the side of her breast, his thumb grazing her nipple. Before she could react to that intimacy, he'd splayed his hand over her back. Pushing her against him, he followed her spine to the rounded curve of her buttocks.

A faint gasp parted her lips when his fingers bit into her soft flesh and he pressed her fully to him. The groan deep in his throat sounded like one of satisfaction when her surprise allowed him to deepen the kiss. She felt the moist warmth of his tongue against hers, the unfamiliar sensation causing her to suck in another breath. With it came the taste of him, his essence. It seemed to fill her. Then, to consume her.

She'd had no idea how quickly desire could ignite. The few chaste kisses Nicole had shared hadn't prepared her for the assault of sensation assailing her now. Nothing in her experience had prepared her for her own reaction, either. Perhaps because, until now, she hadn't experienced all that much. Perhaps, too, that explained the strange sense of disappointment she'd experienced in the clutches of the sea.

Those thoughts were merely nebulous fragments floating on the fringes of her consciousness. She was most aware of the heady vitality coursing through her. It was as if every part of her had become sensitive to the contrasts in Aaron's touch. With a day's growth of whiskers, his face felt deliciously abrasive against her softer cheeks and throat. His mouth and tongue felt incredibly smooth. His hands were cool on her back where they'd snuck beneath her blouse. Yet a pool of heat built where he moved his hips against her. Each subtle thrust constricted the muscles in her stomach, inviting her to return the motion. She started to, but he rolled over her, pushing his hand between them to close over her breast.

Aaron felt her stiffen and eased the bruising pressure of his mouth. The touch of her tongue against his was tentative, the feel of her hands uncertain, though she definitely wasn't pushing him away. It was almost as if she wanted to encourage him, but didn't know how. Or maybe, what she didn't know how to do, was stop him.

He sucked in a stabilizing breath, calling himself a dozen kinds of fool in the process. He wasn't about to take advantage of this woman, though heaven knew his body wasn't pleased with his decision. He'd only meant to comfort her. Or maybe he'd meant to comfort himself. The feel of her molding herself to him and the need she'd seemed to have for his touch had somehow clouded his intentions.

Hell, he thought, lifting his weight to sit beside her. He knew *exactly* what had happened. He'd gone hard when he'd awakened to feel her leg between his and the instant he'd tasted the honeyed-sweetness of her mouth, he'd forgotten all about anything so altruistic as comfort. He'd simply wanted her. The speed with which that raw need had hit had been astounding.

Nicole sat up, too, and hugged her knees to herself. She wondered if he could hear the thud of her heart. She had no idea what to say. Or if she should say anything at all. Aaron's stony silence told her nothing. He sat with his jaw working, his thoughts turned inward as he looked out at the vast stretch of ocean before them.

It only seemed like an eternity before he spoke. Less than a minute actually passed. Yet, with each passing second, she became more aware of what she had been doing. She was sure he was reconsidering it, too.

"I think there's a name for what just happened," she heard him say. "Or at least a reasonable explanation."

She could feel his eyes on her profile. By his silence it was apparent that he wasn't going to share that explanation with her until she looked at him. She wasn't sure she wanted to do that. She'd noticed yesterday that when he spoke, he would study her with an intensity that made her feel invaded, stripped bare. She thought it very unfair of him; especially since he tended to keep all but his surface reactions to himself.

He still waited for her to turn to him. Fearing that she might now see his pity—or worse, his disgust—she couldn't bring herself to do that.

"What is that explanation?" she muttered to her knees.

She sounded as uncertain as she looked. But there was no way she could fake confidence in her present, bedraggled condition. She felt far too vulnerable at the moment to do anything other than try to protect herself. She curled her knees tighter to her chest. It would do no good to pretend she hadn't responded to him so avidly. She might have been a little tentative in the way she'd touched him, but she had most definitely encouraged what he'd been doing.

From the corner of her eye, she saw him absently rub his left shoulder. She noticed when he'd pulled himself from her that he'd favored it a little. It still seemed to bother him, though he said nothing of it. His only concern seemed to be in clarifying what had just taken place.

"Look, Nicole. I don't think I'm overstating it when I say we had a pretty close call last night. We could just as easily have drowned as made it here. We're damned lucky to be alive."

She had no choice. His words brought her eyes warily to his. The quiet intensity of his voice demanded it.

"I was thinking about that when I kissed you. How lucky we were. But mostly I was feeling. I wanted to feel more, and as much as I could. There are a lot of reasons for making love," he said, and caught her chin with his finger when she started to look away. "To escape. To forget. To share. Maybe even to celebrate the fact that you're alive. Maybe that's because your senses are heightened after a close call like that, or the tension built by fear still needs to be released. I don't know what all the reasons are. But I think you were feeling some of the same things I felt, and there's nothing wrong with that. Nothing happened that you have to feel bad about."

And nothing happened that's going to happen again.

He didn't actually say the words. He didn't need to. To Nicole, the message was as clear as the azure sky.

Her glance immediately fell to the sand stuck to her brightly painted toenails. The sea had taken her shoes.

Aaron apparently noticed that, too. But she had no idea what caused his quick frown as he looked from the hot pink polish to the waist-length sable hair tumbling down her back. The neon color on her toes drew his attention again.

Staring at it, he shook his head as one might when too weary to ponder the inexplicable and pulled himself to his feet.

What he'd said made sense, Nicole supposed. It also excused what had happened—for both of them. She was sure he wanted her to know that he'd been reacting only to the situation. Not to her. He couldn't have made that any clearer if he'd tried. If she'd had the presence of mind, she'd have assured him that she hadn't misunderstood his interest. She had no illusions about herself. But he was already walking away. A hundred feet later, he stopped with his back to her at the water's edge.

She struggled to her feet, brushing at the sand clinging to her before hastily tucking the back of her blouse into her torn skirt. She wouldn't think of his rejection, so it didn't matter. The thought uppermost in her mind was that she couldn't believe she'd let a virtual stranger kiss her—or fathom how she could have been so bold as to return his kisses. But then, she wasn't quite feeling her ordinary self in many other respects as well. With the pins gone from her hair, her glasses collecting barnacles on the ocean floor and her thigh flashing with every step she took, she felt more like Tarzan's Jane.

In a way, she rather liked the vaguely primitive feeling.

All traces of that errant thought vanished as her steps brought her closer to Aaron. His gaze raked the length of her body at her approach, but no expression softened the rugged angles of his face. He undoubtedly thought she looked like something the cat had dragged in. By the time she joined him at the water's edge, she felt nothing but uncertain—and awfully self-conscious.

She'd thought she could tie her hair back with her neck ribbon, only she'd lost it somewhere, along with a few of her blouse's more strategic buttons. Trying to appear nonchalant while she held the plackets together, she kept her eyes trained on the water. Not until it had receeded was it apparent how far the tide had been in last night.

An incredibly clear ocean stretched out before them, its shades of turquoise and green startling against the white sand of the beach and the deep blue sky. Rising beyond the drying sand, was a virtual jungle of palm and rubber trees, many of them flattened by the storm. There wasn't a building in sight. No other land, either.

She told herself it was too soon to panic. Just because they couldn't see another island or cay from here, didn't mean there wasn't one visible from the other side of wherever it was that they were. "Maybe there's a village or something farther up the beach."

"Maybe," he mumbled while she shook the sand from her hair. The fine, grainy stuff seemed to have permeated everything. "You up for a walk?"

She was up to anything that would get them out of here and on to the villa. She still wanted to get there before her father did. She wanted a drink of water, too, but fresh water was about as accessible as snow at the moment. She told herself not to think about her thirst, or her twinges of hunger. Long ago, she'd learned that life was easier when she didn't dwell on something she could do nothing about.

Aaron started down the beach, headed in the opposite direction of the one she'd indicated.

"Where are you going?" she called, thinking—hoping— that he'd spotted something.

He didn't so much as glance over his shoulder, though he did continue to rub it as he started along the shoreline. "This way," he hollered back.

"What's down there?"

"How the hell am I supposed to know? I don't even know where we are."

He must have realized how irritated he'd sounded. Still slowly kneading his shoulder, he turned to see her wary expression.

There seemed to be more than impatience to the frown etched in his brow. He looked uncomfortable, as if he might be in pain. Suspecting that the reason he kept at his shoulder was that he'd hurt himself, she ventured a quiet, "Are you all right?"

"I'm fine. Just a bad night's sleep," he mumbled by way of excuse. "Come on. Maybe we can find someone who can tell us where we've landed."

Nicole wasn't going to argue with him. If he said he was fine, then she supposed he must know what he was talking about. Pushing her hair out of her eyes, she took off after him.

After roughly a quarter of a mile, the beach angled to the right, taking them around a small cove. Except for a couple of small inlets and a few wider stretches of beach, the magnificent view remained unaltered. An unbroken expanse of turquoise sea. White sand. Blue sky. The only immediate evidence of civilization to be found was their own footprints, one set following the other.

Nicole knew that Aaron was scarcely aware of her as they walked. He said nothing, yet his pace was easy, his strides measured so she wouldn't have to run to keep up with him. That was his only concession to her presence. His focus was on the sea and the land erupting from it. He was totally absorbed by his surroundings, seeming to draw some kind of peace or strength from them. The tension she'd sensed in him earlier had begun to ease and she'd wondered at his preoccupation. She envied whatever ability he possessed to claim that calming effect, but she also respected his privacy enough to not intrude upon it.

"Whatever this place is, it's beautiful." He spoke quietly, sounding almost as if he were merely thinking aloud. "Nothing man has built can even come close. And a lot of what he has built has taken so much away."

When she'd met him yesterday, she wouldn't have thought him capable of such an observation. Now, she found that his sensitivity didn't surprise her so much as it added to his mystique. "You speak with the soul of an ecologist."

"Nothing so noble. I just can't seem to get enough. I'm kind of like a kid in a candy store. I want to stuff my pockets full so I'll have a lifetime supply of this."

"This?"

"Freedom."

The word threw her. "I'm afraid I don't understand."

"I'm not always sure I do either." His smile was forgiving, his lighter tone designed to change the focus from himself to her. It was a technique he handled well. "Don't you feel better when you're outside?"

"I don't know that I've ever thought about it."

"So think about it now. What else have you got to do at the moment that's more important?"

She supposed he had a point. As they trudged on, she discovered that he also had a way of getting her to admit that she had always loved the outdoors, though her enjoyment of it in the last several years was limited by the activities she pursued. Her leisure time centered around books and art and music, the quieter pastimes she'd been encouraged to enjoy.

"I used to ride," she told him, but didn't bother to mention that her father had sold the horses shortly after she'd turned sixteen. The stables still sat empty, much like the beach house he still owned at Marblehead. She'd often thought she'd go back someday and refurbish it. Her father never went there and she hadn't been since the summer she'd turned eight.

"Were you any good?"

A gentle smile clung to her lips as a wave sucked the sand from beneath her feet. "I was the best in my class."

"I'm impressed."

"Don't be. I was just a child. But it was fun."

The wistful note in her voice seemed to puzzle him. Or maybe his perplexed frown was caused by the way she so quickly changed the subject. She wanted to know how far they had walked. He said he really had no idea because the shoreline meandered so much, then they fell into a considering silence.

The lack of conversation was fine with Nicole. It had been a long time since she'd thought so far back. And now, she remembered that not since she was a child had she walked barefoot along a beach. She hadn't realized the pleasure to be found in feeling the contrasts of warm sand and cool surf. In a way, Aaron's prodding allowed her that pleasure now.

She glanced behind her, expecting to see a meandering path of footprints. What she saw was only a short trail. The gentle waves began to fill the indentations within minutes of their passing. Her glance stretched down the beach to where the prints had been erased completely. Nature had washed away their marks. It was as if they'd never been there.

The farther they walked, the clearer it became that no one else had been there either. Civilization left its stamp when it was present. It was conspicuously absent here. There wasn't a forgotten tube of sun screen, a stray cigarette butt, or a candy wrapper to be seen.

Wherever it was that they were was beginning to appear dishearteningly uninhabited.

That conclusion was accompanied by an embarrassing rumble from her stomach. It was empty. There didn't appear to be an immediate chance of filling it, either.

"Have you figured out where we are yet?"

"Yep," he said without breaking stride. "We're lost."

He didn't seem particularly concerned. At least not as concerned as she thought he should be. She thought better of advising him of that. Instead, drawing on her limited resources, she tried to figure out a course of action that would serve a purpose. Certainly they should be able to do something more productive than trudge along the beach. Tropical survival techniques hadn't been a course of study at Radcliffe, but certain things were obvious.

"Perhaps we should start a fire."

Her suggestion earned her a raised eyebrow, along with a reminder of how he'd wrapped himself around her last night to keep her warm. "Are you still cold?"

Preferring not to dwell on those memories, and the not totally unpleasant sensations they aroused, she managed her most level glance. "No. I'm not cold." The temperature, she guessed, hovered around a very pleasant eighty degrees. "If we started a fire, maybe someone would see the smoke and come to us."

"Got a match?"

The quickness of his response made her hesitate before she answered with a quiet, "No."

"Do you see anything dry that we could burn?"

After yesterday's storm there wouldn't be a piece of dry tinder anywhere.

Meeting his eyes with a touch of defiance, she said nothing as they walked on. She'd only been trying to help.

They'd gone another couple hundred yards when Aaron slowed to a stop. The beach ended in a rocky hill a bit farther down. They could either climb it or the slope rising beside them. The other alternative was to go back the way they'd come.

"Stay here," he muttered and veered off toward the trees. "I'll be right back."

Though she could appreciate that he didn't have a specific destination in mind with their wanderings, it would have been nice to have some idea of what he was doing. If he wanted to scout out the vegetation, all he had to do was say so. And if that was the case, she was going with him. If she was going to be lost, she wasn't going to be lost alone.

"Wait!" she called and trotted right after him.

At her command, he drew to a halt. Hands on his hips, the open front of his shirt flapping in the light breeze, he turned around to see her scurrying toward him.

He saw that she still clutched the front of her blouse, her sense of propriety an unwitting reminder that she wasn't hiding anything from him. He'd glimpsed the tantalizing swell of her breasts when he'd pulled away from her this morning, and he remembered with aching clarity how perfectly they had fit his palms. He also recalled being irrationally intrigued by the lacy ice-blue bra she wore. Except for the intricate embroidery edging it, the thing was practically transparent.

He'd mentally added that incongruity to her preference for Picasso and hot pink toenails. As with those, sexy undergarments just didn't seem to fit the overall picture. Yet, he didn't think she was even aware of her contradictions. She seemed naively unaware of a lot of things.

When she reached him, he waited until she'd pushed her long hair out of her eyes before he politely asked, "What do you think you're doing?"

"Coming with you."

"I don't think you want to do that."

A hint of amusement danced in his eyes. She looked up in confusion.

"Nature calls," he said simply.

Within seconds the confusion disappeared. Her indrawn breath and the way she slowly closed her eyes when she turned away indicated with fair accuracy the moment comprehension dawned.

He addressed the back of her head. "Are you going to find an unoccupied bush of your own? If you are, I want to know where you'll be."

Yesterday, he'd deliberately baited her about the stirrup pots because he knew the discussion made her uncomfortable. She couldn't ease her consternation with irritation at him now. She'd walked right into this. He made perfect sense, of course. They did need to keep track of each other. And after he'd witnessed her seasickness yesterday, not to mention caring for her during it, there was precious else sacred between them.

One thing was for certain, she was definitely experiencing some firsts with Aaron Wilde.

"I'll be in those bushes right over there," she said, and with a dignified set to her shoulders, trudged off in the direction she'd pointed. Had she been prone to such things, she could swear she felt him grinning at her back.

A few minutes later, Nicole sat on the trunk of a leveled palm tree, shredding a leaf while she waited for Aaron to return. She looked out across the vast and empty sea. It looked so benign, so utterly peaceful. Yet, scarcely twenty-four hours ago it had conspired with the forces of nature to upend her neatly ordered existence. Granted, that neatly ordered existence was thrown into occasional chaos by her father's demands. But at least she knew what was expected of her when that happened. Now, she had no idea of what to do. She knew only what she *should* be doing. She should be on Stewart Cay preparing for the arrival of her father and his guests. It looked as if she was going to let him down again.

"You hungry?"

As much as anything else, she was grateful to Aaron for interrupting the track of her ponderings. His question drove all other thought from her mind. She was starving. "What did you find?"

"Breakfast."

She scrambled after him, following the white patch of his shirt through the lush vegetation. As the sun had crept higher, the warming tropical breeze had finally taken the last of the dampness from their clothes. Within a minute, they were damp again. The dense underbrush was still soaked from the rain and the ground, where it wasn't covered with moss and fallen leaves, it was a quagmire of sandy mud. Nicole cringed at first as the goo squished through her toes. Bravely, she forged ahead.

Why, she wondered, couldn't he have brought out whatever it was he'd found.

Pulling her foot from a particularly sticky puddle, she decided she might as well ask. When it came to practical matters, Aaron tended to be quite analytical. No doubt he'd have a perfectly reasonable explanation.

"Because I want you to listen to something," he replied when she posed her question.

Reasonable to him, she amended to herself and replaced exasperation with a fantasy about a flaky croissant and fresh berries with cream as she followed him on into the tangle of undergrowth.

He'd found a breadfruit tree. The spongy, pale melon-colored pulp would have tasted better cooked, for that's the way the islanders usually prepared it, but it was manna from

heaven as far as Nicole was concerned. Even better than the
fruit was what Aaron had found in some of the tree's leaves.

The glossy, dark green leaves were over a foot long and
many of them were cupped upward. Because of that, they
had caught the rain.

Finding a leaf at eye-level that was half-full, she stretched
up, tipping the leaf a bit to let the cool water trickle down
her throat. Some of it splashed down the front of her, running in little rivulets over her neck and between her breasts.
Her collar lay open where the buttons were missing and the
shade-chilled water hitting her bare skin and dampening her
bra was a bit of a shock. She ignored it. She'd tried not to
think of how thirsty she'd been, but now that she could
quench that thirst, she thought of nothing else.

Draining the leaf, she found another, emptying it, too,
before noticing that, all the while, Aaron had watched her.

He was still watching her. Suddenly aware of how greedy
she must appear, she raised the back of her hand to her
mouth to wipe the water from her chin. Something in his
expression stilled her movement. He stood motionless, his
smoky green eyes intent upon hers.

Feeling much as she suspected a doe would if stunned by
a light, Nicole tried to move. The intensity in his eyes held
her. She drew a breath, and promptly felt it catch when his
glance moved to the strip of skin visible between her breasts.
His gaze narrowed as if remembering the feel of her against
him, the touch of his eyes almost a physical thing. Slowly,
she lowered her hand to gather her blouse at her throat.

Aaron leaned against the palm behind him, and let his
glance slide the length of her. When he reached the hem of
her torn skirt, he shook his head, confused as much by her
as with himself. The woman was a definite anomaly. She
clutched her blouse in almost puritanical protection. Yet a
moment ago she'd been drinking from a plant leaf with

purely sensual abandon. As for himself, the sight of her with her head tilted back to expose the elegant line of her throat, her firm breasts straining against the front of her blouse, had managed to elicit the same response that he'd been busy walking off for the past couple of hours.

He raised his eyes to catch her wary glance. She looked like Little Red Riding Hood about to be eaten by the big bad wolf.

With little more than the blink of her silky lashes, that wariness disappeared. She lifted her chin and dropped her hand. "You wanted me to listen to something."

At the reminder, he smiled. The cool reserve she exhibited now had put him off yesterday. Even then, he'd begun to suspect that it was only a facade. He was more convinced of his conclusion when his glance followed her hand to her side.

Her fingers were gently curved, their position quite unremarkable. But he saw the tremor in them. The composure she sought eluded her, but she didn't want him to know that. For now, he wouldn't let her know that he already did.

"I want you to listen for a couple of things." Damp branches and leaves rustled underfoot as he stepped toward her. "Do you hear any birds?"

The question didn't seem so odd after she'd listened for a moment. She shook her head, puzzled. "I don't hear anything."

"I don't hear any either. If there are birds around, you can always hear them, especially after a storm."

He was right. And now that he'd mentioned it, she was aware of their absence. The air should have been filled with their song. "What does that mean?"

"I'm not an expert, but it could mean that we're a long way from any other land mass." He drew his fingers through his hair, muttering to himself as much as to her. "There should at least be a few bobolinks around this time of year. Hell, there are *always* birds in the Caribbean.'' If that's even where they were, he added to himself. They'd been blown around for hours yesterday.

Aaron remembered something an old, mostly drunk, but very experienced sailor had told him one night in a Haitian bar. Aaron had already known that birds were sensitive to changes or disturbances in the atmosphere, which is why they went nuts when the barometer fell and rose before and after storms. But according to that old salt, because of that same sensitivity, their migratory paths avoided the middle of the Bermuda Triangle.

Aaron frowned. Was it possible that they'd been blown that far?

Dismissing the question, he turned to more practical thoughts. ''What else do you hear?''

Nicole listened closer, straining to hear something extraordinary. The sound of an animal, perhaps. Or, hopefully, human voices. ''I really can't hear anything but the ocean. And maybe running water.''

It was that sound that they followed, the rush of water growing teasingly closer as they fought their way through a gardener's nightmare of undergrowth. The ground had ceased to be level long ago. The upward climb was not so much steep as merely tiring. They were about an hour into the interior when the sound became close enough for Nicole to believe that they weren't simply following their imaginations.

Even the prospect of reaching their goal—whatever it was—couldn't prod her any farther at that point. Aaron still had his shoes. She didn't. Her feet were killing her. Resolutely, she plopped herself down on a fallen tree to soak her tired feet in the puddle under it.

Aaron went on ahead, tearing at branches to clear a path for her to follow. There was no danger of losing track of him for a while. She could clearly hear curses alternating with the sound of tearing vegetation.

Shaking her head at the scope of his vocabulary, she took the lapel of her blouse between her thumb and index finger. Gingerly, she pulled at the fabric. It felt stiff, as if the laundry had put extra starch in it. Actually her whole body felt that way. Inside and out. On the inside because of the unaccustomed physical abuse it was taking. On the outside, because of the dried salt water—and all the sand. The minute particles, she had discovered, had permeated even her undergarments during her dunking yesterday.

The aches had just begun to settle into her bones when Aaron's shout put an end to the little pity party she was prepared to indulge in. Certain she was entitled to feel at least a little bit sorry for herself, she moaned a thoroughly unenthused "I'm coming," and trudged on through the thinning trees.

Aaron was waiting for her when she broke through the bushes. Her glance moved from his grin to a grassy area that led to lichen-covered rocks surrounding a nearly mirrorlike pool. "We don't have to worry about fresh water," he told her. "It's spring-fed. We've even got a shower."

The water from the pool spilled down eight feet of boulders to another pool below. By her smile Nicole tried to let Aaron know that she was grateful for his discovery. Now it meant that she could wash away the last twenty-four hour's accumulation of grime. But for some reason she couldn't quite define, meeting this goal made her all too aware of the one they might not reach so easily; that of finding help.

"There isn't anyone else here, is there?"

The flatness of her tone made the question a statement.

Aaron, watching her closely, gave his head a slow shake. "I'm afraid it's beginning to look that way."

"What are we going to do?"

"I'm not sure. But right now, I'm going for a swim. Then, I'm going to relax for a few minutes. Care to join me?"

The instant he started to peel off his shirt, she whirled away from him.

The man was impossible. They were quite stranded and all he was going to do about it was go for a swim and take a nap. Neither would solve their problem.

Not caring to remain while he shamelessly stripped to his skin—or whatever he was doing—she took off toward the trees beyond the second pool. They had climbed to the top of a mountain and the water cascading down the rocks behind her had to be going somewhere.

A glimpse of blue ocean had caught her attention through the trees. Thinking that the mountain must drop off near here, she moved on. From this high up, surely she could see any other islands in the area.

Pushing aside a rubber plant leaf as long as her arm, she peered into open space. Sure enough, water from the pools cascaded down a scarred and rugged wall of rock, the misty spray catching prisms to throw tiny rainbows in the air. It wasn't the beauty of the magnificent waterfall that caused her to pause, however. It was the sight of the jagged rocks below. Like giant blades they thrust out against the surging surf. A chill went through her when she thought of what could have happened to her and Aaron had the sea washed them into that sheer and unforgiving face.

A flash of light reflected off in the distance. She turned toward it, but saw only the ebb and flow of the tide. At the same moment, a wave washed in to the shore beyond, and a flash of sunlight bounced back at her. Another wave, another flash.

The instant she realized what she was seeing, she tore back across the moss- and grass-covered ground. "Aaron!" she cried, praying she wouldn't find him naked. "There's a boat out here!"

Chapter Four

The boat Nicole spotted sat about a hundred yards beyond the tip of a sheltered cove. Aaron, whom she found fully clothed since he'd decided to rest first and swim later, took one look at it, another at their location and decided that the best way to reach the boat would be to follow the ridge. That route would take them twice as long as heading straight down through the scrubby growth on the other side of the hill, but the terrain along the ridge appeared easier to manage.

Nicole had no desire to argue with him, or to subject her bare feet to the punishing rocks visible along the other route, so she forced herself to be patient. Another hour or two didn't matter now that it appeared a rescue was in sight.

Appearances, Nicole soon discovered could indeed be deceiving. The tiring trek down to the cove took considerably longer than she would have thought. By the time the land leveled off to stretch toward the sea, the better part of the afternoon was gone. And the closer they came to their destination, the less certain of their rescue she became.

"I wonder where the passengers are," she said, looking about when they reached the beach. Sparkling sand stretched in a platinum horseshoe around the cerulean water. But no one was in sight. There wasn't a soul to be seen on the sloop's deck, either. "Do you suppose they're below deck?"

Aaron didn't seem nearly so perplexed. With a dull certainty, he muttered, "I'm sure they're not."

"How do you know?"

"Because the people who were on that boat are now on the beach."

Anticipation lit her eyes. She swung around to see what she'd missed. Finding nothing, she turned back to him. "Where?"

Rather than scanning the beach himself, he was cautiously watching her. "Can you see the stern without your glasses?"

Nicole narrowed her eyes on the sloop. She was only slightly nearsighted and by squinting a bit, she could sharpen her focus. Though the boat sat out a ways, the stern faced the shore and the royal blue script on gleaming white clearly spelled out its name.

A vague, sinking sensation centered in the pit of her stomach.

Valiant.

They had found their own boat.

Nicole wouldn't look at Aaron. Her elation met disappointment and the combination made her certain that the stress of the last twenty-four hours was finally beginning to get to her. They had had a way off the island, which is exactly what she wanted. Yet, compelling her as much as the thought of rescue had been the thought of finding other people—of no longer being completely alone with Aaron. Until that moment she'd hadn't let herself acknowledge how completely he both intrigued and intimidated her. Even more confusing was that she wasn't at all sure how she felt about that contradictory combination.

Aaron wasn't suffering any of Nicole's indecision. As soon as she realized they weren't going to be rescued at any moment, his attention focused on the sloop. It listed to port, the angle not boding well for an immediate departure. With a mumbled, "Hang on a minute," he walked straight into the surf.

Not caring to be left behind, Nicole didn't hesitate to follow.

The water was cool and shallow and so clear that it was like looking through glass to the sandy pearl-like bottom. For several feet out, the water came up only as far as her ankles. Another dozen feet and it hit the middle of her calves. Thirty yards from shore she was only in up to her knees, but her progress had slowed considerably. Her skirt was wet to her hips. It stuck to her legs, binding them with the clinging fabric. The small, mincing steps it allowed were getting her nowhere in a hurry.

There was nothing to do but pull her skirt up. As she stopped to gather the sodden fabric above her knees, something slick slithered against her calf.

To her credit, she didn't scream when she jerked back. More startled than frightened, she gasped as a brilliant red mass of undulating, gossamer-like fins scooted off ahead of her. She also promptly lost her balance.

As landings go, she accomplished this one with a certain finesse. Her arms came up and she went down, landing with a splash on her bottom. Water sloshed about her shoulders, surging up onto her face and with a dripping hand she swiped at the droplets clinging to her lashes. She was spitting out salt water, wishing at the same time that she'd caught a better look at the beautiful fish, when she heard the splash of Aaron's long-strided approach.

"Resting?"

Nicole had never learned how to glare. The look she managed, however, came sufficiently close when she glanced up to see him an arm's length away. He stood with his hands on his hips while the water lapped at his knees and the tropical breeze ruffled his sandy hair. His stance had a certain arrogance about it. One that invited challenge. She suffered no doubts that he enjoyed taunting her.

She was tempted to answer that challenge. She willingly acknowledged that something about this man seemed to test her patience. It was the challenge issued by his blatant sensuality that she wasn't sure how to deal with.

He was so unlike the more-civilized males in her life. She couldn't imagine a single one of them standing as Aaron was, grinning like the devil himself at a lady who obviously needed a hand up. Polish and propriety dominated those men's personalities. Yet, even as she thought Aaron the antithesis of the men populating her social circle, she was both fascinated and perplexed by his raw masculinity. It was not something a person could overlook.

With his shirt hanging open, most of his torso was visible. A triangle of golden hair flared over his bronzed chest, the hard muscles sculpted, no doubt, by the kind of physical work no man of her acquaintance would be required to do. She felt certain that he hadn't paid a spa or gym for the privilege of disciplining his body with weights. She'd seen the nicks on his hands, and felt the calluses at the base of his fingers that spoke of manual work. She respected him more for that. The way he'd honed his body made him seem more honest and somehow less vain than a man who used a machine.

Her glance followed the tapering band of hair over the washboard-like muscles of his stomach to where it disappeared below his belt. A splattering of water spots dotted the top half of his once-white pants and his powerful thighs were clearly outlined by much wetter fabric.

Flushing when she realized how bold her perusal had become, she quickly glanced at his face. Nothing in his expression betrayed his reaction to her inspection. He stood watching her while he waited for her to complete it. By his indulgence, it was almost as if he knew that she found him foreign, and possibly exciting in a very unfamiliar and basic way.

If he did realize the fascination he held for her, she was prepared to be quite humiliated. It was bad enough that he found her position amusing.

Thinking him as much like the rogue he looked at the moment, she struggled to her feet. He hadn't offered his assistance, and she adamantly refused to ask for it. In a perverse sort of way, she rather enjoyed being stubborn about that.

She was halfway up when she got his help anyway. With a swift agility foreign to most men his size, he reached out when she started to lose her balance again and caught her under her arms. He easily drew her up, but he lifted her so quickly that she nearly missed her footing. To steady herself, her hands flew to his shoulders. The instant she gripped his left one, he went absolutely still. A second later, his sharp intake of breath preceded as distinct and colorful an oath as she'd ever heard.

Eyes wide, she stumbled back, watching in bewilderment as he grabbed his shoulder. He turned full circle, in the process adding a few expletives that Nicole wasn't sure she'd ever heard before.

"What's wrong?" she asked, too alarmed to be shocked by his profanity. "Did I hurt you?"

Considering his behavior, the question sounded stupid. She couldn't imagine how she could have hurt him—until she remembered that his left shoulder was the one he'd been rubbing off and on all day. When she'd asked him about it earlier, he'd evaded her question. He'd have a little trouble doing that now.

"What did you do to yourself?"

Seeing her outstretched hand aimed for his shoulder, he splashed backward. When she kept coming, he caught her wrist, intent on stopping her before she could inflict more damage. "It's nothing. Nothing," he insisted, gingerly guarding the spot where her hand had landed. "I just bumped it yesterday."

"On what?"

"On the boat," he muttered nonspecifically. "Like I said, it's nothing."

Nicole didn't fancy herself an expert by any means, but she felt fairly certain that a man of Aaron's size and temperament didn't do a rain dance over "nothing." She took a step closer, her tone tentative. "May I see?"

"It's okay. Really."

"Please?"

Her persistence was fueled by concern, and a sense of obligation. He'd hurt himself during the storm, yet he had managed to see to her safety. At the very least, she should see if there was anything she could do to ease his discomfort. Not that she had a clue as to what that anything might be. The offer had to be made, though.

Apparently sensing that she wasn't going to give up until he'd given in, Aaron sighed in resignation and pushed back his shirt. This time it was Nicole's indrawn breath sounding over the distant rustle of palm trees.

An angry red mark, the size and shape of a small horseshoe, sat high on his shoulder. It wasn't black and blue yet,
but it was beginning to turn, and the slight swelling made it
look terribly tender. Without thinking, she reached out to
feather her fingertips below the injury's edges.

"Does it feel as if you broke anything? This is awfully
close to your collarbone."

Her touch was unrestrained, her concern simple and direct. There was no wariness in her inquiring expression, only
guileless consideration for his injury. He couldn't remember the last time anyone had looked at him like that, as if her
only thought were for him.

"I think everything's still in one piece." Though the
shoulder ached like crazy when he raised his arm, everything seemed to work properly. "It's just bruised."

"How did it happen?"

Aaron distinctly remembered encountering a winch when
he'd tried to keep her from being washed overboard. But,
to him, the details didn't matter. "Who knows? We were
being bounced around a lot out there."

She smiled faintly, her glance turning quizzical as she
frowned at her hand. Suddenly aware of what she was
doing, of how bold she must seem, she curled her fingers at
her side. "I'm sorry I hurt you just now. I really didn't mean
to." Almost shyly, she met his eyes again. "Is there anything I can do?"

He quietly scanned her upturned face, seeming to consider alternatives. "I suppose," he finally said, "you could
always kiss it and make it better."

He was teasing her again. She could hear it in his voice.
Oddly enough amusement wasn't in his eyes. He looked
dead serious. At least he did until he smiled at the way her
hand tightened at the collar of her blouse and he turned to
wade on to the listing sloop.

Nicole had but a few moments to wonder whether he had been serious or not—or to consider what she'd have done had he pressed the point. The closer they got to the sloop, the clearer it became that they wouldn't be sailing anywhere right away.

From a distance nothing about the sloop had appeared extraordinary to her. The *Valiant* was simply a boat in the water. Now, she could see that while it was certainly in the water, it wasn't floating. They could walk right up to its side.

The back half of the *Valiant* was over what was essentially a submerged part of the island. From the sharp transition in the color of the water from pale turquoise to sapphire blue, it was apparent that the bow was over a sharp drop-off. All that kept the sloop from floating away was the keel. The force of the storm had rammed it into the downslope of the shoal, so the boat was now stuck.

Unsticking it was not what they wanted to do—or so Aaron told Nicole after she suggested that they give it a push. Instead, they climbed aboard by the diving ladder on the stern—carefully so as not to jar the sloop too much—and dropped the anchor to secure it further. Just above the water line on the landward side was a hole in the bow the size of a turkey platter.

"Can you fix it?"

The question was directed to Aaron's back as he bent over the chart table. He'd headed there as soon as his feet had hit the deck several minutes ago. Mumbling a distracted, "I don't know yet," he kept his frown on the radio. "I'm not even getting static."

"I meant the hull," she clarified, though now that she realized he wasn't getting anything on the radio she was concerned about that, too.

He switched channels with the push of another button. "I need to take another look at it." His concentration on the radio faded to dismissal. Looking faintly bored with the instrument, he turned his back on it.

From where she stood dripping water onto the floor of the galley, she had a clear view of Aaron's profile. He hadn't appeared either displeased or distressed with the radio's dysfunction. And he didn't look particularly concerned about the condition of the sloop. Certainly not as concerned as she was.

"Can you tell where we are?" With all the maps and charts spread out in front of him, she thought surely he should be able to tell her that much.

"Nope," came his maddeningly calm reply.

"The compass works, doesn't it?"

"I guess it does," he mumbled, searching the top of the desk. He was obviously looking for something and not finding it. His scowl deepened by the second.

She hated to intrude on his preoccupation, but she was in the same predicament as he and desperately curious about how they were going to get out of it. For a man who could be so outspoken, he chose the most inopportune times to keep his thoughts to himself. "Then we can use it to get back," she prodded. "Right?"

She sounded as hopeful as a child anticipating a pony ride. Aaron hated to burst her bubble.

"Knowing where north is only helps if you have a basic idea of what lies in that direction. Depending on how far we've been blown off course that could be anything from New York to Newfoundland. We could head west," he continued, still distracted by his search. "But I have no desire to run aground again. None of the electronics on this thing are working and that means no depth finder. If I knew where we were, I could use the charts to avoid the shallows. If I knew where we were, I'd also know how far we have to go to get back. Frankly, the possibility of sailing for a week with only a few day's supply of water and food holds no appeal.'' He turned to a drawer below the chart desk, his voice dropping to a near mutter. "I've done that before and I'd rather not do it again."

When he couldn't find what he was after on top of the desk, he opened a drawer and started shuffling through it. There he found some matches, a flashlight and a foot-long leather case with her father's initials on it. He tossed those items on the table along with a note-pad and pencil. "Find something to put water in, will you? And get some food and blankets together. I'm going to go change."

Nicole stared at him in disbelief. "I thought you were going to take another look at the hole."

"I will."

She felt quite brave asking him, "When?"

The click of the latch on the aft cabin door followed a bland, "Later."

Nicole stared blankly at the brass doorplate. They had a boat with a hole in it and their radio was as dead as a dinosaur. Aaron didn't seem particularly concerned about either. Neither did he know, nor did he seem to care, about where they were. His attitude told her a couple of things. He had nowhere else that he had to be. And he didn't care that she did.

She turned to the closed door, her knock more insistent than she was accustomed to being.

"I have to get in touch with someone at the villa," Aaron heard her call from the other side. "Can't you at least *try* to fix the radio?"

If it hadn't been for the anxiety in her voice, he would have ignored her. Pausing with his hands at the open buckle of his belt, he thought about ignoring her anyway. He'd already tossed aside his shirt and kicked off his sand-filled shoes. A mumbled curse was followed by the rasp of the zipper before he peeled off his soggy pants. This whole mess would be a lot easier to handle if he didn't have her to worry about.

It had been so long since he'd felt compelled to let anyone else know of his whereabouts that her need to do so had escaped him. His agreement with Jake had simply been to leave the *Valiant* at the dock on Stewart Cay. Since there had been no arrangements to meet with anyone there, no one expected him to check in. For all Jake knew, Aaron wouldn't show up for his own boat today because he'd gotten sidetracked somewhere.

"Hang on a minute," he called back, and stripped off his sodden briefs. A moment later, zipping up his favorite cut-offs, he opened the door.

His attire seemed to catch her unawares. Her mouth was open, as if prepared to speak. Instead of pursuing her point, however, she let her startled glance run the length of his body twice before averting her eyes.

"I'm sorry." She stepped back. "I shouldn't have...that is, I'll wait until you've finished dressing."

"I am dressed."

"I . . . oh."

She still didn't look up at him. She kept her attention on his legs, seeming utterly fascinated with his kneecaps.

"Here." He held out a white T-shirt, the kind that had no sleeves and ended in the middle of his chest. It was the only one he had that would even come close to fitting her. "If you wear this you won't have to keep hanging on to the front of your shirt. You're going to need both hands."

After a moment's hesitation, she mumbled a quiet "Thank you" and took it from him. Before he could tell her she could use the cabin, she disappeared into the head.

It didn't take her long to change, or for her to remember what she'd wanted to talk to him about when she emerged a minute later. Smoothing the front of the soft cotton shirt, and looking a bit self-conscious about wearing it, she again asked if he would make an attempt to fix the radio.

"There's no point in my playing with the radio," he told her, finding the topic far less interesting than the way she filled out his shirt. The loose hem hit her at the waist and would bare her midriff if she were to raise her arms.

Finding himself unduly intrigued with the thought, he immediately changed his focus. There wasn't anything he could do to change their situation, but he thought it might help her to know that he understood her problem.

"I know you'd like to put your family's mind at ease, but there's nothing we can do about that right now. Maybe we can figure out a way to signal for help later. In the meantime, try not to worry about your folks. I'm sure they're worried enough."

He expected some acknowledgement that he'd recognized her concern. Rather than easing her anxiety, though, his statement seemed to puzzle her. As she turned to toy with the loose neckline of her shirt, it appeared as if her family being concerned about her was a possibility she hadn't considered.

Actually, Nicole doubted that her father would be anything but vastly annoyed at having to notify the Coast Guard about his missing daughter. Most likely he'd have one of his staff do it, provided Luisa had connected the storm with her failure to arrive. But Nicole hadn't told Luisa how she was getting to the cay. Now that she thought about it, there was always the possibility that the storm had only been at sea and those on shore hadn't been aware of its severity.

Disheartened by her conclusion, she realized it was quite possible that no one yet knew she was missing.

She wouldn't have thought it entirely inappropriate to panic at such a thought. Yet, she wasn't nearly as concerned with the possibility that there might not be anyone looking for them, as she was with the fact that she was stranded with this particular man.

Suddenly conscious of the way she was fidgeting with her neckband, she crossed her arms and held her head high. Other than a skimpy pair of worn and totally disreputable cutoff jeans Aaron didn't have a stitch on. To be honest, all that exposed and beautifully muscled flesh had caught her completely off guard. If she wanted to protect herself from being put at such a disadvantage again, she'd have to learn to expect the unexpected. Besides, if it didn't bother him to stand around half-naked, she supposed it shouldn't bother her either.

But it did. And not in a way that had anything to do with propriety. It bothered her in a way that made her remember all the new and frightening sensations she'd felt when he'd kissed her, when he'd caressed her in places she'd never been touched before.

The more sobering thought was that he'd also made it apparent that her effect on him wasn't nearly so startling.

"There *has* to be some way to get a message to the villa," she insisted, trying for imperiousness when what she really felt was painfully inadequate. "We'll just have to think of something."

"Short of sending smoke signals, I can't imagine what that something would be. But go ahead. You wanted to build a fire before." He held up a small box he'd taken from the drawer. "We have matches now."

Admittedly, she didn't waste much effort attempting to understand his lack of urgency, but she couldn't fathom how he could treat their situation so lightly. Exasperation entered her voice. "You haven't even *tried* to fix the radio."

Patience was etched in the masculine lines of his face. That patience might have been in his voice too, but the clench of his jaw disguised it, making his words sound tight. "There isn't anything I *can* do at the moment. When I said the electronics didn't work, I didn't mean that they were simply being temperamental. I mean we're getting nothing. No juice. No electricity from the batteries. The batteries are dead." He didn't know how much clearer he could make it. "That means no navigation lights, no autopilot, no long-range navigation system, no cabin lights, no electrical refrigeration. The plug's been pulled on everything."

She didn't look convinced. She did, however, appear none too appreciative of his tone. Hers was as controlled as ever. "There must be *something* we can do."

"There is." The duffel bag he'd brought out with him when he'd changed clothes landed with a soft plop on the table. Channeling his irritation by stuffing in the items he'd taken from the drawer, he attempted to curb his annoyance. He knew other people who'd refused to hear what he was saying. Other people who had kept pushing, hoping to make him say what they wanted to hear, rather than accepting the facts.

Taking a deep breath, he forced himself to let go of the tension seeping into him. These circumstances were vastly different from those he'd left behind, but Nicole's failure to accept their situation was making matters more difficult than they needed to be. "We're going to take some supplies from here to the island before the tide changes. After we set up some kind of shelter, I'll come back to see if I can figure out what the problem is with the batteries and take another look at the hole."

She crossed her arms, her stance unyielding. "Don't you think we should be trying to find a way off of the island rather than settling on it?"

"Not until I figure out where we are."

"And when might that be?"

She still had a long way to go to make her hauteur convincing—with him anyway. But there was enough real annoyance in her eyes to give them an intriguing spark of fire. He doubted that she'd ever allowed herself to lose her temper or that she'd know what to think of herself if she did. She seemed to hold herself in check, her emotions bound as tightly as her hair had been.

Now, her dark hair tumbled over her shoulders and down her back in an inviting tangle. If she knew how beguiling she looked, she wouldn't be taunting him this way. He'd never before considered silencing a woman with his lips but the temptation intrigued him.

Equally compelling was the need to dismiss that temptation.

"Hard to say. But if you're in that much of a hurry, there's a broom in the closet. Maybe you can catch the trade winds and fly back. In the meantime," he went on as her eyes widened, "find some containers so we can get water from the spring. I don't want to use what's in the sloop's tanks because it'd be harder than hell to fill them again."

He didn't bother to look up as he added more supplies to the duffel bag. She therefore spoke to the top of his head.

"I don't want to hang around here playing shipwreck with you. We're wasting time," she insisted, her voice rising despite her attempt to lower it. "There's no reason to move things to the island when we'd be more comfortable here. You have to be here anyway so you can fix the boat."

She stepped back as he walked past her. A moment later, he stood at the refrigerator, dropping its meager contents into an ice bucket.

"Why are you doing this?" she wanted to know when he dumped ice into the bucket to keep its contents cold.

"Because we can't stay on the boat. If it breaks loose of the shoal, it'll probably sink. There's already water in the bilge and the pump won't work. Remember?"

The batteries. No power, no pump.

As her voice had risen, so had his.

"Why didn't you tell me that before?"

"I guess I thought you'd have figured it out yourself. But you're so damned concerned about getting out of here, you're not thinking about what that's going to involve. I want out of here, too, but I can't walk on water and short of that, I guess I'm limited to the basics." He shoved the ice bucket toward her. She took it, clutching it to her middle as he glared at her. "The first thing we have to do is make sure we stay safe. That's why we're going back to the island. And I'll fix the damn boat as soon as I figure out what all's wrong with it and see if I've got anything to repair it with. As for where we are, I can't do anything about figuring that out until the stars come out tonight and I've got something to get a fix on. In the meantime, I'd appreciate it if you'd lighten up and help me. While you're at it, take a look around you and relax. It's damn beautiful out there."

For several seconds the only sounds to be heard were the agitated thud of his feet as he marched up the steps to the deck and Nicole's shakily drawn breath. Clearly, he was no more thrilled with their circumstances than she was.

Peeking out the door, she saw him with his hands on his hips, looking back toward the island. To her way of thinking, he'd picked a devil of a time to admire the scenery, which is what he'd just insisted that she do.

He was right in assuming that she'd been too preoccupied with their problem to notice the island's true beauty. *He* noticed, though, and even now, he seemed to be drawing some peace from its lush tranquility. She suspected that he'd asked that of his surroundings before; that nature calm him. He wasn't expecting nature alone to accomplish that task. From the slow, controlled rise and fall of his shoulders, she could tell he was making the effort to calm himself.

Quietly, she moved closer, stopping several feet behind where he stood at the stern. "I'm sorry," she said to his back. "You're right, I wasn't thinking. I didn't want to admit that we might really be stuck here for a while. I hate to let my father down again." She turned around before he could. "I'll get the containers for the water."

She hurried back down the stairs to gather a few other necessities from the cabin. Though far from pleased with the situation, nothing gave her more pleasure than having a purpose. They would spend at least one night on the island. Even if Aaron could repair the sloop today—a circumstance she would regard as miraculous considering the size of the hole in the hull—they had to wait until night to figure out where they were.

Glancing around the cabin, she tried to think of what all they would need. If there was one thing she did know how to do, it was organize.

Aaron entered a few minutes later to see her struggling with the wide cushions from the bunks. "What are you doing?"

The cushions were six feet long, which meant they were awkward for her to handle and probably too short for Aaron. Propping the second one next to the door, where she'd dragged the first she started back for blankets.

"I thought we could sleep on those," she said, absently pulling at her wet skirt. The fabric still clung to her legs, wet and itching and annoying her with each step. Having spent most of the past twenty-four hours in various stages of "drenched," being dry again sounded like heaven.

That thought reminded her to grab towels from the head.

"Why don't we just sleep on blankets?" Aaron asked, frowning as she tugged again at the soggy fabric stuck to her knees.

Nicole glanced at him over the towels. "On the ground?"

It was a fair indication of her tolerance that she appeared more curious than shocked by his suggestion. He wouldn't have been surprised if she'd thought the idea barbaric.

"You can pretend you're camping," he told her, hoping to add to the appeal.

"I've never been camping."

He didn't think she had, which meant she hadn't ever cooked over a camp fire either. His breakfast of breadfruit and rainwater had long since worn off.

"Can you cook?"

She followed his hopeful glance to the propane stove. The appliance seemed fairly straightforward. The switches were marked On and Off and had gradients in between. "I suppose," she replied gamely. "But I'd need something to prepare."

Aaron reached into the ice bucket for his cupcakes and handed her the yogurt that wouldn't keep without refrigeration anyway. They lacked ingredients and she obviously hadn't spent much time in a galley, but he had to admire the fact that she'd appeared willing. Now that she'd accepted that staying put for a while was her only choice, she didn't seem opposed to carrying her own weight with the other tasks, either. She just plunged right in.

With the cupcakes and yogurt gone, their food supply was now down to one muffin that was going stale in a hurry and the two crates of delicacies destined for Stewart Cay. Some of those provisions weren't going to make it that far.

Nicole added four tins of pâté de fois gras, two of truffle, which was a specialty of the club's chef, a box of lime water crackers, and two bottles of Dom Perignon to the pile of blankets and gear they'd stacked on the aft deck. Despite the inconvenience, Aaron thought being shipwrecked with an heiress had its finer points. At least the menu for dinner wouldn't be breadfruit. He'd had it prepared every way imaginable, but never had managed to develop a taste for the stuff.

It took a while to load the raft. Aaron couldn't raise his left arm without it hurting so, one item at a time, Nicole handed blankets and pillows and one of the blue sail covers down to him while he stood in the chest-deep water. When their supplies were in the raft, Nicole climbed down the diving ladder on the stern and slipped into the water herself. With the rope Aaron had attached to the plastic oarlocks, they dragged the raft back to the island.

Other than to question the necessity of an item, little had been said as they'd worked. Nicole was preoccupied with setting up a decent shelter of some sort. Aaron, she hoped, was busy figuring out a way to get them out of here. Pulling at the tenacious material of her skirt so she could walk, she trudged onto the shore and scanned the vast and empty beach.

"You sure you don't have anything else to wear?" she heard him ask from behind her. "You're going to break your neck in that thing."

"Will you please stop worrying about it? I'm fine."

She turned to see sculpted muscle rippling along his shoulders as, with his back to her, he gave the final tug that landed the raft on dry land. Unbidden, her glance slid lower to where water sluiced down his thighs, the little rivulets flattening the hair on his powerful legs.

Neptune rising from the sea, she mused.

Immediately chagrined by the fanciful thought, she averted her eyes to survey the foliage for a possible homesite. "How about right over there?" she asked, pointing to a sheltered area near the trees.

She expected him to veto her suggestion, as he had every other one she'd made. Instead, she heard him mumble, "Looks good," and turned to see him scowling at her skirt.

"I don't suppose you'd consider wearing a pair of my shorts, would you?"

The glance she shot him was quite droll. "No, I wouldn't. This will dry out soon."

She thought he'd dropped the matter when he picked up the heavy blue canvas sail cover and started toward her. Preparing to get an armload of supplies and follow, she started to the raft, tugging at her skirt as she did.

"Hold it." The instant they started past each other, the canvas hit the sand, and his hand locked on her wrist. "Turn around here for a minute."

She barely managed a surprised, "What for?" when she saw him withdraw a pocketknife from his pocket. A moment later, he'd squatted in front of her. "What are you doing?" she asked.

"You're going to be in and out of the water a lot in the next day or two and it's driving me crazy watching you struggle with this thing. It's already ruined," he said, thinking that all the unattractive garment had going for it in the first place was the tear in the side that allowed occasional glimpses of her nicely curved leg. "So I won't be hurting it any. Ever wear a mini?" he asked, grabbing a handful of fabric above her knees. The blade slid cleanly through the material.

"Of course not. You can't—"

"Oh, but I can," he interrupted and pushed his hand between her legs to grasp the back of her thigh when she tried to pull away. The contact froze her on the spot. "Hold still," he ordered. "I don't want to cut you." Releasing his grip slowly to make sure she wasn't going to bolt, he took hold of the two new edges he'd made and tore through the soggy fabric. The bottom half of her skirt disappeared with a dull ripping sound. The front half anyway. Taking her by the hips, he turned her around and finished the alteration.

"There." Looking enormously pleased with himself, he folded the knife back into itself and pushed it into his pocket as he rose. "That's better."

Standing back, he surveyed his handiwork. The skirt was a shade shorter than he'd intended, but the length looked good on her. Amazingly good.

Chapter Five

The sun slid like a giant red ball below the horizon, its golden pink haze backlighting the darkened water. Overhead the twilight sky grew inky and one by one, stars popped out.

Aaron stood silhouetted against that pastel backdrop, his back to where Nicole had stopped rummaging through the duffel bag to watch him. He'd been drawn by the sunset, then absorbed by it. And because of the way he'd left her and strolled to the shore alone, he'd seemed reluctant to share it.

She didn't pretend to understand him. He was both kind and cool, amazingly sensitive and wickedly teasing. He encouraged her to speak her mind. Yet, in many ways, he seemed to be a very private man and a remarkably honest one.

He had quite logically explained away what had happened between them this morning and had made no attempt to repeat it. As for his comments yesterday when he'd put his arm around her while Mother Nature was putting them through the blender, he was no doubt just being nice. He could afford to flatter her if he thought he was going to die.

Disgusted with the course of her thoughts, she turned back to the duffel bag. The color was leaving the sky, the faded twilight allowing night to encroach. It grew darker with each passing second. The flashlight was, of course, on the bottom.

"Can I borrow that?"

Aaron hunched down when she held out the flashlight. Flipping it on, he directed the beam into the duffel bag and took out a pad and pencil along with the leather case monogrammed with her father's initials. He handed the flashlight back to her, asking her to hold it for him while he took the sextant from the case and made a couple of quick adjustments.

She knew by now that Aaron wasn't too reliable when it came to explaining what he was doing. With him, a person either had to be a mind reader, or prepared to ask questions. Her curiosity now overrode her diffidence. "What are you looking for when you look through there?"

The moon had yet to rise and evening claimed all but the small space illuminated by the flashlight. That pale light allowed the cautious curiosity in her expression to be seen as she indicated the three-inch long brass telescope supported above a calibrated metal arc.

"I usually look for Betelgeuse."

"Beetle juice?"

"It's the brightest star in Orion," he said, smiling at her confusion. "It became visible a couple of minutes ago."

She rose when he did, intrigued as much by that easy smile as with what he was doing. "Where?"

The pencil clenched between his teeth, he jerked his head in the general direction of the sky and mumbled, "Up there. Wanna help me?"

She did. Partially because she wanted to know how he was going to determine where they were, but mostly because he headed back toward the shore and it was kind of creepy alone in the dark. There may not have been any birds around, but she had seen a respectable number of bugs. Some of them seemed to find the tropical humidity conducive to large and rapid growth.

It soon became apparent that Aaron could have accomplished his task quite easily without her. Her job was to write down the numbers he called out after he'd looked through the sextant, along with the corresponding time. They had to use his watch. Hers, she'd discovered, hadn't been waterproof. After giving her three sets of numbers, he held the instrument toward her. "Do you want to try?"

A quick smile answered his offer. Then, she hesitated. "I don't know what star to look for."

"Just spot the brightest star in Orion through here—" he pointed to the eyepiece on the tiny telescope "—and then move this arm until the image of the star touches the horizon line. That's this here."

He made it sound so simple. "I'm afraid I don't know where Orion is. Or even what it looks like. There are so many stars up there, I don't know if I could pick it out even if I did."

"Can you find the Big Dipper?"

Everyone could do that. "That hardly counts."

"Sure it does. I met a guy on Crete who couldn't even spot that. He had to rely on his crew for bearings. At least you can recognize shape. All you have to do to pick out a constellation is eliminate the stars that aren't in it. Just see what you want to see." At her dubious consideration of his suggestion, he smiled. "Come on. I'll show you what to look for."

Earlier that afternoon, while Aaron had gone back to check out the boat more thoroughly and bail some of the water from the bilge, Nicole had made two neat and very separate stacks of blankets and pillows at opposite ends of the blue canvas sail covers she had spread over the sand. Aaron now sat down on the nearest one while she stood over him and aimed the light on the pad. A series of dots were drawn over the pale yellow page.

"This is Orion," he said, indicating the dots on the pad. "And this star here, is Betelgeuse." He touched the pencil tip to one of the larger dots. "It's actually Orion's left shoulder. These three are his belt and these," he went on, "are his sword. It's raised above his head like so. Now—"

He reached up, took the flashlight from her and turned it off. A moment later, he folded his hand around her wrist and pulled her down beside him. Turning her so she sat in front of him, he pointed over her shoulder to a spot well above the horizon. He'd left his free hand on her other shoulder and he was so close she could feel his chest against her back. "Can you see it?"

She hadn't realized how cool she was until she felt the heat of him seeping into her. She shivered. Even as she did, she knew she couldn't fully blame it on the difference in temperature. Aaron's presence had that effect on her. Something about his nearness enlivened her nerves and gave her an awkward, giddy feeling deep in the pit of her stomach. The sensations were a little disconcerting and amazingly difficult to ignore.

Maybe, she thought, looking out in the direction he indicated, she reacted as she did because she wasn't accustomed to being touched. No one she knew used casual contact as part of normal conversation the way Aaron did.

Beyond a handshake or the polite touch of a man's hand at her waist while dancing at one of the innumerable charity fund-raisers she organized, people kept their hands to themselves.

Aaron seemed to think nothing of his actions, as if touching were simply a way to facilitate an explanation—or to communicate without words. The pressure of his fingers increased ever so slightly, seeming to draw her back toward his chest.

"I'm really terrible at this," she said, certain the contact meant nothing to him.

"Come on." His tone gently cajoled, but the slight squeeze he gave her shoulder jolted her clear to her toes. "You haven't even tried yet."

That was true, and, in this instance, totally unlike her. While she hesitated where people and relationships were concerned, she normally tried to learn all she could about everything else. Even as a child she'd wanted to know the how and the why of things and within an instant of a question arising, she'd be in her father's study precociously demanding an answer—until her questions had become bothersome and he'd begun brushing her off with a distracted, "Go look it up." Nicole had always felt horrid for having made her father frown at her—and a little confused because he'd once encouraged her inquisitiveness. Even with her enthusiasm dimmed by her father's increasing abruptness, she would do as he said and turn to books for the answers. Invariably, she had found what she was looking for, but when she had, there had seldom been anyone around with whom to share her discovery.

That had been long ago. Over the years, much of her natural curiosity had been buried beneath the demands of daily living. One did not have time to stop and smell the roses when ordering them to be cut and arranged for a dinner party. At the moment, though, she had the time and she found that she very much wanted to see what Aaron was trying to show her. If a person were to stop and consider it, the night sky held all manner of mysteries. Entire religions were formed around the constellations and ancient civilizations had been rooted in the myths surrounding their namesakes.

"Look for the brightest star," she heard him remind her.

She concentrated a moment more, then reached for the pad and flashlight. After studying his drawing, and waiting a few seconds for her eyes to adjust to the darkness, she tried again.

This time, she saw them—the three stars that made up the belt and the bright one that Aaron had first seen.

"I think I see it," she said, her voice bearing a hint more excitement than the event probably deserved. "I *do* see it." She turned with her smile still betraying the pleasure she felt at her simple discovery. "Will you show me another?"

Aaron wouldn't have thought it possible for a grown woman to look as innocent as she did at that moment. He could easily see the anticipation she tried to temper, along with her faint embarrassment when her smile grew more brilliant. Her eagerness couldn't be hidden. It was too real. Or, possibly, too new.

He'd caught the briefest glimpse of that guilelessness once before. It had been veiled somewhat by the tasks at hand, but that same interest had been sparked at the idea of sleeping on the beach. She'd acted as if she knew she shouldn't be too crazy about the thought, but rather liked the prospect anyway. Now, she wasn't able to stifle her pleasure.

That she seemed so surprised by her own enthusiasm told him more about her than he probably had a right to know. He had felt that same freeing excitement when he'd first discovered the simple pleasures he'd once been too busy to notice. At first, he'd felt guilty doing nothing but enjoying the peace and beauty of an evening sky. He'd actually once bought into the idea that a thing was of value only if it cost you something. The more it cost, the more "valuable" it was. No thought was given to what was free and available to anyone who took the time to look for it—the song of a bird, the colors in a sunset, the clean smell of the sea.

Having money and wanting more had cost him dearly. He'd paid his dues, though, and he was now free. Nicole wasn't. He'd have bet his boat on that, and his boat was just about all he had left. He was almost as sure that money wasn't Nicole's motivator. But he was beginning to feel quite certain that something with the same allure and potential to destroy had a hold on her.

The allure she had for him was a more immediate concern. As he'd watched her, caught by the enchanting innocence of her smile, he'd let the silence stretch on too long. In that silence, he heard her sweet, shuddering intake of breath.

The moon had cleared the tops of the trees, cloaking them in its ethereal light. That pale illumination softened the harder angles of his features, but nothing could soften the intensity of his eyes. His glance caressed her face as he studied her, her breath catching as he focused on her mouth. Each beat of her heart grew louder. Surely, she thought, he could hear it.

"I'll show you more," he said in response to the request she'd made of him nearly a minute ago. "I promise. But right now, I think I'd better see if I can figure out where we are."

She nodded, for a moment seeming unsure what to say. "I didn't mean to keep you. I'm sorry."

"You don't have anything to apologize for," he returned, obviously puzzled by her apparent need to do so. "I just have to check my sightings or I might not get an accurate position. It won't take long."

The smile she gave him was much weaker than she intended. It was a little perturbing to know that she'd let herself be so transparent. He probably knew that she'd wanted him to kiss her again.

The corner of his mouth jerked in a smile. Before she realized that the savvy thing to do would be to return it, he was on his feet.

From behind her she heard him rustling around with his blankets, then the click of the flashlight and the crackle of paper as he unfolded a map. He'd probably have explained how he was going to determine their location if she'd had the nerve to ask. All her nerve had been used up when she hadn't turned away from him a few moments ago.

She stretched out on her blanket, keeping her back to him as she pulled her other one over her. She was sure he'd have forgotten his promise by the time he finished.

It only took Aaron a couple of minutes to confirm his calculations and he'd called her name twice before he realized that Nicole had fallen asleep. He didn't bother trying to deny his disappointment. He'd wanted to explore the constellations with her, if for no other reason than to see the delight in her expression when she picked one out. He was actually a little surprised that she hadn't stayed awake. Even if the stars hadn't been a compelling enough reason to keep her from drifting off, he'd have thought her desire to know where she was would have kept her awake. Obviously, her exhaustion had preempted that concern.

In a way, he figured it was just as well that she had fallen asleep. He couldn't give her an exact location. Tomorrow, he'd take a look at the more detailed charts still on the sloop. Surely one of them would show the island they were on.

She slept curled in a little ball, one hand beneath her cheek and the other clutching the blanket at her throat. Even in repose, her guard was in place. Stifling the urge to brush a lock of hair from her forehead, he turned away, moving quietly so as not to disturb her. She'd put in a long day and, except for her initial impatience with their circumstances, she hadn't complained much. That had thoroughly amazed him. He had trouble imagining any woman not complaining about being stripped of modern conveniences—especially one raised, no doubt, with every luxury money could buy.

He folded the map and stretched out a few feet from Nicole to lie with his hands behind his head. He was tired, too, and it was easy to let his mind drift as he stared up at the vast night sky. As a young boy, he'd spent many an evening doing this same thing; looking up at the stars. Orion had been his favorite and he'd pick it out, imagining himself the great hunter and fighting imaginary battles with his sword. He never lost. He always won. Always.

Maybe, he thought, that was where it had all started, where the seeds of competition and aggression had taken root. Heaven knew his family had nurtured those traits. Second-best was never good enough for a Wilde and he'd been taught that first was the only thing to be.

He'd since learned that being his own person was an even tougher goal to accomplish. But once that goal had been reached, it certainly beat being chased by the other rats on the treadmill. It took incredible energy to be number one, and the position could be usurped at any time. He'd tumbled many men himself as he'd clawed his way to the top. But the thing he had now that he didn't have then, was something no one could ever take from him. His freedom.

Those thoughts were merely Aaron's more nebulous mental wanderings. He was quick to remind himself to appreciate what he had, but he didn't spend a lot of time analyzing anymore. He'd been through all that and now simply cherished each moment as it came. It was becoming apparent to him, though, that Nicole had been as far removed from his aggressive, winner-take-all upbringing as he was from her amazing naïveté. Despite the air of aristocratic hauteur she affected on occasion, her basic manner was shy, almost self-effacing. What confidence she possessed was mostly external. That lack of self-confidence bothered him most.

She'd been so quick to apologize when they'd argued this morning. She'd had every right to be upset about their circumstances and no apology had been necessary. And just a while ago, she'd said she was sorry when she thought her request of him to identify another constellation had been an imposition. The main reason he'd had to move was because he'd been so tempted to taste the softness of her mouth.

He wished he hadn't remembered that. It took little enough effort to recall the thoughts evoked by the scent of her hair when he'd leaned over her shoulder. The guarded invitation in her eyes when she'd smiled at him had nearly stolen his breath away. She was an utterly beguiling combination of sensuality and innocence and, if he were to guess, she wasn't terribly comfortable with either.

He wasn't very comfortable at the moment himself. And as protected as he was beginning to sense that she had been for most of her life, she'd probably faint if she knew how hard he was now, just from remembering how well she'd fit beneath him this morning. Long-legged and slender, he could easily imagine how it would feel to have her wrapped around him.

Flipping on to his side, he released a long low breath and tried not to think about that.

Aaron often slept lightly, a habit developed while spending months alone at sea. It seemed, though, that he awoke more often than usual that night and every time he did, he was immediately conscious of the thought that had followed him into his dreams.

Nicole Stewart was as far removed from the role of seductress as a female could get. Yet she tantalized him in a way no woman ever had.

By the time the sun had crept above the horizon and warmed the ever-present breeze, Aaron had forgotten all about the hours of sleep he'd missed. After wading out to the sloop, he'd checked the charts there, then brought them back to show Nicole. She'd taken one look at him, another at the charts, and seemed to know that the news wasn't good.

Still dripping from his excursion, he tossed the charts on his blanket and dug around in his bag for a towel and a T-shirt. Nicole sorted through their supplies, setting out their breakfast.

Stuffing his arms in the shirt, he pulled it over his head and down his chest. "I don't suppose there's any coffee in that box. I checked the cupboards on board, but there isn't any there." He bent over, toweling off his wet legs as best he could with his cutoffs still dripping onto them.

Nicole had never watched a man dry and dress himself before, so she tried not to appear either fascinated or flustered, though she was actually a bit of both. Thankful that she had somewhere else to look, though she knew she wouldn't find what he'd requested, she turned her scrutiny to the contents of the crate. "There isn't any here either," she told him. "I'm sorry."

"It's not your fault we don't have coffee," he muttered. He sat down to spread the charts over the blanket. "I think you'd better see this."

She didn't like the sound of his statement. She hadn't liked the guarded expression that had been on his face since he'd come back from the boat a few minutes ago either. There was a certain caution to both, as if he knew she wasn't going to like what he had to say.

The crackers and imported lingonberry preserves that would be their breakfast were set beside him. Adding two cloth napkins to the meager fare, a casual attempt at a form of civility that didn't seem to apply here, she sat down across from him.

He raised his eyes to find her cautiously watching him. "Do you want to know where we are?"

She nodded, suddenly less certain than she'd thought she'd be. "I know we were blown off course, but we couldn't have been blown very far. Could we?"

"I don't know what you consider 'far.' In terms of manageable distances, we're not in bad shape. I figure we're a little over a hundred miles north and east of where we want to be."

"A hundred miles?"

She repeated the figure calmly, as if it bore no significance to her one way or the other. The distance wasn't Aaron's major concern anyway. "We were in a wind moving basically northeast. That's the same direction the Gulf Stream flows. The current is probably as responsible for taking us this far as the wind was. It usually runs at about three or four knots and that's always taken into account when crossing it. But sometimes, it gets to running faster, and if you've got a wind pushing you, too..."

He let his explanation end with a shrug. The look of concern remained to shadow his features. He sat across from her, staring down at the various shades of blue on the map. "I didn't hear a single airplane yesterday. Did you?"

Nicole was caught unawares by his comment and his question. Only for a moment, though. Aaron seemed to notice things, or their lack, the way most people took them for granted. Always, too, he seemed to have a purpose for his observations.

"I don't know if I did or not," she admitted, knowing she tended to overlook her surroundings in favor of her more immediate concerns. Just last week she'd stopped at a new street vendor for an ice-cream cone on her way home from the museum. The vendor, she later learned, had been in that same location for over a month, which meant she had walked past him a half dozen times without noticing.

She made herself sound more certain. "I must not have." Even if she did tend to be a little myopic at times, she would have heard a plane. That would have meant a possible rescue. "No, I'm sure I didn't."

Unaware of the mental gymkhana she'd run to come up with that answer, Aaron contemplated the struggle of a tiny sand crab as it burrowed beneath a palm frond lying a few feet away. "This is supposed to be the busiest part of the Atlantic ocean. Shipping lanes run through here and it's one of the most popular areas in this hemisphere for blue-water sailing. But, I didn't see a ship or a boat or hear a single airplane all day yesterday. Nothing this morning, either."

"And no birds," she said quietly.

"Yeah." He made a sound that was half snort, half chuckle. "No birds. That's the spooky part."

"I'd appreciate it if you wouldn't use that word." She set aside the cracker she'd been nibbling. The ominous undertones of their conversation had dulled her appetite. "I'd appreciate it, too, if you'd tell me what you think all this means."

"I'm not sure what it means. I only have a suspicion." He hesitated, not appearing too comfortable with whatever it was that had occurred to him. "Have you ever heard any stories about the Bermuda Triangle?"

For a moment she did nothing more than stare at him. He looked as serious as a judge contemplating a sentence. No smile softened the austere lines of his face, and his eyes, as he waited for her to answer him, were dispassionately calm. He wasn't teasing.

"Do you believe in the inexplicable?" he prodded.

Finding herself drawn to the sense of mystique surrounding him, she had to admit that there definitely were some things that defied reason. Based on some of his comments, it was obvious that he was an educated man; one who was well traveled and, curiously, without roots. The combination was most intriguing.

All she told him, however, was that she found such stories a little short on credibility. "I've heard it's an area where ships and crews are supposed to have vanished without a trace. But I doubt anything has happened there that can't be scientifically explained."

"Here."

"I beg your pardon?"

"Here. You said you didn't think anything had happened *there* that couldn't be explained. It's *here*. We're in it. Look."

Picking up his pencil and ruler, he drew a line from Melbourne, Florida, northeast to the island of Bermuda, then one down to Puerto Rico, and back to Melbourne. About two inches out into that triangle were the three intersecting lines drawn in pencil that corresponded to the coordinates he'd obtained last night using the sextant. The place where all three lines intersected was where they were.

Nicole refused to find anything extraordinary about their location. "All of the Abaco Islands, which is where Stewart Cay is located, and half of Grand Bahama Island is in that area, too," she pointed out. "On the edges of it, anyway. I've been to the cay dozens of times and nothing strange has ever happened. Nothing really strange is happening here." She looked back to the chart. "Everything seems normal."

"Almost."

"If you mean the birds and the planes, I'm sure there's a reasonable explanation—"

"That's not what I'm talking about. I mean the compass. The triangle is only one of two places on earth where it points to true north. Everywhere else, it points to magnetic north. Since we're in the middle of the triangle, we'll need to take that into consideration if we can get the sloop repaired. Otherwise, we'll miss our destination by miles."

If we can get it repaired, he'd said. "Where's the other place?"

"Off the coast of Japan. An area called the Devil's Sea."

"How appropriate."

He smiled slightly at her muttering, then settled back to openly study her. It seemed that he was now more interested in her skepticism than in the chart. "You really don't believe some phenomenon could be responsible for some of the weird things that are supposed to have taken place here?" he asked. "We've all heard the explanations and some of them aren't so far-fetched. I think we can safely dismiss the ones about sea monsters and extraterrestrial landing zones, but what about the theory that there are enormous pools of natural gas frozen under the floor of the sea. Every once in a while a tremor or a rise in temperature causes a lot of gas to escape and, as the big bubbles break into smaller ones on their way to the surface, it makes the water lighter and whatever is sitting on it would suddenly sink. The same theory works for airplanes that disappear. The gas plume erupts above the surface, causing engines to stall and the plane plunges into water it can't float on. It makes a lot of sense if you think about it." Paper crackled as he took a cracker from the package. "You need for things to make sense, don't you?"

Her eyes had followed the movements of his hands. Now, he raised the one nearest her, startling her as he reached over to run his knuckles down her cheek. In the moments before his smile turned teasing, she could have sworn she saw his sympathy for her reluctance to indulge her imagination.

"It's probably just as well that you think the way you do," he told her, pulling his hand away to reach for the preserves. "Now I don't have to worry about you panicking when you take a closer look at that map. I don't think you noticed, but there's no island there. Looks to me like we're sitting on what should be about three-hundred-and-seventy feet of water."

She'd suspected it before. Now, as she watched him pop the preserve-laden cracker into his mouth and load up another, she was positive of it. He actually enjoyed baiting her.

She pulled the map closer, wishing she had her glasses. Surely, somewhere under those lines he'd drawn was the tiny printed speck that represented their island.

Despite his willingness to allow for the peculiarity, he seemed to appreciate her skepticism. "I know. I even erased my lines and looked again myself. There's nothing there."

"Maybe you erased the island."

A certain indulgence softened the harsher lines of his face. "I don't think so. The island's not on any of the other maps, either. I checked."

Not knowing what to think of all that he'd said, or of the easy familiarity in his touch moments ago, she rose to pace the perimeter of the tarp. Being near him bothered her. Not only in the physical sense, but in an emotional sense as well. She didn't like feeling off-balance.

"It's nice that you can be so blasé about all of this. Personally, I'm finding it quite inconvenient. I've got a dozen things to do and absolutely no way to get them done. I'm getting farther behind schedule by the minute."

"Tell me," he began, his calm all the more maddening because her own composure was suffering. "What if we can't get off this island? What if we're stuck here? Do you think your schedule will even matter then?"

"We're not going to be stuck here."

The certainty in her voice evoked his strangely sad smile. "You won't even consider the possibility, will you?" His voice was curiously flat, his expression wry as he capped the preserves and handed them to her. "What frightens you the most about not going back?"

Nicole didn't know if it was the scope of his question or the implication that she may, indeed, have become a permanent resident of an uncharted island that made an immediate answer impossible. She simply stood there, gripping the jar as she stared back at him.

He rose to hand her the crackers. "Think about it."

A moment later, he started toward the shore.

Her voice stopped him on his second step. "What about you?" It wasn't like her to challenge, but his question caused her enough consternation to want to know if he shared her anxieties. He had a way of asking her to face situations she didn't know how to handle, or would as soon not think about. "Aren't there things you'd miss?"

"I'm not talking about *things* Nicole. We can make do without possessions. I've got the feeling you aren't all that caught up in your father's wealth anyway. I'm talking about the part of yourself that you fear you'd lose without all

those trappings. What would you be without the people who
see you in the roles you play? As far as I'm concerned, there
would be worse ways to live than in a place like this. But I
promised myself that I'd sail around the world at least once
and I've still got half of it to go. I'm not going anywhere
until I get that boat fixed, though. Right now, I'm going to
try to find something to patch it with so I won't have to keep
bailing water. If you've got any ideas as to what that something might be, I'd appreciate hearing about it.''

She should go with him to help. Though he wasn't complaining about it, she knew his shoulder still hurt, and
bruised as it was, he shouldn't bail water. Knowing that, she
still couldn't bring herself to follow him just now.

She sank back down on the blankets as he walked away.
The possibility of remaining here with him was at once
frightening and wildly exciting. Certainly the most exciting
circumstances *she'd* ever been presented with. It was also,
she rationally reminded herself, far too premature to consider, even if it was a lot more interesting to think about than
to come up with an idea for patching the boat.

As for the question he'd asked—and bluntly told her to
consider—she had no intention of pondering. There was no
reason to think about what she'd fear most about not going
back. She already knew what it was.

Chapter Six

The moss-laced grass felt cool and damp beneath Nicole's feet, the sun deliciously warm on her face. Savoring the clean, salt-tanged air, she took her time as she worked her way down the hill to the shore. A path of sorts had been formed by the tropical rains that washed the island and she followed it between a profusion of purple and orange bird of paradise and brilliant red hibiscus. All but a few of the sturdier palms and breadfruit trees respected the meandering right-of-way. She skirted or ducked under those, never leaving the path she'd taken to the top.

The hike up to the fresh-water spring Aaron had discovered had taken over an hour. The climb down took just as long because the weight of the water jugs she carried made the trip more difficult. Nicole didn't mind. Until a couple of days ago the most strenuous activity she engaged in was hailing taxicabs. It had come as something of a revelation to her that she actually enjoyed exertion. It was good that she did, too. The present circumstances demanded a certain physical approach.

After spending the morning bailing water until her arms ached, she'd left Aaron frowning at the hole in the hull and headed back to their camp. Since they had used what fresh water they'd had cleaning up that morning and since the containers needed to be refilled, Aaron had suggested she could take care of that task while he tried to reinforce a broken rib in the sloop's frame. Their earlier discussion had left her less inclined to engage in conversation and he'd apparently grown tired of her silence. Filling water jugs had sounded fine to her, especially since it had provided her with an excuse to remove herself from his disturbing presence.

It had also provided her with an opportunity for a shower. She'd taken her soap and shampoo with her and, while at the falls, had scrubbed away the accumulation of salt and sand. It had felt like heaven. Doing so out in the open, however, naked beneath a waterfall that overlooked the Atlantic, had felt . . . strange.

A smile struggled free. That had definitely been a first.

It felt terrific to be clean again, but she'd have felt even better if she'd had a change of clothes. Aaron's T-shirt and her recently altered and insanely short skirt comprised her limited wardrobe. The skirt and top were absolutely all she wore at the moment, too. She'd washed out her under things and rolled them up in her towel.

About fifty feet from their camp, she stopped to hang both the towel and the lacy pastel garments over a branch in the sun. She hoped they'd be dry soon. It felt peculiar to be without them; daring actually.

The thought of going without underwear would have held little appeal before. Now, though a little reluctant to admit it, she found the experience both liberating and disturbing—especially her lack of a bra. The soft cotton of Aaron's shirt against her bare breasts was really quite comfortable. But the fact that it *was* Aaron's shirt covering her so intimately made her feel vaguely restless—and very aware of how the fabric brushed against her nipples as she moved. The subtle contact reminded her of how Aaron had touched her, and how she wished he would touch her again. That was what disturbed her the most.

With a shake of her head to clear it of such thoughts—wondering, too, if there might not be some merit to Aaron's suspicion that something in this area made things, and people, act abnormally—she lugged the water jugs through the bushes and sea grass leading to the beach.

She had intended to put the water with their box of provisions. But as her steps slowed and her puzzled glance swept the sparkling sand, neither the box, nor the blankets she'd shaken out and folded, were anywhere to be seen.

Confused, she looked out toward the sea.

Any other boat would bob slightly with the surf's gentle surges. The *Valiant* sat firm in the pale-blue water, its unnatural stillness confirming that the keel remained embedded in the sandbar. Its position from where Nicole stood also told her that she was in the right place. But where, she wondered, were their things?

That question had no sooner posed itself when the rustle of dry palm fronds met the sound of a tersely muttered oath. Feeling her heart jump, she jerked around.

Aaron's eyes narrowed on her startled expression. "It's about time," he informed her, his tone as flat as the horizon. He emerged from the vegetation, a fierce scowl darkening his face as he absently kneaded his shoulder. "Where have you been?"

"I went to fill these," she said, and held up one of the jugs. He knew where she'd gone. It had been his idea that she go. "You knew that."

"That was hours ago. You should have been back by now. And don't say you're sorry," he cut in when she started to do just that.

Confusion swept her delicate features. Stung by his abrupt remark, she set the heavy jugs in the sand and stepped back. "All right," she returned, her voice quiet. "I won't."

Her capitulation did nothing to improve his mood. If anything, it seemed to increase his agitation. "What took you so long?"

"I wasn't aware that it had been all that long. I went to the spring and came back." If he hadn't been scowling at her as if she were an irresponsible child, she might have expanded on that explanation. Not particularly enamored with his attitude, she decided it was none of his business what she'd done there. "It takes a while to hike to the top, you know."

"You hiked up to the spring?"

The question was as confusing as his interrogation. He was obviously irritated with her, but she had no idea why. "Where else was I supposed to get water?"

"To where the falls come down the rocks," he told her. "That's where I thought you'd gone. It certainly would have been easier."

Around the bend and up and over a lower part of the hill was a stream formed by the falls. While it was true that the water there was a little closer, it was less accessible for her. The ground on that side of the island consisted exclusively of rocks. Sharp ones.

She couldn't have showered there, either.

Exasperated, trying not to be, she met his unyielding gaze. "It might be easier for you, but I don't have any shoes."

That seemed to take a little of the wind from his sails. His glance darted to her bare feet with their hot pink toenails, his expression losing some its harshness as he lifted his eyes back to her face. Even without the scowl, he didn't look overly pleased with her at the moment.

"Did you need me to help you with something?" she asked, thinking that might explain why he seemed so perturbed. Maybe he'd been looking for her to help him and had become irritated when he hadn't been able to find her.

That didn't seem to be the case. He shook his head, tension shadowing his expression. Instead of his shoulder, he was now massaged the side of his neck. "I just didn't want you wandering off somewhere and getting lost. It'll be dark in a few hours."

His words were grudging, as if the thought of having to track her down might require more energy than he had. The fact remained, however, that he'd been worried about her.

"Why didn't you say so?" Her exasperation calmed by his reluctant concern, she tried for understanding. "I can't read your mind, Aaron."

She couldn't read his mind, but she was beginning to suspect what lay at the root of his enigmatic mood. Her glance settled on his shoulder. He'd no doubt used his arm more than he should have. "You overdid it today, didn't you?"

Too stubborn to confirm her suspicion and too honest to deny it, he didn't answer at all. That lack of response told Nicole all she needed to know.

Bailing out the boat wasn't easy. Had the electric bilge pump worked, there wouldn't have been a problem. But the battery had been damaged beyond repair and there was no hope of getting power to it. It wouldn't have been that big a deal with a hand pump, either, but they didn't have one. They'd had no choice but to take water from beneath the floorboards by using a bucket. Their relay system—one filling the bucket, the other hauling it on deck to dump it over the side—worked fairly well. But until the hole was plugged, it was like trying to bail out the ocean, especially since every once in a while, a wave would wash in another gallon of water.

Aaron had undoubtedly irritated the injury to his shoulder. Pain, she was certain, could easily account for his present, crummy mood.

As much as she wished she could help, there was little she could do to ease his physical discomfort. The bruise would simply have to heal on its own—if he'd rest long enough to let that happen. She hadn't consciously thought in terms of "owing" him for taking care of her when she needed him. But it did seem that it was now her turn.

"Have you thought of a way to fix the hole?" she asked, when what she really wondered was whether or not he would let her take over for a while. He was awfully independent.

"I've got some ideas. For now, I've got the life raft jammed against the inside of the hull. It'd never work at sea, but it's keeping most of the water out for the time being."

His use of the life raft explained where it had gone. And now that she thought about it, she remembered him mentioning earlier that they should move their camp into the protection of the trees in case the clouds billowing on the horizon turned threatening. A sliver of blue tarp visible through the lower shrubs behind him indicated that he'd done just that.

Picking up the water jugs, she hoisted them to her hips and headed into the bushes. "I guess that does it for today then." Leaves rustled as she pushed through the foliage and bent to put the water beneath the protection of a low palm where Aaron had put their blankets. He obviously intended for them to sleep beneath its leafy canopy tonight.

His voice, edged with disbelief, followed her. "What happened to your all-fired rush to get out of here?"

She'd had a feeling he might ask that question. The trouble with the answer was that she wasn't quite sure what it was that had lessened her determination. Maybe it was simply the serenity of the island. The pressures and stresses she normally felt had no place here. There was no rushing a sunrise or sunset and the tasks of meeting simple, basic needs—of making sure they had food and water and a place to sleep—made the pace of the life she led in Boston seem so harried. Or, possibly, the reason she didn't feel quite so compelled to hurry back to the demands of that life was because, for the first time, she felt just a little bit free.

Her smile felt as if it came a little easier than usual, too. "Like you said," she reminded him, "we can only do one thing at a time. Right now, I think we should catch dinner. Interested?"

He gave her a dubious look. "In dinner, or in catching it?"

"In dinner. I'll take care of the rest. Do you like crab? I saw some by the inlet."

His skepticism increased. "Do you know how to catch them?"

"No," she admitted, undaunted by the technicality. "Do you?"

The late-afternoon sun picked out the hints of silver in his wheat-colored hair as he nodded. "I've done it before."

"Then, will you show me how?"

He didn't show her. He told her. And a half-an-hour later, she was staring into the water in search of their meal.

"Will that really work?"

"I don't know why it shouldn't," he said from his perch on a boulder behind her. "Seems pretty straightforward to me."

She'd made it clear that she wanted to do this by herself and Aaron obligingly withheld any offer of assistance—other than the verbal variety.

"Just drop the bait and when one comes from under its rock, snag it with the net."

It sounded as simple as it was—or could have been had Aaron not been watching her as if she were the evening's entertainment. Not particularly enamored with the idea of her prospective dinner mistaking her toes for bait, Nicole had stayed on a short outcropping of flat rock just above the incredibly clear water. It was about three feet to the bottom and she could clearly see pincers peeking from between the submerged rocks.

The problem wasn't with reaching them. The handle of the fishing net Aaron had retrieved from the sloop—along with a pot to boil the crab in—was long enough. It was just that to reach down there, she had to bend over. She was already terribly conscious of how Aaron's eyes kept straying up her legs to her hips.

"I'm getting awful hungry," he prodded, leaning back to chew on a piece of sea grass.

His mood had improved tremendously. Meeting the teasing in his eyes, she gave him as bland a look as she could manage and turned to her task. Sitting on the edge with her legs tucked beneath her, she dropped a small piece of pâté into the shallow water and promptly forgot about Aaron's gaze raking her backside as an orange-colored crab the size of a dinner plate scooted out sideways from its shelter.

Nicole leaned out, catching that one and another that darted out after it to claim a share of the bait. Though the abundance of sea life surrounding the island would have made it nearly impossible not to catch *something* edible, she felt terribly proud of herself. She'd never caught her own food before. That sense of accomplishment was unabashedly betrayed by the grin lighting her face when she held her heavy, dripping and crustacean-laden net out to Aaron.

"Dinner," she announced and felt her breath catch when she saw the pure pleasure in Aaron's eyes. A hint of something electric lingered in his glance. But only long enough for her to wonder if she'd seen it at all.

As he lifted himself to stand in front of her, her only thought was that he seemed to have enjoyed watching her as much as she'd enjoyed herself. She was grateful for that, she supposed. At least he wasn't as edgy as he'd been a while ago. She didn't know which was worse; his frowns or his smiles. Both played their own kind of havoc with her senses.

Nicole had never honestly given her senses much thought before. To her, they were rather like a heartbeat or breathing; essential in their function, but easily taken for granted because they were always there. Being with Aaron somehow made her pay attention to all she had been too busy to notice before. Possibly, because he demanded it.

Because of him, she'd become more aware of subtleties that had eluded her until now. She was more attuned to her surroundings—and to him. She noticed little things, such as the rough-tender feel of his callused hand as he clasped hers to help her over the large flat rocks. She found, too, that she appreciated the colors of the sunrise, and the inky darkness of an evening sky. When his eyes smiled into hers after she finally managed to build a fire of dry grass and breadfruit tree twigs, she discovered that sea-green was nature's most seductive hue.

They sat on a blanket in the sand, the fire crackling as they washed down succulent chunks of crab with a bottle of vintage champagne. Her legs tucked beneath her, a linen napkin on her lap collecting bits of shell, Nicole took another sip of the sparkling wine. "Somehow," she said, "this doesn't seem like being shipwrecked."

Aaron merely smiled at her wistful tone and held up the bottle. "More?"

A moment's hesitation preceded her quiet, "I shouldn't. I don't usually have more than one glass of wine."

Indulgence marked his expression. He still held the bottle. "You haven't answered me. You said you shouldn't, which means that you still could. And you said you don't usually, which means that you could on occasion. How about a simple yes or no? Do you want more?"

Had she ever had a second glass? At the moment, she couldn't remember. Whatever the case, she was positive she'd never had a third.

"Yes, please," she said and watched an expression of curiosity move into his eyes.

He said nothing as he refilled her glass, then added more to his own. By the time they finished their meal and washed up after burying the shells, the first bottle of champagne was gone.

At Nicole's request, Aaron opened another.

The sun hung above the horizon, an hour away from sunset. Leaning back on his elbow on the blanket, he stared out at the *Valiant* anchored in the calm sea. Even from here, he could see the two-foot wide gash just above its waterline. Beyond them, a quarter of a mile away, a rocky ledge jutted from the island. Covering its rugged angles were fallen slabs of shale. It was his guess that the hull had met one of those jagged boulders before the storm had tossed the ship farther down the shore and stuck the keel in the sandbar.

He'd mentioned that theory to Nicole as they'd eaten and they'd both agreed that the damage could have been worse, all things considered. A companionable silence had eventually settled between them. Aaron didn't want to disturb it. After his remarks this morning about how she should face whatever role it was that she was playing and then coming down on her as he had when she'd returned from the spring this afternoon, he figured he'd best keep his mouth shut. With a few minor exceptions—basic survival being one of them—who she was and what she did was really none of his business.

That was what his logic told him. And that logic would probably have worked just fine if he hadn't been so fascinated with the little transformations he could see taking place within her. She was like a butterfly slowly emerging from a cocoon; not sure she wanted to venture out of that safe shell, yet lured by the vastness of what lay beyond its confines. Her wings were far from developed, though. Leaving that shell in too big a rush could result in all manner of disaster.

She didn't seem to notice when he surreptitiously moved the bottle of champagne out of her reach.

The shadow of the sloop wavered in the rippling turquoise surf. Nicole, her bottom lip caught between her teeth as she pushed her breeze-blown hair away from her face, seemed to be contemplating the *Valiant*, too.

Her musings confirmed his suspicion.

"My father's going to have a fit when he sees that. Even if we can get there before the regatta, there won't be time to fix it properly before the race."

"There will be other races."

She gave a soft, rather unladylike snort and took another sip of her wine. "You don't know my father. He doesn't appreciate being prevented from doing what he wants. He's entered the *Valiant* for the past five years, and won his class all but the first year. The reason he had it refitted this year was because he wanted to beat his best winning time."

It seemed that her father was a man who competed with everyone, including himself. To be fair, Aaron had to admit that he'd been guilty of possessing that same drive, but it bothered him that Nicole would think her father would even care about his boat considering that her personal safety had been at stake. "Don't you get along with him?"

"We get along fine," she returned, looking very much as if she couldn't understand why he'd asked such a question.

It occurred to Aaron that yesterday she'd been puzzled by his remark about how he was sure her family was worried about her. The thought had seemed to catch her off-guard, as if the idea of someone being concerned about her was a totally foreign possibility. Was that because she didn't have any other family? he wondered. That would explain part of her reaction. Since she'd spoken only of her father, maybe he was all she had.

She confirmed that suspicion when he asked about brothers and sisters.

"It's just my father and me," she told him, seeming fascinated with the bubbles on the inside of her glass. "It almost always has been."

Aaron couldn't begin to explain why, but he didn't care for that idea at all. The impression he'd gotten of Harrington Stewart so far was far from favorable.

"What exactly is it that your father does?" he asked, not bothering to be subtle about his curiosity. "He must be into something fairly lucrative to own an island."

She held up her glass, still entranced by the way the bubbles clung tenaciously to the sides then suddenly broke free for a rapid race to the surface. Lowering it again, she smiled vaguely at his understatement.

To say that her father's concerns were "fairly lucrative" was like comparing a Fortune 500 company to a lemonade stand. Harrington Stewart was worth millions. "Shipping,

IT'S FUN! IT'S FREE!
AND IT COULD MAKE YOU A
MILLIONAIRE

If you've ever played scratch-off lottery tickets, you should be familiar with how our games work. On each of the first four tickets (numbered 1 to 4 in the upper right)—there are PINK METALLIC STRIPS to scratch off.

Using a coin, do just that—carefully scratch the PINK STRIPS to reveal how much each ticket could be worth if it is a winning ticket. Tickets could be worth from $5.00 to $1,000,000.00 in lifetime money.

Note, also, that each of your 4 tickets has a unique sweepstakes Lucky Number...and that's 4 chances for a **BIG WIN!**

FREE BOOKS!

At the same time you play your tickets for big cash prizes, you are invited to play ticket #5 for the chance to get one or more free book(s) from Silhouette. We give away free book(s) to introduce readers to the benefits of the *Silhouette Reader Service™*.

Accepting the free book(s) places you under no obligation to buy anything! You may keep your free book(s) and return the accompanying statement marked "cancel." But if we don't hear from you, then every month we'll deliver 6 of the newest Silhouette Special Edition ® novels right to your door. You'll pay the low members-only price of just $2.74* each—a savings of 21¢ apiece off the cover price—plus 69¢ for shipping and handling!

Of course, you may play "THE BIG WIN" without requesting any free book(s) by scratching tickets #1 through #4 only. But remember, the first shipment of one or more book(s) is FREE!

PLUS A FREE GIFT!

One more thing, when you accept the free book(s) on ticket #5 you are also entitled to play ticket #6 which is GOOD FOR A VALUABLE GIFT! Like the book(s) this gift is totally free and yours to keep as thanks for giving our Reader Service a try!

So scratch off the PINK STRIPS on all your BIG WIN tickets and send for everything today! You've got nothing to lose and everything to gain!

Here are your BIG WIN Game Tickets, worth from $5.00 to $1,000,000.00 each. Scratch off the PINK METALLIC STRIP on each of your sweepstakes tickets to see what you could win and mail your entry right away. (See official rules in back of book for details!)

This could be your lucky day – GOOD LUCK!

THE BIG WIN — TICKET 1
Scratch PINK METALLIC STRIP to reveal potential value of this ticket if it is a winning ticket. Return all game tickets intact.

LUCKY NUMBER

1J 840781

THE BIG WIN — TICKET 2
Scratch PINK METALLIC STRIP to reveal potential value of this ticket if it is a winning ticket. Return all game tickets intact.

LUCKY NUMBER

3R 842423

THE BIG WIN — TICKET 3
Scratch PINK METALLIC STRIP to reveal potential value of this ticket if it is a winning ticket. Return all game tickets intact.

LUCKY NUMBER

50 840546

THE BIG WIN — TICKET 4
Scratch PINK METALLIC STRIP to reveal potential value of this ticket if it is a winning ticket. Return all game tickets intact.

LUCKY NUMBER

9U 839929

FREE BOOKS — TICKET 5
We're giving away brand new books to selected individuals. Scratch PINK METALLIC STRIP for number of free books you will receive.

AUTHORIZATION CODE

130107-742

FREE GIFT — TICKET 6
We have an outstanding added gift for you if you are accepting our free books. Scratch PINK METALLIC STRIP to reveal gift.

AUTHORIZATION CODE

130107-742

YES! Enter my Lucky Numbers in THE BIG WIN Sweepstakes and tell me if I've won any cash prize. If PINK METALLIC STRIP is scratched off on ticket #5, I will also receive one or more FREE Silhouette Special Edition® novels along with the FREE GIFT on ticket #6, as explained on the opposite page.

(C-SIL-SE 07/90) 335 CIS 8164

NAME _____

ADDRESS _____ APT. _____

CITY _____ PROVINCE _____ POSTAL CODE _____

Offer limited to one per household and not valid to current Silhouette Special Edition® subscribers.
©1990 HARLEQUIN ENTERPRISES LIMITED

PRINTED IN U.S.A.

Carefully
detach card
along dotted
lines and
mail today!
Play your
<u>all</u>
BIG WIN
tickets
and get
everything
you're
entitled to—
including
FREE BOOKS
and a
FREE GIFT!

**Business
Reply Mail**

No Postage Stamp
Necessary if Mailed
in Canada

Postage will be paid by

SILHOUETTE READER SERVICE ™

THE BIG WIN SWEEPSTAKES

P.O. Box 609
Fort Erie, Ontario
L2A 9Z9

Canada Post
125
Postes Canada

mostly," she finally said. "Oil and grain. That sort of thing. And diamonds. The market, of course," she added, because everyone seemed to be into that. She understood very little about it though. Her trust fund was handled by her father's experts and she put most of the ridiculous sums she received for her living-expenses into regular savings accounts. "I can't remember attending anything lately where the Dow Jones averages haven't been a major topic of conversation. Or pork bellies," she tacked on with a smile. "It's amazing how big they are in the commodities market."

Aaron tried to smile back, though it was difficult to share her faint amusement with the topic. How well he remembered being sucked into those discussions, or instigating them himself. But he didn't want to think of that now. Having pigeonholed the inimitable Harrington, he moved on.

"Jake said he's from Boston. Is that where his offices are?"

"Actually, we live across the river." She took a sip of her champagne, catching the drop that clung to the edge of her glass with the tip of her tongue. "In Cambridge," she clarified, and glanced up to see that he was following her every move.

Suddenly self-conscious, she turned her attention to brushing the sand from the edge of the tarp and started to answer the rest of his question. Before she could, Aaron cut her off.

"We?"

"My father and I."

The slight frown accompanying her response made it appear as if she found his incomprehension inexplicable. And actually, he didn't quite know what to make of what she'd said. He hadn't given the matter any specific consideration, but if he had, he'd have thought she'd have her own place. A brownstone on Nob Hill, perhaps. Or an apartment at one of the more exclusive addresses. It never would have occurred to him that she'd still be living with her father.

"Have you always lived at home?"

"Except for when I was away at school."

"College, you mean?"

"I lived at home while I was in college. Radcliffe," she added. "I went to boarding schools off and on before that."

Prior to that, Aaron learned as the rest of her champagne disappeared and the sun sank a little lower, she'd had governesses. Two very stuffy ones and one she'd adored but whom her father hadn't liked because the woman, Selina, wasn't a "proper" influence.

She didn't say what it was that Selina had done to prompt her dismissal, and she didn't mention her mother, other than to add that the first governess had been hired shortly after her mother had left them.

He thought both omissions odd, but it was her reluctance to talk about her mother that he found more curious. The most he could get out of her was that her mother had left when Nicole was eight and that she had died a few years later. He let the subject drop. He had the feeling that Nicole didn't talk about herself very much, and he didn't want to give her a reason to clam up now that she was.

The subject of school had been safe enough, so he went back to that, asking her how she'd felt about living away from home while she'd been growing up. The thoughtful silence that preceded her answer gave him the impression no one had ever asked her such a thing before.

Seeming both pleased and unsure of how to respond to his interest, she sent him a cautious glance. "Do you really want to know?"

"Yeah," he said, finding the look in her eyes impossibly vulnerable. "I really want to know."

Her smile was soft, its essence almost childlike. She turned away before she answered him, as if the words she spoke were as much an admission to herself and a response to him. "I didn't like it very much."

Aaron couldn't help but marvel at her understatement. He also couldn't help feeling certain that she'd endured those years without complaint. There was a quiet strength about her, a survivor's instinct. He'd seen it at work himself, though he doubted she recognized it. Her diffidence seemed too ingrained. "I bet you never said that to anyone at the time."

Her shrug was dismissive, her eyes fixed on the little pyramid of sand she was building at the edge of the blanket. "It wouldn't have done any good. The circumstances were what they were and nothing I could say would change them. My father always sent for me on holidays," she added, quick to defend the man who had raised her. "At least, he did when he was home. A lot of his interests were outside the country." The pile of sand grew higher. "I really didn't get to see him very much, but I imagine things were difficult for him, too. He was a busy man and a child can be . . . Well, I suppose a child can be quite demanding. He did the best he could."

The lightness in her voice sounded forced and her smile, when she looked back to where Aaron lay watching her a few feet away, was unnaturally bright. "What about you?"

The change of subject was abrupt, but Nicole didn't care. She didn't want to talk about herself anymore. It made her uncomfortable. She wanted to know about him. As long as she had the courage to ask, she would.

"What do you want to know?"

She thought about that for a moment. Having grown increasingly curious about his silences concerning his life, and with his example—and the help of three glasses of champagne—bolder in her own approach, she started with the thing she understood least. "Why do you live on a boat?"

A look of profound indulgence swept over Aaron's unshaven face. "Because I subleased my apartment."

His response was direct, if not particularly enlightening. She tried again. "Why did you do that?"

"I got tired of it." He hesitated. "I got tired of everything."

She took another sip of her champagne. It had to be the wine fueling her persistence. Normally, she'd have dropped the matter right there. He'd sounded either defensive or weary. She couldn't tell which. Either way, this was obviously not his favorite topic of conversation. "Everything?"

"The way I was living. With what I was doing for a living. You name it, I was tired of it."

"What did you do for a living?" she asked, feeling very much as if she should hold her breath.

He smiled then, his casualness at odds with the intent way he watched her. "Nothing so extraordinary. I was a broker for my father's securities firm. He wasn't real pleased when I walked off the floor."

She didn't imagine that he was. Yet, she certainly admired his courage. "You just—"

"Walked out," he completed for her, then gave her a grin so wicked she thought for certain that the ground tilted beneath her.

Or maybe, she mused, thinking she should be alarmed by the sensation, what she felt was merely the effect of the champagne. She'd heard it could have deleterious effects on the equilibrium.

"I guess you could say I'm the black sheep. The present one, anyway. There have always been black sheep in the Wilde family."

She considered his statement as she stared down at her empty glass. Then, as if she'd come to some profound conclusion, she gave him a definite nod—and shoved back the hair that had fallen into her eyes. "If I could, I'd be a black sheep, too."

His smile was indulgent. "You would, huh?"

She nodded again and looked for the bottle. It had somehow gotten on the other side of Aaron. She leaned over, snagging it from where he'd shoved it in the sand to keep it from tipping over. Her fingers had barely closed around its neck when Aaron's hand folded over hers.

"Are you sure you want to do that?"

"Do what?" she returned, aware of little other than the heat of his hand on hers.

"Have any more to drink. I suppose you could tell me its none of my business how much you have, but if you get drunk, I'm the one who has to take care of you."

That should have been a sobering thought. Instead, the idea of him taking care of her seemed rather nice at the moment. "I've never been drunk before," she said, enunciating carefully.

"Trust me," he said, taking the bottle from her. "I have. If you drink much more of this, you'll have a hangover that you won't believe. Champagne can be nasty stuff."

"I've never had a—"

"I know." Sympathy joined what looked suspiciously like amusement. "You've never had a hangover before."

A look of utter amazement lit her eyes. "How did you know that?"

His chuckle made her frown. "Because you just said you'd never been drunk. It's sort of a necessary prerequisite."

He hadn't let go of her hand. That, she was sure, had as much to do with her inability to think clearly as did the alcohol. Feeling quite proud of herself for reaching that conclusion, she mumbled a faint, "Oh," and pulled her hand away.

She was immediately sorry that she'd done that. She'd liked the feel of his strong hand wrapped around hers.

"Do you want to go for a walk?" he asked after she'd sat there for several seconds staring down at her empty glass while she mentally kicked herself for acting so abruptly.

"No." She raised her eyes to his, and swallowed hard. "But I would like for you to kiss me."

It was impossible to tell what thoughts her reckless statement prompted. For several excruciating seconds, he said nothing. He simply sat there holding her glance while she bit her bottom lip and the breeze tossed the silken strands of her hair about her face and shoulders.

He caught one of those strands with his fingers, drawing it slowly away from her cheek. Within the space of a few frantic heartbeats, he leaned forward and touched his lips to the corner of her mouth. Before the warmth of his breath on her cheek could even register, he sat back again.

She closed her eyes and lowered her head. Chaste and quick. A kindly kiss designed to fulfill the wish of a pathetic and slightly inebriated woman.

Propelled by humiliation, she turned away and began to rise.

Aaron's fingers snagged her wrist. Confusion edged his tone. "Hold it! Where are you going?"

"For a walk." Which is what she should have told him she'd do in the first place.

She was on her knees, trying to pull away. The effort was futile. The gentle tug of his hand on her arm canceled her attempt and brought her back down on the blanket with a soft thump. Still holding her wrist, he raised his free hand to cup her face and turn it toward him. His touch was as insistent as his tone. "Talk to me, Nicki. What happened? You asked me to kiss you and I did."

"I shouldn't have done that."

"You mean you didn't want me to kiss you?"

"No." She shook her head, the motion making it feel fuzzier than it already was. "I mean, yes. I wanted you to to, but I shouldn't have asked."

"Why not?"

She focused on his face, unable to believe the sincerity she saw there. The man was a louse for making her say this. "Because you didn't want to do it. Because I feel like a fool for asking you. Will you let me go now?"

His response was a terse expletive, followed immediately by a shift in positions. Taking her by the shoulders, he drew her against him so abruptly that she had to grip his arms to keep from toppling over him.

"I'll make you a deal," he muttered tightly. "You don't tell me what I want and I won't presume to second-guess you. You said before that you can't read my mind. Well, I can't read yours either. You're going to have to tell me what you wanted."

"I can't," she whispered, not sure she even knew anymore. She felt overwhelmed, completely out of her element.

His words became gentle. The heat in his eyes did not. "Then show me."

Show him?

"You kiss me," he told her when she hesitated. "Show me what you wanted."

In the waning sunlight, she could clearly see the tension etched in his strong features. That same tension pulled at her, making it impossible for her to move even when he eased his grip on her arms.

She didn't want to move anyway. Compelled by a heady sense of recklessness, she raised her hand to his cheek, cupping it as he had hers only moments ago. His hand had been steady, though. Hers was trembling.

Slowly, uncertainly, she inched forward.

The touch of her lips to his was tentative at best, and wholly experimental. Though kissing someone seemed fairly straightforward, she'd never taken the initiative before, so she didn't know what he would expect. His mouth felt firm beneath hers, yet soft and incredibly warm. She pressed a bit harder, hoping he would open his mouth as he had yesterday. To encourage him, she hesitantly touched the tip of her tongue to his top lip. He had done that to her and just remembering how his tongue had felt in her mouth made her insides turn liquid.

A low, faintly guttural sound rumbled from deep within his chest. Encouraged by that vaguely primitive groan, she let her thumb caress the hollow of his cheek.

"Is that all you had in mind?" he asked, his voice a raw whisper when she pulled away.

Feeling herself grow soft at the feral gleam in his eyes, she managed a totally honest, "Not quite."

"Maybe we'd better try again."

This time, he met her halfway. The kiss was long and slow and deep and in the space of those luscious, lingering moments, he somehow managed to reduce conscious thought to little more than a series of fleeting impressions.

Her only coherent thought when long moments later the kiss turned feverish and he drew her down on top of him, was that he was wrong. He *could* read her mind. This is what she'd wanted—to feel again his strength and the raw, elemental awareness she'd never before known had existed. In his arms she felt alive and vital.

Under any other circumstances, Aaron would have been more than willing to take what she seemed to be offering. It had been over a year since he'd been with a woman; longer than that since he'd felt anything beyond the need for only simple physical release. But he wasn't about to take advantage of a slightly inebriated woman whom he strongly suspected had never been with a man before.

She pressed her lips to the side of his neck, the warmth of her breath as tantalizing as the feel of her fingers drifting over his chest. Her untutored touch was every bit as seductive as a more practiced one. More so really, because she seemed to be learning from him. By following his lead, she quickly perfected the feather-light strokes she ran down his side. Of her own accord, she carried that touch to his shoulder and placed a gentle kiss to the bruise beneath his shirt before tucking her head against the side of his neck.

"You saved my life," she murmured so softly that he barely heard her. "I've never thanked you for that."

Gratitude, he thought. So that's where this is coming from. "No need," he whispered, feathering his lips over the delicate shape of her ear.

She said nothing else as his hands moved in slow circles along her back and over the seductive curve of her hips. Loath to end what was little more than a refined form of torture, he knew he had no choice but to move her away. He should have done so long before now. Each second he delayed made pulling away from her that much more difficult.

Trailing his fingers down her spine, his touch drifted to her bare legs to caress the back of her thigh.

She made a faint, almost kittenish sound and his hand moved higher, sneaking beneath the short hem of her skirt. Higher still as his palm molded the firm curve of her bottom. A few moments later, questioning his sanity for subjecting himself to this agony, he went utterly, completely still. She wasn't wearing any underwear.

She also wasn't moving anymore.

It seemed that consuming nearly an entire bottle of champagne had not only made Nicole bolder, it had also put her to sleep.

Chapter Seven

Honest, Nicki," she heard Aaron say with a thoughtfully subdued chuckle, "you could feel worse. Probably not *much* worse," he added while she squinted at the cup of the tea he'd made for her. Coffee might have been better, he'd said, if they'd had it. All he'd been able to find on the sloop was a box of tea bags. "But at least you passed out before you could finish the other bottle. Just think of how bad you'd feel if you'd managed to polish off that."

Considering such a circumstance was not something Nicole cared to do at the moment. As it was, had she the energy, she would have found her behavior last night appalling. Lacking that energy, she could concentrate only on the dull throbbing in her head and on her desire that Aaron go away. No one should be allowed to be philosophical around a person who's head felt like an echo chamber for the percussion section of the Boston Symphony.

Other than to sit up, she hadn't moved from where she'd slept. The plaid blanket Aaron had covered her with had fallen to her waist. Crossing her legs Indian-fashion beneath it, she watched him move toward her. Despite the faint chill in the salty air, he wore only the tattered cutoffs she assumed he'd slept in.

"Here," he said, bending toward her. "Eat these. They'll make your stomach feel better."

She took the crackers he offered. When he straightened, her gaze fixed on the sinewy muscles of his legs. It didn't seem worth the trouble to tip her head back to meet his eyes. She also didn't care to see the amusement she knew she'd find there. He hadn't come out and said it, but there was an I-told-you-so-attitude about what he was doing that she found monumentally irritating.

"It's not my stomach. It's my head."

His tone was mildly sympathetic. "Drink the tea. Part of your headache is from dehydration. Wine will do that to you."

The mere mention of the drink that had done this to her almost made her stomach turn. Taking a bite of cracker, she dutifully washed it down with the strong tea. Aaron sounded very much as if he knew what he was talking about when it came to these remedies. Though she hesitated to think of why he was so knowledgeable about the subject, and despite her wish that he'd leave her to suffer her indignity alone, she nonetheless appreciated what he was doing for her.

She only wished he'd stop looking at her as if she were a prime case of arrested development. What difference did it make that she was only now discovering things most eighteen-year-olds considered old hat?

The ever-present breeze rattled the palm fronds overhead, knocking loose a few of the thread-like fibers that edged the leaves. One of them landed on the fringe of her blanket and she picked it up to pull it through her fingers.

Aaron apparently realized that she was going to be lousy company for a while. After checking his canvas deck shoes to make sure nothing had spent the night there, he knelt to put them on. "If you'll be all right here for a few hours, I'm going to walk to the other end of the island and see what's there. I'll see what I can find us for lunch, too. I think it'd be a good idea to save the food we have in case we need it later."

Even as bad as she felt, she understood the implication in his casually delivered statement. There was a possibility that the sloop couldn't be repaired; that when their food supply ran out, they would be completely dependent on what fare the island offered. At best, should he manage to fix the hull, they faced a two- to five-day trip to their destination.

Later, when the pounding in her head stopped, she might indulge in a little panic at those thoughts. For now, all she did was tell him she was fine, a harmless little lie he didn't seem to believe anyway, then lay back down to sleep off her very first—and most assuredly her last—hangover. Some experiences, she'd discovered, were not necessarily worth having.

But some, she found herself thinking a few hours later, definitely were. Showering beneath a waterfall was one of them.

Water from the spring-fed pool at the top of the hill tumbled in a crystalline cascade over a knifelike ledge of slate. Eight feet below, it sliced into a larger pond of sparkling clear water bordered by mossy rocks and ferns as delicate as handmade lace. Surrounded on three sides by an emerald jungle and with the falls facing an infinite expanse of sapphire sea, the setting offered a sense of protection as well as a feeling of unfettered freedom.

Maybe, Nicole thought, skirting a patch of tiny yellow flowers peeking through the sweet-smelling grass along the pond's edge, it was that combination which so intrigued her about the idyllic place. The sense of protection and freedom. Certainly those same qualities were what drew her to Aaron. In many ways, he seemed to encourage her new-found sense of discovery, while at the same time keeping a watchful, though slightly wary, eye on her.

She stopped at the edge of the water to set down her soap and the undergarments she'd rinsed out yesterday.

She wasn't going to bother denying her attraction to him. Nor would she attempt to rationalize her behavior last night. Were she prone to do so, she was certain she could easily blame her actions on the extraordinary circumstances she'd found herself in. But Nicole wasn't in the habit of looking for excuses for herself. She took responsibility for what she did and what she felt and, though the thought terrified her, she had to admit that she was inexorably drawn to Aaron—despite the fact that he represented everything she found frightening and foreign. She felt as if she were standing at the edge of a precipice knowing she was about to fall, but unable to pull herself back.

Nicole needed security. She needed to know who she was and what was expected of her. Perhaps that was why she had been content living with her father for so long. Working for him, taking care of his household, she always knew her position and where she belonged. She had a routine and schedules and duties and those, by their very nature, gave her stability.

But Aaron had walked out—as her mother had—on the very kind of stable life she so cherished. He hadn't given her any of the details, but he'd freely admitted that he'd abandoned everything and everyone to become a drifter. He was a man who had turned his back on responsibility, whose home was never in the same port for more than a month, and who clearly wanted no ties.

Shaking her head to dispel the disquieting thoughts, she unfastened her skirt. Immediately, she hesitated. With Aaron off checking out the end of the island they'd yet to explore, she was quite alone, but she was hardly accustomed to disrobing outdoors. Even so, as she finally slipped her skirt over her hips, she noticed that she didn't experience quite as much hesitation as she had when she'd first undressed to bathe yesterday. Moments later, when she pulled the T-shirt over her head and tossed it aside, she even let herself admit that the feel of sunshine on her bare skin was heavenly. Not nearly so wonderful though, as the feel of Aaron's hands had been.

Bracing herself for the chill, she stepped into the shallow pond and moved toward the waterfall. She'd heard that too much alcohol sometimes made people unaware of what they were doing, or that it made them unable to later recall what they had done. It appeared that multiple glasses of champagne did not affect her in such a way. She may have lost a fair proportion of her inhibitions, but she could remember with heart-stopping clarity everything that had happened, and how it had felt. At least she could remember everything up until the time she'd fallen asleep—or passed out as Aaron had so charitably phrased it. But what she recalled now, what she hadn't been able to forget all morning, is that she'd wanted him to teach her how to make love with him. It wasn't wise. It wasn't practical. But it was what she wanted—and she'd never let herself want before.

She was hardly an expert on the subject, but after the way he'd touched her, she thought he wanted her, too.

With a deep breath at that thought, and a gasp for the chill, she stepped beneath the cascade. The water slid over her long limbs, raising a layer of goose bumps over her entire body. Dealing with the faint shock of cool water, and rather surprised at how quickly it helped to clear the last traces of fog from her brain, it was several moments before she noticed that she was no longer alone.

When her skin adjusted to the cooler temperature, she tipped her head to let the water smooth her dark hair away from her face. Since the force of water had plastered her hair to the narrow line of her back, she stepped away from the fall and raised her arms to lift her hair from her neck so she could wash it.

She couldn't do that without her shampoo.

Preoccupied as she'd been with thoughts of Aaron—and wondering if she shouldn't be making a hasty emotional retreat—she'd forgotten to bring the bottle with her. It lay fifteen feet away with her clothes.

She glanced in that direction, resigned to the inconvenience of having to retrieve it. An instant later, resignation was about the last thing she felt.

Her gaze locked on Aaron's gray-green eyes.

Aaron didn't move and she couldn't seem to. He stood beside her discarded clothes, his face devoid of all expression. Her own features had gone utterly still. Feeling as if she were operating in slow motion, she lowered her arms, leaving them at her sides. It seemed foolish, even hypocritical somehow, to try to cover herself now.

If it hadn't been for the heat in his eyes, she might have thought he found nothing remarkable about the way he'd found her. But that heat flickered brightly as his glance moved along her shoulders to settle on her water-slicked breasts. Her dusky nipples, already taut, grew pebble-hard beneath his visual caress.

She saw his mouth open slightly, as if he'd just drawn a deep and difficult breath. When his tongue unconsciously touched his upper lip, she felt her own breathing alter.

Something hot and liquid formed inside her chest. That sensation intensified, moving downward with his glance as he drew it over her stomach and along the length of her legs. Slowly, his eyes returned to meet the unashamed vulnerability in hers.

Her heart felt as if it had stopped beating. Something raw and heavy filled the air between them, swirling around her like the mist from the roaring waterfall. That tension taunted and teased, threatened and promised, and Nicole was aware of nothing so much as the elemental hunger Aaron had awakened inside her.

Moments later, it was as if a door slammed shut. Aaron closed his eyes, his expression tortured and bleak. Without a word or a gesture, he turned to walk away.

It was almost evening before Aaron finally saw Nicole again. She sat on the beach around the curve of the inlet not visible from their camp. His relief at having found her was carefully masked.

He saw her look up at his approach. Hugging her knees, she immediately turned back to look out at the darkening sea. Clouds had long ago blocked out the sun and the air was chill without its warmth. All afternoon, it had felt to Aaron as if it might rain.

He tried to keep his tone light as he hunched down beside her. "Don't you think it's about time you came back? It'll be dark soon."

Curled up into herself as she was, he didn't know if she was cold or if the position was merely self-protective. He did know that she'd been left pretty defenseless. She didn't even try to mask her insecurity with the haughty bravado he'd so often seen her fall back on.

"I'll be there in a while."

She hadn't looked at him and the flatness in her voice made him feel worse than he already did. Walking away from her this afternoon was about the most difficult thing he'd ever done—and one of the most necessary.

There had been a time in Aaron's life when he'd have taken what she'd offered without a second thought. He knew how to use people, manipulate them. But he wasn't going to take advantage of her innocence. He couldn't do that to her.

He sat down beside her, cringing a little inside when he saw her stiffen. She didn't move away, though, nor did she do anything else to acknowledge his presence. She was hurt and it was his fault. He'd hurt people before and it hadn't mattered. It did now, and he didn't like the feeling at all.

"Nicki," he began and she immediately cut him off.

"Don't call me that. My name is Nicole."

"Nicole," he corrected, not feeling the time appropriate to question her sudden preference. "About this afternoon—"

"I don't want to talk about it."

"I do," he returned and caught her by the arm when she started to get up. "And I want you to listen. I didn't mean to walk up on you like that. I thought you'd just gone up to fill the water jugs and I was going to help you bring them back down. I wish to God now that I hadn't."

There was more truth in his words than she was likely to believe. The memory of how she'd looked draped in the cascading water, her head tipped back in abandon, taunted him even now. But it was the memory of how she'd appeared when she'd stepped from the crystalline fall, her lithe body glistening in the sunlight and her arms raised to lift her heavy hair, that might very well haunt him forever.

"But my seeing you isn't why you've avoided me all day, is it?" he prodded. "The problem was my leaving."

He didn't need for her to acknowledge him. As attuned as they'd been to each other, he was painfully aware of the nature of their current problem. In the past six hours, he'd thought of little else.

"Nicki," he went on, because, despite her protest, that was the name that suited the woman he'd come to know, "I left because it would have been a mistake to stay. If I'd touched you, we'd have wound up making love." His voice became gentler, making his next words a statement rather than a question. "You've never made love before, have you?"

Her head was lowered, her hair falling in a dark veil over her shoulders. "No," she whispered into the breeze.

She made the admission sound like a failure, as if she were blaming herself for being undesirable. The woman clearly didn't understand her power, or the seductive pull of her innocence. It filled him with a fierce possessiveness, yet at the same time, he wanted what she'd given no other man. The intensity of that desire was a little frightening.

He knew the skin of his hands was rough, so he kept his touch gentle as he tipped her face toward him. "You know nothing about me. And chances are when we leave here, you'll go on with your life and I'll go on with mine. I can't promise you anything."

She could feel no more devastated than she had at the moment Aaron had turned from her at the falls. But what she felt, too, was an odd kind of sympathy for him. He was being completely honest with her, trying to make her see what she obviously chose to overlook.

There was no reason to make it any more difficult for him. "It's okay if you don't want me. I understand."

Something raw and thrilling entered Aaron's eyes. It seemed to intensify as his glance moved to her mouth, warming her much as the heat of his palm warmed her neck when he slid it beneath her hair and drew her forward. His voice was a low, guttural hiss. "I do want you, damn it. I want you so bad that I hurt. I just don't want the complications. This may all seem a little like *Paradise Lost* to you, but you have to live with the consequences of whatever happens here. So do I. And I don't need the guilt of knowing I caused you to do something you'd regret. Regrets are damned hard to live with."

His expression hardened. She held her breath, wondering what he meant to do. But instead of kissing her as she hoped, he withdrew his hand from her neck, seeming to not trust himself with the contact. A moment later, he draped his forearms over his raised knees and looked out to the sea. Whatever had prompted his certainty about regrets had pulled him farther from her.

Nicole hugged her own knees tighter. Later, she told herself. Later, she could feel foolish for not having considered the more practical realities of their situation. She wasn't surprised that Aaron had thought of them. He was one of those rare individuals who was his own master, who knew the difference between what he could control or change and what he had to accept—and had the strength that acceptance required. She wanted very much to know how he had come by his wisdom. But for now, she wanted to feel only the relief of knowing that he hadn't really rejected her.

He'd also protected his precious freedom, but she could hardly fault him for that. Having tasted a little of it herself in the past couple of days, she understood its allure—and the price he'd paid for it. She'd recognized the loneliness behind his smiles. It was there as he smiled at her now.

"Hell of a mess we've got ourselves in, huh?"

She met the teasing light in his eyes, relieved at his attempt to diffuse the strain between them. "Hell of a mess," she agreed and watched his eyebrow arch when he heard her swear.

"Come on." Lifting himself to his feet, he held out his hand to help her up. The instant she was on her feet, he released her, careful to keep the contact brief. "We've got a long walk ahead of us. We should go before it gets much darker."

He was very careful not to touch her now. But that was only part of the cause for the faint frown that shadowed Nicole's expression as she swatted the sand from her skirt. She knew she'd walked for miles while trying to sort out her thoughts this afternoon, but she was sure their camp was just beyond the curve of the beach. "Aren't our things just around there?" she asked, indicating the direction from which he'd come.

"Not anymore. I found a cave that will keep us dry if it rains. It's farther from the sloop, but we'll be more comfortable there."

The air was cooling rapidly and the shiver that ran through Nicole was partly from the chill. Mostly, it was trepidation. A cave sounded a lot more permanent than open beach or a canopy of palm trees. And just this morning, subsistence living had become something of a necessity.

The first drops of rain kept her from dwelling on what that all might mean.

The clouds had formed a solid ceiling, dimming what was left of the evening light to a pale pearl gray. The sky didn't look nearly as ominous to her as the one that had brewed itself and the sea into a sloshing cauldron. But it promised a solid drenching to anyone foolish enough to take her time gaining cover.

A sporadic drizzle followed them to where their camp had been that morning, but the drops grew more constant as they hurried through the knee-high grass that bordered the rock ledge containing their new dwelling. Within minutes of Aaron leading her to the small cave, nature turned the waterworks on full force and was putting on a rather impressive light show. Fortunately, the wind was little more than a stiff breeze. Otherwise, it could have driven the rain right in with them.

As it was, the interior of the grotto-like chamber was fairly dry, protected as it was by its outcropping of rocks overhead and enormous ferns and hibiscus along its entrance.

Nicole stood at that opening hugging her blanket around her while she watched the gray sky turn black. Her perspective on storms had changed in the past few days. They were beautiful to watch, but only from a distance. She was enormously grateful to Aaron for having found this shelter for them, and had told him so. He'd shrugged the accomplishment off as luck. He'd found it while looking for her.

"I wonder how long this will last?"

Behind her she heard the click of the flashlight as Aaron turned it off. The shadows fled from the craggy rock walls, the darkness hiding the neat beds Aaron had made for them on the tarps and the box storing their meager supplies. The tube of maps, which might very well prove useless, had been propped in the curve of the wall.

She felt him stop beside her, then saw his strong profile in a fleeting burst of illumination. "Depends. Tropical storms can last minutes or hours. I saw one last for three days."

"When was that?"

"Last summer. I was off the Azores heading for the Canaries."

He'd mentioned once that he'd promised himself he would sail around the world, and that, so far, he'd only made it halfway.

"Where will you go when we leave here?"

She knew that the premise of her question was shaky. But right now whether or not they got off the island wasn't the point. He'd said she didn't know him, but he was only partially right. She knew that, with her, he was honorable and honest, qualities not necessarily possessed by many of the men she'd once thought more "civilized" than he. Now, she wanted to know the part of himself that he guarded. She wanted to know what his hopes were, and his dreams. She'd never allowed herself to dream, but she was sure that Aaron did. She had the feeling that his dreams had somehow sustained him.

The distant roll of thunder could be heard over the steady fall of rain. He was watching the storm, as she was. "Australia," he returned. "I'll pick up my sloop and head through the Caribbean to the Panama Canal before it's closed off to us. I want to be in the Pacific before the end of September." A droll note entered his voice, along with a hint of a smile. "Once I get below the equator, the weather should be better."

"Don't you get tired of sailing? I can understand why you'd like it on the clear days, but day's like these—"

"Days like these are why I do it."

"I don't understand," she said, when he fell silent.

Except for the infrequent flashes of lightning, it was difficult to see much of anything. When Aaron moved from the arch-shaped opening, it was impossible for Nicole to see him at all. She could hear him moving farther into the cave and knew by the muffled rustle of blankets that he'd either sat or laid down on his bed.

For a moment, she thought he meant to ignore her quiet appeal to understand.

"It's days like these on the sea that have helped me put things in perspective. There isn't a whole lot that matters to you when all that's keeping you alive is your own wits and the whims of nature. Life itself becomes more precious than anything else." A considered silence filled the dark and cozy space. "But you already know that."

A note of intimacy shaded his last words, telling her he knew he didn't have to explain any further. They shared something most other people wouldn't comprehend. Having survived the storm that had landed them here, she knew what it was like to face her own mortality. More important, she knew how having done that could change the significance of a person's concerns.

"What were you trying to put into perspective?"

A cool, cynical chuckle preceded a flat, "My life. It was pretty screwed up. Royally screwed up, in fact."

Darkness held the illusion of anonymity. Maybe, Aaron thought, that was why he responded to her quiet, "How?" without qualifying his response.

"I had everything. The right Manhattan apartment. The right suits hanging in my closet. The right art hanging on my walls. The owners of the right restaurants knew me by name and I had my 'power-lunches' at the right tables." His self-derision became more acute. "I was even engaged to a woman as caught up in all that as I was."

A flash of lightning provided enough illumination for Nicole to see that Aaron was sitting with his back to the rocky wall. Her bed was only a few feet from his. She moved toward it, as careful to avoid him as he had been to avoid her.

"What happened," he heard her ask as she worked her way through the darkness.

He had never verbalized these thoughts, though for months they had been his constant companions. Now that he was about to, he didn't know if he even knew where to start—or why it was so important to him that Nicole know the kind of man he had once been. She could be repelled by the knowledge. It might be just as well if she were. But now that he'd said as much as he had, he found that the words came with surprising ease.

Aaron had been taught early on that money and power were what made a man—and his own father respected no man who was not a success. Aaron, being his father's son, was therefore determined to have it all. But somewhere in his ambition to succeed—to prove that he was a man—he became blind to what was happening to himself. It wasn't until Lynn, his fiancée and a financial whiz in her own right, had said she wanted them to buy a summer home in the country that he began to take a look around himself.

Aside from the fact that he preferred the beach to the country, they hadn't needed a summer home. They both spent so much time at their respective offices or wining and dining clients that they were rarely in the apartment they'd shared. And then he'd started looking around the apartment itself, at all the things—expensive, trendy and useless things—he had acquired and started to ask himself why he kept pushing himself to have more. More money, more power, more *things*. Those had become his only goals and they had made him into a person he no longer recognized. He didn't like the man he had become, the one who walked over and on people to get what he wanted.

"When I tried to talk to Lynn about this, she looked at me like I'd just shaved my head and said I'd feel better after a good night's sleep. That's when I told her that I was serious about making some changes, and she told me that if I wanted to make any changes, I'd have to make them without her. She liked her life exactly the way it was. We split a few days later.

"Three weeks after that, I was in a deal that would have made a lot of people a lot of money, myself included. But part of the deal meant selling a block of stock that would put a small mill in Indiana into bankruptcy and that would have put about fifty people in an already depressed area out of work. There was no way I could stop the sale. If I wouldn't put in the call, another broker would. But I couldn't do it. I walked out two hours before the closing bell, bought a sailboat and never went back.''

And he'd named that boat *Salvation*. It was entirely possible, Nicole realized now, that it had been just that.

The rain had eased, its patter on the wide-leafed plants gentler now. Nicole sensed that Aaron was looking toward the shadowy opening, seeking in nature the peace he always seemed to find there.

''I'd always dreamed of sailing around the world,'' she heard him say. ''And after leaving all that behind, it seemed like a good way to rediscover who I was. A man learns what he's made of when he has only himself to rely on.''

She had the feeling that he'd glossed over much of what had gone on in his life before. But she knew the type of man he must have once been. There were many of them in her father's circle. It was difficult, though, for her to reconcile the picture Aaron had drawn of himself with the man she now knew.

''What about your family? What did they say when you left?''

''Dad blamed it all on Lynn. He said the competition between us was what got in the way and that I'd be back to work in no time. Mom said she didn't care what I did as long as I was happy. It took a while, but they've accepted what I've chosen to do, though I know neither one of them really understands why I haven't gone back yet.''

''Why haven't you?''

His tone became more casual, some of the tension she'd sensed in him seeming to dissipate. "Because I haven't been to Australia yet."

She smiled into the darkness. "Do you know what you'll do after that?"

"Not really. I haven't thought that far ahead."

She could appreciate that. She tended to avoid thoughts of the future herself. Mostly that was because the future had always promised to be no different than her present, or her past.

"Doesn't it get lonely relying only on yourself?"

She could feel his hesitation. When he finally spoke, it was with a certain caution. "That depends on what kind of loneliness you're talking about. I'd rather be alone than with someone for the wrong reasons."

Quiet filled the cave, the silence seeming to confirm that the conversation had somehow concluded itself. The rain had eased up even more and after a moment Nicole could easily hear Aaron moving around. He seemed to be stretching out on his blankets.

"We should probably get some sleep now," he said, his voice muffled as if he'd turned to face the rocky wall. "I'd like to get an early start in the morning."

His last statement effectively altered the course of her thoughts. "An early start with what?"

"I think I've figured out a way to fix the hull. But I'll need your help."

"What are you going to do?"

He didn't seem interested in talking anymore. About anything. Saying only that he'd tell her about it later, he fell silent.

Nicole didn't question him further. He could explain his idea to her in the morning.

She figured he probably would have, too. If the sloop hadn't broken away from the shoal.

Chapter Eight

Nicole closed her eyes and prayed for patience. If Aaron told her one more time to pull it tighter, she was going to let go of the darn thing all together.

She gave another tug on the sail. "I'm pulling it as tight as I can," she called from where she sat braced on the bow. "That's as far as it will stretch."

His voice came from beyond the port side of the sloop. He was in the water, trying very hard not to lose his own temper. She wished he would. It might help clear the air. Despite the constant activity, the tension between them had been as thick as espresso all morning.

He must have dived back under the bow. For a moment she heard nothing but blessed silence—followed by the sound of him breaking the surface and a not-so-mild curse.

"There's still a bulge underneath."

"I'm not surprised," she said, refusing to tell him she thought this idea harebrained even though he'd never hesitated to poke holes in her suggestions. Granted, they had to do *something* since the shoal had loosened its grip on the keel, but she didn't think this was the answer.

Gripping the heavy, laminated fabric, she tugged it with her as she crossed the polished teak deck to peer over the edge. The metal bow rail ran two feet above the deck and by lying on her stomach, she could easily slip under it to see what Aaron was doing.

The shadow of the sloop wavered in the gently rolling surf, the line of its tall mast slicing across the rippled pattern of the sandy ocean floor. The water was as transparent as crystal and a pumpkin-orange starfish was clearly visible among a sporadic scattering of shells. A few feet from it lay the secondary anchor Aaron had dropped.

Aaron himself stood in the chest-deep water, pushing his wet hair back from his forehead. He looked frustrated and perplexed and vastly annoyed with this latest turn of events.

Laying on the sail to keep it from slipping, Nicole doggedly drew her attention from the beautiful contours of his iron-hard torso to offer her unsolicited opinion of their progress.

"I really don't think that tying a sail around the hull to cover the hole is going to work."

Aaron's scowl remained fixed. "It's worked before."

"You've done this?"

"I haven't. But this is how sailors used to patch cannon-ball holes in their ships. Once we're underway, the force of the water will hold the sail snug against the hull."

"Won't it leak?"

Exasperation edged into his impatience. "Geeze, Nicole. Of course it'll leak. Just pull on the damn thing, will you?"

She'd grown accustomed to his swearing. It was his use of her more-formal name that told her the situation was disintegrating rapidly.

When they'd awakened this morning, his manner had been distant and coolly polite, as if he meant to maintain civility but intended to avoid all but the most necessary conversation. Nicole had been left with no choice but to think he'd said all he needed to say last night and after what had happened yesterday, he intended to prevent further complications by avoiding her as best he could.

She'd almost convinced herself that he'd chosen the wiser course when she'd noticed the sloop bobbing in the surf. The realization that the keel was breaking away from the shoal had turned his polite indifference into total preoccupation with stabilizing the sloop.

Now, his taciturn attitude was becoming intolerable.

"If you're so sure this'll work, why didn't we do it before?"

"Because," he bit back, "I was hoping to come up with a better idea. I'd have preferred a more solid patch, but that hole's on a curve and everything on this boat that I could use to fix it with is flat. Even if I could manage to bend cabinet doors or decking, we don't have a hammer and nails or glue or tape or anything else to make that kind of a repair. This is all I can think of." His voice dropped to a mumble, his thoughts focused on the sloop rather than on her impatience with him. "This is liable to leak like crazy if we have to tack, but if I can keep it with the wind and fairly level we should make it."

"If we keep bailing," she added at his less-than-certain assumption. "Should" didn't sound anywhere near as definite as she'd prefer him to be.

"It won't sink, if that's what you're worried about."

The memory hadn't had time to dim. Too easily, she could recall being beneath the sea, needing to breathe but inhaling water when what she'd needed was air. She'd awaken at night feeling that panic. Each time she had, her first thought had been to turn to Aaron. He could make her feel safe. But she had stayed where she was, because she knew he didn't want her any closer.

"Of course, I'm worried about it," she said quietly.

Aaron closed his eyes at the apprehension in her softly delivered statement. He'd been so caught up in his own private battle that, until now, he hadn't considered how she might feel about going back out on the boat again.

Making promises wasn't something he did easily. But he didn't hesitate to offer her this one. "I won't set sail until I'm sure this will hold."

He was telling her that he wouldn't take any unnecessary chances, and she believed him. If he felt comfortable sailing the sloop this way, then she would try not to worry about it any more than was absolutely necessary.

"What about your shoulder?" she asked, thinking it a proper concern. "Will you be able to handle the boat?"

She'd noticed that he didn't favor his left arm as much as he had earlier, so she thought his injury must have improved a little. Logic dictated that if he hadn't had the strength he couldn't have roped the sail to the bow as he had—and strength was necessary to handle sails and winches and to steer. Still, the bruise looked awfully painful to her, and it had darkened to a sickly blue.

Her concern warmed her eyes and when Aaron raised his own to meet them, he felt the tension within him shift. She made being indifferent impossible and that was what he'd hoped to be with her. When that had failed, he'd turned his irritation with himself outward and used her to vent his frustration. He was only fooling himself if he thought he could be around her and not want her. He was only human after all, and about as far as a mortal could get from being a saint.

"It'll be fine," he told her, the ache in his shoulder nothing compared to the deeper ache she caused within him. His inability to stop thinking about her frustrated him even more. "But I'll need you to take over once in a while."

"You want me to sail?"

"You have a problem with that?"

It was impossible for her to guess why the testiness had slipped back into his tone. Hating the way they were acting with each other, she kept her own voice as even as she could. "I have no problem with doing what I can. I'm just not sure what I can do. I've always been a passenger."

"How badly do you want off this island?"

He obviously expected her answer to be immediate and certain. A few days ago, Nicole would have expected the same. Finding herself hesitating, she skirted his question. She'd once feared being stranded with him. Now, she wanted nothing more. The irony of it seemed appropriate, if not terribly practical.

She scooted up, her hair swinging forward as she secured the end of the line she held to a cleat on the deck. It wasn't tight enough, but he could take care of it himself. "Maybe this will work better if you pull. Trade places with me."

"What are you doing?"

Ignoring him, she lay flat on her stomach and slid under the railing to swing herself over the edge. With her legs dangling down the side, she took a quick breath and pushed off to slip feet first into the water. She went clear under, emerging a foot from where Aaron stood by the sail-covered hole. Ropes were lashed across the hull, holding the heavy cloth in place.

"You didn't have to come down here," he told her, deliberately reaching for one of the looser ropes. By keeping his hands occupied, he might be able to keep them off of her. She was close. Too close. And far too tempting.

The morning sunlight captured the translucence of her skin, the beads of water that clung to her lashes accenting the darkness of her eyes. A rivulet of salt-water snuck toward the edge of her mouth and with the tip of her tongue, she captured it, unaware of the seduction in the motion.

Droplets flew like diamonds as she flipped her hair away from her face. "I'm obviously not able to pull the ropes tight enough for you, so you go up and do it. I'll take over down here. Just tell me what I'm supposed to do."

The muscles in his jaw jumped. "Go on back up. You were doing fine."

"Right," she muttered. "That's why you've been yelling at me all morning."

"I haven't been yelling at you."

"The hell you haven't."

She hadn't meant to phrase her comment quite that way. But she wasn't going to say she was sorry for her less-than-ladylike language. It seemed to irritate him when she apologized and right now he was definitely irritating her. Reaching past him, she grabbed one of the loose ropes floating near the repair. It had already been tied to the other side and now needed to be stretched around the bow and tied on the other side.

"Are you going to go topside so I can give this to you?"

He looked from the rope in her hand to the very real annoyance in her expression. Three days ago, he wouldn't have believed her capable of acting with such open challenge. But then, three days ago, he couldn't have imagined her standing naked beneath a waterfall looking like Botticelli's Venus, either.

"Well?" she prodded.

He drew closer, his motion causing the water to surge over her shoulders. She had to stand on tiptoe or tread water, and she moved back, thinking he meant to pass.

He didn't move on by, though. He stopped right in front of her, leaving only inches of aqua surf to waver between them. A vaguely predatory light moved into his eyes, his glance sweeping her face. He'd already memorized every fragile angle and plane of her features. He knew about little things, such as the tiny mole under the curve of her jaw, and that her left eyebrow was a bit longer than her right one. And about more intimate details such as the subtle nuances of color in her brown eyes and how the flecks of gold in them seemed to disappear when awareness darkened them. He knew too, the way her mouth softened and opened slightly to allow for a more deeply drawn breath when that awareness sharpened.

The flecks had disappeared and now the inviting curve of her mouth parted.

Taking a stabilizing breath. Nicole sought a little more distance and held out the rope. Aaron's eyes were locked on hers, his glance penetrating and hard. All he'd have to do was curve his hand around her neck to draw her to him. She didn't think he'd do that, though. He'd given her more than enough reason to believe that he wouldn't touch her.

He raised his hand, reaching toward her, and the breath she'd drawn stuck in her throat. She slowly released it a moment later.

He'd taken the rope.

It took the rest of the morning for them to finish. A truce of sorts had been drawn, along with a tacit acceptance of the underlying strain that made casual conversation impossible. Nicole wished desperately that she could undo the circumstances that had caused this cautious dance they wove around each other, but she couldn't change yesterday any more than she could predict tomorrow—and she tried to avoid thinking about that too.

She dreaded being confined with him on the sloop. But she saw that situation as unavoidable unless she wanted to be left behind. Once it had been determined that they could soon leave, Aaron had focused steadily on that goal. She attempted to do the same, accompanied the entire time by a gnawing ambivalence about her feelings for Aaron, seeing her father, and the uncertain trip home.

Despite Nicole's initial misgivings, the jerry-rigged repair looked as if it would work. As added insurance, Aaron resecured the rubber raft against the inside frame. That raft wouldn't have done any good alone. The force of the water while they were under sail would push it from the hole without the patch on the outside. But between the sail and the raft, most of the ocean should stay where it belonged and not in the bottom of their boat.

She sincerely hoped it would. On their fourth trip back from gathering the supplies they'd taken to the island, Aaron announced that there was no reason for them to stick around any longer.

"I charted a course for us a couple days ago," he told her, swinging himself up the diving ladder on the stern to drop the freshly-filled water containers onto the built-in bench. Nicole stood below him, holding the last blanket above her head so the waves wouldn't soak it. Shuttling supplies had been much easier with the raft. "We still have a few hours of daylight left, so we might as well use them."

The boat rocked slightly now that it was free. Looking up to take hold of the ladder after Aaron took the blanket, she caught a glimpse of a thin red gash on the side of his foot as it disappeared over the edge. The water sluicing off of it was tinted pink by his blood.

She hurried up the ladder, reaching the top just as he started down the steps to the cabin. Grabbing the water jug he'd left behind, she started after him. "What did you do to your foot?'' she asked, the moment she stepped through the door.

His brow furrowed sharply at her question. "I didn't do anything to it," he told her, clearly unaware that he was tracking faintly pink puddles across the floor. He set the container he carried in the galley sink and tossed the blanket onto the navy-striped sofa across from the table. Though Nicole had shaken the blankets out, sand still clung to the fringed edges.

"If you didn't do anything to it, why are you bleeding?"

She knew he'd been preoccupied. She also knew that she now had his attention. Truly puzzled by her question, he looked at the foot she'd pointed to. His incomprehension turned to dismissal.

"It's probably just a shell cut," he told her, totally unconcerned. "Have you seen the chart case?"

The watertight tube containing the navigational maps lay on the sofa. "You just threw the blanket on it. Aaron, you're bleeding."

"It's okay. I'll wipe up the floor in a minute."

Nicole watched in mild disbelief as he uncovered the metal tube and twisted open the cap. Obviously, he couldn't feel the cut and the bleeding was far from profuse, but there was bound to be sand it and it should be cleaned.

"I don't care about the floor," she said, and too late, realized what her statement implied.

She saw Aaron's hands go still and he slowly raised his head. His eyes met hers, direct and probing. She didn't care about the floor. She cared about *him* and in the faint smile he managed, she knew he cared about her, too. The day hadn't been easy for either of them.

"Got an adhesive strip?" he asked.

First-aid supplies were in a kit strapped to a wall in the head. The large white metal box was marked appropriately with a red cross, and Nicole retrieved it while Aaron unfolded the maps on the chart table.

She was still wet to her neck and she shivered slightly as she reentered the room. The sun hadn't yet had a chance to warm the space, only now reaching the long, narrow window that ran the length of the cabin. Thinking she should grab a couple of towels since Aaron was still dripping, too, she set the first-aid kit on the table—and felt her breath catch when she glanced up and found him watching her.

Her T-shirt. Wet, it was nearly transparent, and the filmy little bra she wore under it hid nothing.

She turned away before he could and gave the clinging fabric a surreptitious pull. "Can you manage this yourself?" she asked, popping open the metal latch on the kit.

His voice sounded huskier than usual as he assured her that he could. Sitting on the sofa, he propped his foot on his ankle. The cut was along the outer edge of his foot. Realizing he couldn't get to it that way, he bent his knee in the other direction and started to tear the wrapper from an adhesive strip.

"Aaron," Nicole drawled over the crackle of paper. "You need to clean it first. You can see the sand in it."

"I'll do it later."

"By then you might have an infection."

He didn't appear pleased with her logic, but he couldn't refute it. Deciding that the cut was in too awkward a place for him to tend the way she seemed to think he should, he scooted back on the sofa, extended his foot and held out the bandage.

Nicole said nothing as she sat down to lift his foot onto her lap. It only took seconds for her to realize that there was something terribly intimate about both the position and the silence, and she found herself searching for something to say.

She thought about asking if he was one of those people who seemed to be constantly injuring himself, then dismissed that idea because she felt sure he wasn't careless. The bruise on his shoulder was the result of an extraordinary incident, and a shell cut was something she could easily have gotten herself. She thought too about asking what he did when he hurt himself or became ill when he was at sea, then decided not to ask because the answer was obvious and she hated the thought of him being alone and needing help when there was no one there. So instead of making conversation, she concentrated on keeping her hands from shaking as she tended the small wound, carefully swabbing away the sand and applying antiseptic. In spite of the effort, her hands shook a little anyway. Aaron was watching her. She could feel it. He had to know how disconcerting she found his scrutiny.

Aaron's eyes narrowed on her slender neck. She'd pulled her hair around, draping it over her other shoulder to keep it from swinging forward. Her head was bent to her task and as she smoothed the edge of the small bandage, her attentions were brisk but gentle. He had the feeling that she was trying to be impersonal. If so, her attempt failed miserably. He could feel the faint tremor in her hands and see the tension in her shoulders.

That tension was in her smile, too, when she raised her head a moment later.

"There," she said, her voice falsely bright. "I think that should do it." The medical kit lay on the table and she replaced the antiseptic she'd used and latched the lid. A lipped shelf was built into the wall behind them. Turning as Aaron dropped his foot from her lap and sat forward, she reached behind him to put the kit on it. "I'll put this away later. I'm going to go and dry off. You wouldn't happen to have another shirt I could borrow while this one dries, would you?"

He doubted that she realized the provocation in her innocent request. Most women would know full well how such a comment would draw his attention back to what he couldn't ignore anyway. Nicole wasn't that skilled. Her actions were as open and honest as they'd been yesterday, when she hadn't turned from him at the waterfall. She didn't engaged in the intricate games men and women played with each other; the ones that taught a person how to maneuver and exploit—and how to hide vulnerability. When it came to the attraction between them, all she knew how to do was to go with what she felt.

His glance moved from the wet fabric molding her breasts to where she'd pulled her lower lip between her teeth. He saw her slight shiver. Heaven help him, he wanted to go with what he felt, too.

"You're cold," he said.

"A little." She gave him a shaky smile. "But I wouldn't be if I had a dry shirt."

She was doing her best to keep the subtle strain from her voice, to keep the conversation light. But there was no denying the awareness pulsing between them. It was pointless to even try.

Needing to touch her, he brushed the tips of his fingers along her temple and slowly pushed his fingers into her hair. It felt like silk and smelled of spring. Just as she did. "Then maybe I'd better get you one."

The flecks of gold in her eyes vanished, intensifying their darkness. She leaned closer. "Maybe you'd better."

"Yes," he whispered, achingly aware of how her nipples strained against the thin fabric. "I definitely think I should."

"When?"

He told himself he'd only kiss her; just taste her to remind himself of her sweetness. "In a minute."

She felt soft and willing and the sound of her trembling breath when he grazed her bottom lip with his was the sweetest sound he'd ever heard. Her lips parted as he angled his mouth over hers, welcoming him when his tongue slipped inside.

The kiss was long and deep, causing heat to gather in the pit of her stomach. The warmth of his body seemed to seep into her as he pulled her to his side and the cold fabric clinging to her skin was forgotten. Needing him nearer, she slipped her arms around his neck, excitement tingling her nerves as her breasts flattened against his chest. He felt strong and hard and hungry and as she pressed closer, his kiss became more urgent.

She felt his hands work over her back to her hips, then felt his fingers against her cool skin when he slipped under her T-shirt. His mouth still covering hers, he started to pull it up. The fabric was too wet to slip off easily.

He held her away from him, his eyes glittering. In a voice rough with desire, he told her to lean back, so he could remove her shirt, then stopped her when she started to do it herself.

Nicole looked up in confusion.

That confusion was immediately replaced with feminine comprehension. A question had suddenly clouded the need tightening his expression. He was remembering what he'd said to her yesterday. But that was then and this was now. And right now was really all they had.

She reached out, tenderly touching his cheek. He hadn't shaved for days and his shadowy beard felt rough on the softer skin of her face. She didn't care. She just didn't want him to pull away. "Don't stop," she whispered, and saw something primitive flare in his eyes.

That searing light remained as he raised his hand to run his knuckles over the side of her face. He carried that caress along her neck and opened his hand flat at the base of her throat. Slowly, her breath coming with much more difficulty, she felt his hand slide farther down.

The lacy pattern of her bra was visible through the shirt and the transparent fabric did little to hide the shadow of her erect nipples. With the tip of his finger he traced the shadow, teasing the bud tighter. A tingling sensation started there, seeming to shoot straight down when he molded his hand over her and gently lifted her breast.

Something dark and wildly exciting filled her as his head bent. He took the rigid nipple into his mouth, sucking it through the wet fabric. Slipping her fingers through his hair, she held herself to him. The jolt of pleasure filling her was almost painful. But what she wanted was to feel his mouth on her bare skin.

As if reading her thoughts, he pulled back. Almost impatiently, he worked her arms from the sodden shirt and pulled it over her head. It landed on the floor with a soft plop and before she could begin to wonder at his impatience, it was gone. He grasped her by the waist, his hands nearly spanning it as he pulled her closer. "You are so beautiful," he said in a hushed and ragged voice.

She hadn't felt at all embarrassed by her nakedness. The reverence in his eyes wouldn't allow it. Yet, his words made her flush. "You don't have to say that, Aaron. I know..."

"Don't." He stroked the damp tendrils of hair from her face and smoothed them from her shoulders. She was fined-boned and delicate, her body small and feminine. She wasn't a beauty in the classic sense, though she was far prettier than she realized. But he meant what he said. He wouldn't play games anymore. "There are all kinds of beauty, Nicki, and you're beautiful to me. And special," he added, though he wasn't prepared to admit what that meant. "That's why I want you to be very sure you know what you're doing right now."

She touched the bruise on his shoulder. It hurt her when he was hurt. She supposed it was only natural that she feel that way. After all, she loved him.

She didn't know when she'd come to that realization, but there was no question in her mind. Her feelings for him were that simple—and that complicated. "I know what I'm doing. More or less," she added, her smile a shade more nervous that she'd have liked. "Since I've never done this before, I'd appreciate it if you'd show me what to do."

He'd already taught her so much. And after all they'd been through together, after all they had shared, it seemed only right that they should share this, too.

It was the bond forged between them that made it impossible for him to deny her. He couldn't deny what he himself wanted so badly anyway. Pulling her down to lie beneath him, he told himself that later he'd think about just how much he wanted from her. And why.

The sofa was long, but it was narrow and its corded fabric felt coarse against her back. Nicole scarcely noticed. All that mattered was Aaron. He kissed her temples, her eyelids and her mouth, then trailed his lips down her throat to the softness between her breasts. His breath was hot against her cool skin, and the heat building in her threatened to turn her blood to steam.

She became attuned to every nuance of his touch, wanting to bring him the same delicious pleasure. They played an enticing game of follow the leader, exploring, teasing, giving. There was no room in his arms for the shyness she'd expected to feel. Even when he stripped off the rest of her clothes and discarded his own, she didn't experience any hesitation. He made it easy for her to give, just as he made it easy for her to forget that anything existed beyond this island paradise.

Time suspended itself. Tactile sensations took over. She felt the crispness of his hair as she pushed her fingers along his scalp and the smoothness of his skin over the rope-like cords of his back. She felt the coarse texture of the hair on his legs rubbing against hers and the powerful muscles of his thighs when she let her hand drift there. He seemed to need her touch as much as she wanted his and she knew there was nothing she wouldn't do to please him.

The breeze came through the open window, carrying with it the soft sound of water lapping against the sloop. The only other sound was the quick intake of Aaron's breath when he leaned away and her hand ventured low on his rock-hard abdomen.

"Oh, sweetheart," he all but growled. "You touch me now and this is going to go a lot faster than either of us wants."

His hand slid over her stomach, his eyes on hers as he cupped the downy curls between her legs. She tensed and he bent to kiss her. His mouth was warm and full on hers, reassuring as he waited for her to become accustomed to his touch. When she relaxed, he grew bolder, parting her to gently stroke, and she tensed again. The sensations he elicited made her arch against his hand and the soft sounds his lips captured seemed to please him somehow.

He told her that he didn't want to hurt her, that he'd try to make it easy for her. Not knowing what to expect, knowing only that she loved him, that she trusted him, she accepted his weight as he lowered himself to settle his hips against hers.

"Wrap your legs around me," he whispered. Instinctively, she arched toward him. "Easy, honey. Easy," he repeated, thinking he'd go mad with the urgency gripping him.

He eased forward, knowing he had to take her slowly. Sweat broke out along his back, the feel of her body giving way to accept him an exquisite agony. She was damp, too, and he brushed his palm over the glint of moisture on her forehead as he pushed again. The sound she made was faint, a small whimper caught by his kiss and when the uncomfortable moments were over, he slipped his hand between them, stroking her while her body became accustomed to the invasion. He felt her slowly become fluid and groaned aloud when she began to move her hips.

He could no longer be patient. She wouldn't let him.

Nicole's fingers dug into his back. His skin was smooth and covered with a fine sheen of perspiration. The sting of pain she'd felt lessened, and she cupped his tight buttocks, feeling them clench as he thrust deeply. She didn't need his patience now. She simply needed him. She suspected she always had.

She arched against him, learning the rhythm he was teaching her. He was guiding her, leading her to a place she thought she'd die if she didn't reach soon. Even as she raced toward it, she felt frightened by the intensity of the pressure escalating within her. She whimpered his name, gripping his back. His mouth moved to her ear, his words of encouragement urging her on, and in the moments before she became lost in a sea of overwhelming sensation, she knew she felt whole for the first time in her life. She was part of him. And when he shuddered against her, he became part of her.

The realization lingered, though reality returned a little slowly.

Nicole had no idea how long she lay with Aaron's head pressed to her shoulder. She'd become conscious of his weight, of how much heavier he felt now that his muscles were relaxed, and of the calmer cadence of their breathing. She'd have been content to lie there forever, stroking his hair, but he raised himself up to his elbows and she had to pull her hand away. A moment later, he'd rolled them onto their sides and tucked her head beneath his chin.

"This better?" he asked, alluding to the fact that she hadn't been able to draw a decent breath with him crushing her.

"The other way was fine, too." She hadn't minded not being able to breathe nearly as much as she minded him pulling away from her.

A smile entered his voice. "The other way was fantastic."

The sloop moved gently with the ebb and flow of the surf. Beyond the window, she could hear the steady drone of the ocean. She ducked her head farther into his chest, pleased and a little embarrassed with his assessment. She felt content and sated and pleasantly tired. "I could fall asleep like this," she said, wondering what it would be like to awaken in his arms.

She found out exactly what it was like later that night and again the next morning. Aaron didn't think it was a good idea to fall asleep on the sofa because it was so cramped, and after a while led her to one of the beds. They were both tired. They'd worked hard for nearly twelve hours, ever since shortly after sunrise, and should have fallen right to sleep. It was a long time before that happened, though. And when they did, they slept straight through to morning.

Over the years, Nicole had read countless stories that ended with the people in them riding off into the sunset. She had never dreamed that she'd find herself doing the equivalent of that when she and Aaron set sail with the sunrise.

She'd often wondered what happened to those people; what fates they met beyond that painted horizon.

For the next three days, she thought that there must be some special magic in that setting. The barriers had fallen. She and Aaron laughed and argued, shared long conversations and comfortable silences. He taught her the basics of sailing and how to play cards, and, for the most part, he was serious when he helped her study her books on the Moche for the museum tour. They made love, too; during long, lazy afternoons, under starlit skies and with the sun breaking pink in the morning.

She'd never been so happy, or felt so free. But within an hour of entering the waters off the Abaco Islands and sighting Stewart Cay, Nicole had to remember that there was no such thing as happily ever after.

Chapter Nine

Twenty miles northeast of the Bahama Islands and Stewart Cay, the *Valiant* encountered a Coast Guard cutter. According to the officer aboard, Search and Rescue had been looking for signs of the vessel for five days. As Nicole watched while Aaron compared coordinates with the cutter's navigator, it became apparent that they'd been looking in the wrong place.

No one had considered that the *Valiant* had been blown as far out as it had, or after the survivors of another boat caught in that same storm had been found, that it would even be afloat. The hurricane had hit so quickly that several vessels had been disabled. One had broken up, the officer mentioned, and another had capsized.

That was when Aaron told the officer about the island that had saved their lives—the one that didn't appear to be on the officer's chart, either. The seasoned skipper simply noted the account for his records. Because of seismic activity along the ocean floor, islands formed and vanished in a relatively short while. Sometimes, seemingly, overnight. He'd learned long ago not to question the gifts of the sea.

The officer's main concern was the patched hull. It had held surprisingly well and since neither the sloop nor its passengers appeared in any immediate danger, the cutter left them. But the officer radioed in so other patrols in the area could keep an eye out for the injured-but-able vessel and to let Nicole's father know that they had been found.

Knowing that call had been made left Nicole feeling oddly depressed. She was relieved that her father would know of her safety, but she was no longer all that anxious to be reconnected to a world in which Aaron wanted no part. He had said nothing of a tomorrow, or what might happen between them now, and she was afraid to ask. It was all so new, so tentative. For now, the best she could do was as Aaron did and take each moment as it came.

Having decided that much, she promptly dismissed the encroaching sadness she felt, and gave him a breathtaking smile when he pulled her between him and the wheel so he could hold her while they steered together. She'd become a pretty fair sailor, he told her as he nuzzled the side of her neck.

Nicole made herself forget about everything else. Aaron was still hers for a few more hours.

The hours dwindled to minutes. As they neared the jig-saw pattern of islands and shoals that changed the deep blue sea to shades of azure and turquoise, Nicole became increasingly quiet. When Stewart Cay came into view, she fell completely silent.

Even from beyond the breakwater, she could see the villa. It wove like an opalescent string of pearls through the tropical vegetation. Multi-leveled and rambling, with deep fucia bougainvillea embracing its walls, the white, stuccoed structure peeked from a profusion of palms. Long verandas with low railings and short urn-shaped supports jutted out from each tier, and covered walkways connected one level to another.

Always before, Nicole had looked forward to coming here. She loved the villa so much that a few years ago she had spent an entire summer redecorating its interior, which had been filled with the dark heavy woods of a mediterranian decor. Now, the spacious rooms were light and airy with white wicker and the pale pastels so unlike the traditional appointments of her father's formal, Colonial home in Cambridge. In this warm and humid climate, the casual atmosphere she'd created invited relaxation, which was probably why her father's cosmopolitan friends practically tripped over themselves to be invited here.

Several of those guests, dressed in the whites and bright colors of the tropics, could be seen moving about the veranda as Aaron brought the sloop past the man-made breakwater toward the cay's dock. The sun sat high in a sky striped blue and white by long wispy clouds, and the steady wind carried them smoothly from the open sea to the calm, protected water. Little was said as Nicole and Aaron worked together to bring the sloop in; she handling the sail as he had taught her, while he guided it toward the pier where two other sloops were already tied.

The next few minutes blurred into each other for Nicole. They were still a ways from the dock when she saw Luisa's Jamaica-born husband, Jerome, and a handful of guests hurriedly thread their way down the switch-back stairway leading from the villa to the boathouse her father had had built when he'd first bought the island.

Nicole turned to Aaron. *It was too soon to come back. She wasn't ready.*

Her anxiety showed clearly in her expression as she fought the wind for control of her hair. "Aaron?" she said, then let the breeze carry off his name because she didn't quite know what she wanted to say, or what she could say that would make any difference.

A strangely sympathetic smile settled in his eyes. But all he had time to say was a quiet, "I know," before tossing a line to one of the dozen hands waiting to catch it. There was no time now for the words that hadn't been uttered. Until now, they hadn't been necessary. And now it was too late. She and Aaron were no longer alone, and it suddenly felt as if nothing would ever be quite the same.

Jerome's deep voice boomed over the water. "Steer her here. Throw me your line. You okay, Miss Nicole?" he asked in his musical accent.

His question was echoed by the others, and their demand to know how she was quickly became as overwhelming as the clutch of hands wanting to assist her from the sloop. Aaron's hand had been at her back and she'd pulled into him, only to be pulled away by those wanting to say they had helped. Once she was out of the sloop, Jerome and a couple of men Nicole knew she'd met but whose names she couldn't recall at the moment, gathered other lines from Aaron and secured them to the pier while she tried to smile at the woman coaxing her away.

With a polite touch to her arm, Doris Parmenter-Perkins quietly suggested that Nicole might want to come with her. "The men can probably muddle through without our help," she said, mercifully avoiding the kind of questioning Nicole knew she was about to face. *What happened? How did you survive? What did you do all that time? Who is that beautiful man?*

She could practically hear the questions now. And she would, in due time, provide her father's guests with fodder for the conversations that had probably gone stale with speculation by now. At the moment, she was grateful for Doris's thoughtfulness.

Fifty-and-holding, was the way the lovely, silver-haired widow liked to describe herself. Doris was on the social register, a member of the best country clubs, and on the A-list for every fashionable function from Washington to London. She was also an exceptional hostess in her own right. Doris and Nicole's father had known each other for years and were often a couple for social events because they knew many of the same people. Nicole was a little surprised to see her now, however. Last she'd heard, Doris had been seriously dating an ambassador.

They stepped from the floating dock to the steadier one supporting the white clapboard boathouse. Reaching the end of the dock, they started up the wooden steps to the villa. With a quick glance back, Nicole saw Aaron brace his hands on his hips as he watched them move away. Standing as he was, the wind teasing his perpetually wind-blown hair, he looked a bit like a pirate who'd just had his plunderings stolen from him. Nicole shivered at the thought of just how untamed he could sometimes be.

Doris caught the look, and the shiver. "Are you sure you're all right?"

"I'm fine. Really." Her bare foot hit another step and she stopped. She looked back toward the sloop, but Aaron had just turned away to go below.

"He'll come up with the men," Doris said, seeming all too aware of her concern. "Jerome will take care of him." A quick shake of her head preceded her deceptively mild observation. "You must have had quite a time of it out there."

Feeling as transparent as cellophane, Nicole's abashed glance swung to Doris. The woman didn't seem to notice that her comment was open to a variety of interpretations. In fact she seemed quite unconcerned with what she'd just said as she continued up the steps. It was then that Nicole realized the older woman might very well have been referring to the condition of what was left of her clothes.

Nicole wore the skirt Aaron had altered and, since she'd washed it out in the fresh-water pool before they'd left the island, the blouse had lost its buttons. Tied beneath her breasts, its sleeves rolled up to her elbows, the blouse provided more-or-less adequate cover. Actually, when she'd put it on this morning, Aaron had told her it looked as sexy as hell and had proceeded to make dressing impossible.

Though she wouldn't have traded the memories of the morning for anything in the world, sexy was definitely not her style. Suddenly, she felt conspicuous and unimaginably tacky next to the smartly attired society maven. Somehow she had to get to her room and change before she ran into anyone else.

"We had some close moments," she said, because Doris seemed to be waiting for a reply to her earlier comment. "But we managed all right."

"Your father will be relieved to hear that."

"Where is he? And everyone else," she added, because it had been her responsibility to prepare for the guests' comfort. A responsibility she hadn't met.

"Harrington is in the library. Everyone else has gone down to the pool for Luisa's piña coladas. I asked her if she'd mind setting out lunch early to give everybody something to do while you got settled. I thought you might want to talk to your father alone—" her hazel eyes smiled, "—and freshen up before you encountered the madding crowd. They're all anxious to know how you are. I'll tell them you look . . . remarkably well," she decided to say.

They had reached the top of the stairs and paused by one of the many arched wooden doors along the terra-cotta-tiled walkway that encircled the building. Doris smiled again when she turned, only this time her smile was for Aaron.

He approached with Jerome, who was scowling at the width of Aaron's shoulders. Jerome was easily as tall as Aaron, but built on longer, leaner lines. Nicole was fairly sure he was trying to figure out what size the man wore so he could find him a change of clothes. He was carrying Aaron's shaving kit. Seeing the women waiting for him, he excused himself to put it in one of the guest rooms.

"Ah, here's the man of the hour. Mr. Wilde, I'm Doris Perkins." She held out her well-manicured hand, the pale peach polish on her nails a perfect match for the silk wrap she wore. Although she still smiled pleasantly, a note of hesitation slipped into her tone. "I'm a friend of Nicole's father," she added, that same caution in the glance she angled toward Nicole. "It's a pleasure to meet you."

The subtle guardedness that had so surprisingly slipped into Doris's manner was gone in an instant, charmed as she was by Aaron's smile. He gave a slight, continental nod as he took her hand. "I'm a friend of Nicole's," he returned, identifying himself in the same manner she had, then told her that the pleasure was his.

The wing of Doris's eyebrow arched in approval. It took an urbane and confident man to so skillfully assert his position while at the same time appearing to simply be meeting the formalities. Doris tipped her head down the veranda. "Mr. Stewart is most anxious to meet you. He's waiting for you now, so I won't keep you any longer. Until later, Mr. Wilde. And, Nicole, please let me know if I can help you with anything."

Nicole felt certain she now knew why Doris was here. Her father loved to entertain, but absolutely loathed all the details it involved. That's why he'd called Doris. The woman could have organized Bedlam if she'd been called upon to do it. She'd been requested to fill Nicole's shoes, and now that Nicole was back, she was being very careful to let her know that she was turning the reins back to their rightful holder.

They had stopped within inches of the door leading into the library. Even as the tap of Doris's high-heeled sandals on the tiles faded away, the door opened. Nicole nearly groaned right along with the hinge. She'd wanted another moment alone with Aaron and time to change her clothes. But as her father's frame filled the doorway, she knew that what she wanted didn't matter anymore.

Sixty-seven years of expecting the same perfection of himself that he demanded of others made Harrington Stewart a formidable man. There was a formality about him that even his casual attire—linen slacks and an open collared shirt—couldn't reduce. Accustomed to having his slightest wish immediately acted upon, he didn't take kindly to delay.

"Nicole." Harrington's voice was smooth and polished, and just as insistent as always. He stepped back, ushering them in to the white paneled room with its glass enclosed bookshelves and pieces of alabaster and malachite sculpture on individual pedestals. "Thank God you're all right."

Aaron would have thought that the man would open his arms to her. All the distinguished-looking, silver-haired gentleman did was stand there with his hands at his side, as if waiting for her to explain herself now that he'd spoken. He did look her over quite carefully, though, his shrewd eyes seeming to check every visible pore in her skin for signs of harm.

Nicole stood in front of him, a half-smile on her lovely lips, and her own hands clasped in front of her. For a moment, Aaron thought she might initiate some physical contact. She didn't. She simply assured her father that she was, indeed, just fine, and turned to Aaron to introduce him.

The gesture proved unnecessary. Harrington knew who he was. As with anyone Harrington Stewart wanted to know something about, he'd already pulled together an impressive catalog of information.

He held out his hand. "So you're Aaron Wilde. I've heard about you from Jake Wilton." His grip was firm, and as measuring as the look in his eyes. "I owe you a great deal, young man. Come. Sit down and tell me how this all came about. Or perhaps you'd prefer to rest first? Forgive me for seeming so anxious." He flashed a strained smile. "I imagine you're tired after such an ordeal. And probably hungry, too. I'll have Luisa bring a tray to your room and you can fill me in on the details later if you'd like."

Thinking the man far more solicitous of him than he was with his own daughter, Aaron watched him turn to her.

"Are you sure you're all right?"

"I'm fine, Father. I'm just sorry I worried you," she said, deepening the frown already etched in Aaron's brow. "I'm sorry, too, that I wasn't here to make sure everything was ready when you and everyone else arrived. There was no sign of a storm when I left and, by the time it had built up, it was too late to turn back."

"It doesn't matter, Nicole." The statement seemed part assurance and part dismissal. "The important thing is that you're here now. We'll talk after you've tended to yourself. I know you wouldn't want anyone to see you like this. I'm sure you'll feel better once you're more presentable."

Her long, unbound hair fell forward as she looked down at the pattern woven in the cream and peach Dhurri rug under her bare feet. Her toes curled, as if trying to hide the bright polish on them.

Puzzled by her father's lack of sensitivity and Nicole's accepting reaction, Aaron moved his glance to her face. Beneath the golden tan she'd acquired, her skin seemed to go ashen. Her voice, however, was steady and cool, her manner almost regal when she raised her head again and met the faint disapproval in her father's eyes. From the way she'd kept the neck of her blouse bunched in her hand, she'd already seemed uncomfortable with her appearance. That her father found it unacceptable, no matter what the reason, was just as apparent.

"I'm sure I will," she told him. "Please excuse me." With an almost formal nod to Aaron, she started for the door. Before she reached it, she turned back to her father. "Is Dr. Culver here?"

Genuine concern snapped Harrington's attention from Aaron. "I believe he's taken his wife and gone over to Cooper's Town for the day. Are you hurt? The Coast Guard indicated that there'd been no injuries."

That was because they hadn't told the Coast Guard everything. "I'm fine. But Aaron has hurt his shoulder."

"My shoulder's fine," Aaron cut in.

She met his eyes, a quiet concern resting in hers. "It wouldn't hurt to have Dr. Culver look at it. Will you let him?"

Aaron wasn't worried about the bruise, though for her, to put her mind at ease, he'd have said he'd see the man. He wasn't given a chance to answer, though. It was Harrington who responded.

"I'll see that he's taken care of."

After a quiet, "Thank you," she promised her father that she wouldn't be long and left the room.

Before the door clicked shut, Harrington was on the phone to summon someone to show Aaron to his quarters.

Aaron sank against the wall, the fatigue suddenly settling into him and sucking what energy he had from his bones. The ever-present worry that the patch on the boat might leak too much; two near-sleepless nights spent making sure that it didn't; the insidious, draining feeling that he was losing what he hadn't yet had a chance to attain, all combined in a weariness he had no desire to fight.

After taking Harrington up on his offer of a drink, he was asleep within two minutes of entering his room.

It was nearly eight o'clock before Aaron stepped out onto the open hallway overlooking the villa's inner courtyard. The distinctive beat of reggae music drifted upward, mingling with the soft din of conversation from the guests gathered around the tiered fountain below. Wearing the white dinner jacket and shirt and dark linen slacks Jerome had procured for him, Aaron felt much as he had at the last cocktail party he'd attended. Distant, removed. The one thing he didn't feel was bored.

"Aaron?"

Nicole's voice, oddly hesitant, came from behind him. A smile immediately formed on his lips, but when he turned from the rail, his smile faltered. He almost didn't recognize her.

Her beautiful hair no longer caressed her shoulders. She'd pulled it back, securing it in an intricate knot at the back of her head. The elegant line of her neck was completely concealed by the high collar of her pale gray silk dress, the skirt of which completely covered her shapely calves. Having seen the way her father's implied criticism of her earlier attire had affected her, Aaron reasserted his smile. He wouldn't do that to her.

"Are you just now making an appearance?" he asked, wondering if he still had the right to touch her.

He stepped forward to take her hand meaning to assure himself that despite the reserved way she held herself, she was still the same soft woman he'd held only a few short hours ago.

With a furtive glance over the edge of the rail to the guests below, she stepped out of his reach. His hand fell to his side.

"I was just coming to get you," she said, looking uncomfortable despite her pleasant smile. "Dinner will be a little later than normal tonight. Luisa had planned on serving fish, but Doris thought we'd had enough of that so she substituted a tenderloin. We're gathering for cocktails now."

She sounded vaguely impersonal, as she might to any acquaintance encountered on his way to dinner. Or maybe, Aaron thought, it was caution he heard in her voice. She seemed unsure how to act. She was also treating silence as if it were dangerous.

"I saw Dr. Culver a while ago," she hurried on to tell him. "He said you were very lucky not to have broken anything. I'm glad you're all right. Did you get any rest?"

"I did." The polite inquiry goaded him somehow. She didn't have to *act* at all around him. "But I'd have slept better with you."

A hint of pink suffused her cheeks. "Please don't say things like that, Aaron."

"Why not? It's true."

"But someone might hear you."

"I'm not going to embarrass you, Nicki."

Her gaze flew to his face, wide and seeking some kind of assurance he didn't know how to give. "I didn't mean to imply that you would. It's just that we're not alone anymore."

As if to prove her point, a door opened farther down the hall. Nicole moved away just as one of her father's attorneys, dressed in flowing yellow, and the woman's law professor husband, wearing a tropical white dinner jacket, stepped into the open hall.

"Nicole!" the woman exclaimed the moment she looked up. Nicole had, over the years, met many of her father's business associates. Ellen Conroy was one of the more affable. No one mistook her open friendliness for naïveté, however. She was one of the sharpest tax attorneys in the country. "We were worried sick about you. And your poor father. I've never seen him so distressed as he's been the last couple of days."

You couldn't prove it by me, thought Aaron, hoping that Nicole wouldn't blame herself for that doubtful circumstance. He had hardly believed it when she'd apologized to her father for getting caught in the storm—as though the bad weather had been her fault. What bothered Aaron even more was that the man hadn't even put his arms around her. She could have drowned. Her father might never have seen her again. Yet, he'd done damn little to indicate that her safe return even mattered to him. To her anyway.

Nicole demurely thanked the lady for her concern and, after introducing Aaron, graciously accepted Ellen's husband's offer of an escort.

Finding Ellen attached to his own arm, Aaron followed them down the curving staircase. His frown remained fixed firmly on Nicole's back while Ellen, oblivious to his displeasure because she was watching the steps, told him how most of the guests had heard of Nicole's disappearance before their arrival for the regatta. Apparently, Harrington had come to the island to await word of her circumstances. His friends had decided to come anyway and wait with him.

Naturally, they all wanted a firsthand accounting of the storm.

To induce Aaron's cooperation with that matter, someone asked what he'd like to drink. He said he'd take a bourbon, rocks, and a moment later, a crystal glass of ice and amber liquid was handed to him. With the drink came the introductions, and a blond woman's breathy, "Tell us what happened. We're all just dying to hear about it."

Of the fourteen guests staying at the villa, half stood in a small knot by the bar, the other half around Aaron by the fountain. Their curiosity revealed itself in varying degrees, none daring to look as intensely interested as he or she really was. Their sophistication demanded a certain blasé approach to even the most intriguing matters. Having displayed that same studied ennui himself on numerous occasions, Aaron knew exactly how the game was played. Only now, his own cynicism increased in direct proportion to Nicole's withdrawal.

He directed his response to the petite blond who'd identified herself as "Kim, Congressman Holt's companion." In this particular group, she was the only one who didn't look as if she had relatives who'd come over on the Mayflower. Cute and savvy, she had the look of a climber, one who wanted to belong at any price. It had been she who'd first addressed him.

"There's not that much to tell." He took a sip of his drink, casting a surreptitious glance toward Nicole who stood with her back to him talking with the other group. She was easily close enough to overhear. "A storm came up and we were washed into an island. The boat was damaged, so Nicki and I fixed it as best we could and—here we are."

"Nicki?" a man to his right repeated.

"He must mean Nicole, dear," the woman next to him whispered, then offered Aaron a smile to coax more out of him. Aaron remained silent.

He knew Nicole was listening. She'd stiffened the moment she'd heard him use her nickname, then seemed to hold her breath in anticipation of whatever else he'd say.

Apparently, she didn't trust him with the more intimate details of the eight days they'd spent together.

"Maybe you'll fill us in on the details during dinner." The blond woman made the suggestion after another inquiry resulted in an equally cryptic reply on his part. Since the saga of the storm seemed to provide little conversation, she came up with the next most logic topic. "So, what is it that you do, Mr. Wilde," she inquired. "I heard someone say you were a stockbroker."

"*Was,*" he corrected, taking a sip of his wine. His eyes were still on Nicole. Her father had just joined her and she was beaming at his compliment about how nice she looked. "I *was* a broker."

"And now?"

He gave her his most charming smile. "Now, I'm not."

"Aaron is doing what most of us only fantasize about." Her politician friend edged in, either to prove his ability to access information or protect his claim on the blond. Aaron didn't know and he didn't care. He'd just cut off his view of Nicole. "He's left it all behind to sail around the world."

"How exciting! You have your own yacht then?"

"It's not a yacht, Kim. He has a modest sailboat. A thirty-six foot sloop, if I remember correctly." The congressman, a man in his mid-fifties with an apparent predilection for younger, impressionable women, met Aaron's eyes evenly. "He lives on it."

"Well, he'd have to if he's sailing around the world." Looking pleased with herself for having figured that out, she brightened her smile for Aaron. She clearly failed to grasp the irresponsibility her companion found inherent in Aaron's choice of accommodations.

Aaron lifted his glass to the man. It seemed good old Jake hadn't spared many details. "I see Harrington's been sharing information."

"He shared his concerns with me," the politician replied, his tone amazingly diplomatic. "Naturally, he wanted to know something about the man his daughter's safety depended upon. He was relieved to know the extent of your sailing ability."

Aaron spoke mildly, voicing what the man would not. "But not too crazy about the rest of it." Ice cubes clinked as he took another sip of his bourbon.

"He's most indebted to you," came the noncommital reply. "I've known Nicole and her father for years. She adores him and Harrington is very protective of her. We all are."

The exchange was remarkably civil. But the warning was there. Aaron was an outsider. He didn't belong. And the veiled warning was intended to let Aaron know that while he was welcome, that welcome was temporary.

Harrington himself made that abundantly clear a few minutes later. He'd left Nicole with Doris so the guests wouldn't pester her, and had asked Aaron to join him in the library. They still had nearly an hour before dinner and, away from the chatter, they could talk.

Surprisingly, Harrington didn't ask for details. He seemed satisfied with whatever accounting Nicole had provided him earlier and now only wanted to settle up with Aaron.

"I'm indebted to you," he said, using the same term his friend had only a short while ago. "And I always pay my debts."

Aaron's response was immediate. "You don't owe me anything. None of what happened was your fault. It wasn't anyone's, for that matter."

Harrington looked impressed. "That's very big of you, but the fact remains that you saved my daughter's life. She tells me you dove in after her when she was swept overboard."

Leaning against the back of the long white sofa bisecting the room, Aaron crossed his arms. Did she also tell you she wanted to make love with me out of gratitude for that? he wondered, unable to imagine the diffident young woman downstairs doing such a thing. "That's between her and me."

Harrington acted as if he hadn't heard Aaron. "Then, there's the matter of the boat. You managed to save it, too. I want to show my appreciation, so I've done a little research."

A piece of contemporary sculpture, white marble and variously curved, sat on an onyx pedestal beside the wet bar. Pacing between it and where Aaron leaned idly against the sofa, Harrington quickly capsulized all he'd learned of Aaron's background and qualifications. He knew where he'd gone to school, when he'd graduated, and the date he'd walked away from the Exchange. He even knew something Aaron hadn't; that his ex-fiancée had married another broker. Aaron silently wished her well.

"I'm telling you this so you'll know I'm aware of your circumstances. I won't be so crass as to offer you money, but I insist on repaying you in whatever small way I can. I can always use people with an understanding of commodities and the international trade market. I have an opening. It's in my London office, but since you don't appear too attached to any place in particular at the moment, I don't think that should pose a problem for you. You'd have a decent flat, of course, and membership in the racquet club. And a car. I believe there is a Jaguar there now, but if you'd prefer something else, that's fine, too. The salary is negotiable."

As Harrington spoke, Aaron had slowly stood up straighter. Every muscle in his body reacted to the tension coiling in his stomach.

"Did Nicole ask you to do this?"

The man looked shocked, then suspicious. "Of course not. This isn't the sort of thing I'd discuss with her."

Some of his tension eased, though not enough to take the hard edge from his expression. "I appreciate the offer," he lied. "But I don't want a job."

"Young man, I'm offering you a chance to reestablish yourself."

"I know what you're offering." And Aaron wanted no part of it. What Harrington was proposing was a chance to go back to exactly what he'd left, to an "acceptable" life-style. The fact that the job was also on another continent probably had added appeal for Harrington. Aaron was pretty sure he had no idea of what had happened between him and his daughter, but the man wasn't going to take any chances.

The word *protective* was taking on a whole new meaning.

"As I said, I appreciate the offer. But I'm declining. Thanks, anyway."

It was apparent that Harrington was not a man accustomed to having his gestures refused. Nonetheless, he acknowledged Aaron's decision with a tight nod then looked at him with the same curiosity he might exhibit over a tablet of hieroglyphics. Interesting but, to him, indecipherable.

"May I ask why you would turn down such an offer?"

"It's just not what I want to do."

He had no intention of reentering the world he'd left—the one where a person hadn't arrived until he had at least one ulcer and an occasional migraine. He'd been there and, having managed to escape, valued his sanity too much to return. Right now, he'd be willing to bet that at least a third of Harrington's guests ate antacid tablets like dinner mints. Another third probably spent as much time talking to their analyst as they did their families. Keeping up with the Joneses was an exercise in stress-to-excess, especially when the Joneses belonged to "society."

"You don't think you're being irresponsible?"

The question wasn't an attack. It seemed prompted only by simple curiosity.

"Quite the opposite," Aaron replied evenly. "Walking away from what was destroying me was probably the most responsible thing I've ever done."

The door had opened a moment ago. Grateful for the interruption, Aaron turned toward it. He could no more make a man like Harrington Stewart understand what motivated him than he could turn back the clock. Yet, seeing Nicole standing in the doorway, he wished he could do just that.

He caught a shimmer of awareness in her eyes when they met his and, for an instant, he thought he might see her lovely smile, the one that held such delight. But the shutters came down and her guard went up as she demurely touched her throat. Stepping into the room to tell them that dinner was ready, her glance cautiously avoided his.

It seemed to Aaron as if she were pretending she scarcely knew him; as if she wanted no opportunity for their familiarity with each other to show. When she ducked her head as her father passed in front of her, Aaron couldn't help but wonder if she might not now be ashamed of all that had happened.

"Aren't you coming," he heard her ask.

Nicole looked up, scarcely trusting herself to meet Aaron's glance without giving herself away. Just now, when she'd caught his eye, she'd actually felt the knock of her heart against her ribs. It had vibrated all the way up to her collar. But the look he gave her in the moments before he preceded her out the door, nearly chilled her to the bone.

Chapter Ten

I'd like some more wine, please."

The dinner conversation, underscored by the clink of silverware against china, muffled Nicole's request. Talk of Saturday's regatta had finally replaced that of her return. Nonetheless, she was aware of how two pairs of male eyes had narrowed on her. Her father seemed perplexed by her uncharacteristic indulgence. Aaron seemed intrigued by it. She ignored them both and leaned back so the waiter could refill her glass. It was her third, and she really had no intention of drinking it. She just wanted it there.

Still very much aware of Aaron's and her father's scrutiny—and of the subtle tension that had accompanied the two men out of the library—she turned her attention to the other twelve people seated at the long, graciously appointed table. None of the guests had seemed to notice the strained atmosphere. They were all too busy speculating about who might win the race.

The general consensus was that, if the *Valiant* hadn't been damaged, all money would have been on it. She was the fastest forty-five footer in the Caribbean, according to Ellen Conroy, and she felt it a pity that Harrington wouldn't be entering the race this year. Her opinion was echoed by several others, and good-naturedly refuted by those entering the regatta themselves.

One of those entrants was Dick Holt. Though he was as close to her father as anyone could be, they both possessed a fierce competitive streak. Neither hesitated to use it against the other.

"You know, Harrington, you could always bump up a couple of classes and enter your Gulfstar. Of course," Dick added, baiting his old friend, "you'd have to pull a crew together. I don't know how you could possibly do that at this late date. The rules don't allow professionals, so you can't use your captain, and finding an experienced non-pro who's not already entered would be impossible."

Harrington's eyes glittered. "Nothing's impossible, Holt. You were reelected."

Good-natured laughter rippled along the table as the congressman adroitly dodged the dig. "Does that mean you're entering?"

"It means I may not be out of it yet." Too astute to let personal prejudice prevent him from succeeding, he turned to the man seated across from his daughter. "What about you, Aaron?"

The quiet chatter faded to a sudden and expectant silence.

For most of the meal, Aaron had said very little, answering questions posed to him but initiating little discussion on his own. Nicole had come to know that his silences were sometimes a way of stabilizing himself and that his surface conversation was just that. It seemed to her tonight that he was intent on simply getting through the evening, though probably no one but she realized it.

He dropped his napkin beside his plate and sat back in his chair. To the others he appeared interested in the banter. To her, he looked ready to break the glass in his hand. "What about me?"

Harrington leaned back, too, comfortable in his little domain. "I've got a sixty-foot sloop out there that takes three to handle. You interested?"

Aaron idly contemplated the question. "You said it takes three."

The arching of a grayed eyebrow noted the detail and Harrington inclined his head toward the attentive woman seated to Aaron's right. "Doris has sailed with me before. She's pretty good."

"I'm *very* good," came the smooth correction. Doris smiled warmly at Nicole's father. "I expect you to remember that."

As the guests laughed at the remark, Nicole couldn't help but notice the light in Doris's eyes. It was the same sort of look she greatly suspected had been in her own eyes with Aaron at times, especially when he teased her.

She couldn't see the slightest hint of humor in Aaron's eyes now. Taking a sip of her wine, she turned her attention to Doris. Since Doris had kept her company most of the evening, leaving Harrington to mingle with his guests, it had only been in the last half hour or so that she'd been able to observe the woman and her father. Though she couldn't quite put her finger on it, there was a subtle difference in the way they moved around each other. Now that she thought about it, several of the guests were acting strangely, too. The women in particular. They kept bouncing glances between the two as if waiting for something to happen.

Too caught up with the business of trying to be pleasant while Aaron all but ignored her, she didn't bother trying to figure out what was going on. She could do that later. Right now she saw an opportunity too good to pass up.

Eager to see that her father got what he was after, and to draw Aaron out, she leaned forward. "You'd be perfect, Aaron. Why don't you do it?"

"Why don't you?" he returned blandly. "You know how to handle a winch."

She hadn't expected that. "I couldn't."

"Of course you could." She had sailed the *Valiant*. She could certainly crew. "You can do anything you want to do."

He was serious. He was also challenging her. For the briefest instant, she thought about tossing the challenge back. But with the women waiting to see how she would respond to the gauntlet and her father not appearing too pleased with the turn in the conversation, she didn't think it wise. It seemed to her that he was talking about more than just sailing.

"I have to stay here," she said, her responsibilities easily excusing her. She added a quiet smile, hoping to ease the tension only she seemed to sense. "When the winners come back, they'll want to celebrate."

To remove the possibility of Aaron pursuing the matter further, Harrington cut in. "Nicole isn't a sportswoman. Never has been," he added, catching Aaron off-guard with the lie. Nicole had once loved to ride. She'd told him so herself. And she took to sailing as if she'd been born on the water. He glanced toward her, but she said nothing, letting her father's assessment of her interests stand. "She always handles this end of the event. It's what she does best. Now, what do you say?" he prodded. "You willing to handle the sails for me?"

For a moment, Aaron ignored the question, his attention on the woman intently studying the pattern of her wineglass. This wasn't the first time she'd let her father speak for her. It was the first time, though, that her acquiescence had been so obvious. That she wouldn't meet his eyes now told Aaron she knew he was as aware of that fact as she was. It also seemed to him that she had made a choice. Or, maybe, more accurately, a choice had been made for her.

Harrington was waiting.

Few men said no to him. Aaron had already done it once tonight. He had nothing to lose by doing it again. "I'm afraid it isn't possible. I have to leave in the morning."

Harrington didn't look pleased but, to his credit, he said he could understand that Aaron might not be too anxious to pit himself against the sea so soon after his ordeal. He then turned to Ellen's husband, a relative newcomer in the group, to elicit his aid. Nicole scarcely noticed what else was said. Aaron had looked straight at her when he'd announced that he was leaving and when he'd seen her go pale, he had pointedly glanced away.

The evening went downhill from there.

Nicole was at the silver service pouring herself another cup of coffee after the dessert. Cognac had been set out on the buffet. From the corner of her eye, she saw another china cup being held toward her to refill. She reached for it, her smile faltering when her eyes locked on Aaron's. The cup was his.

She turned back to the task, her hand trembling ever so slightly as she poured the steaming coffee. It was the first time all evening that they hadn't been surrounded by a half-dozen other guests. "You're drinking it black. Right?"

She set the cup on the linen runner. It seemed safer than trying to hand it to him.

"You didn't tell him about us, did you?"

She shouldn't have been surprised by his blunt accusation. She'd always known him to get straight to the point. Yet, here, among everything she regarded as real and familiar, his incisiveness was far more unsettling than it had been before.

Nicole hadn't wanted to acknowledge it, but there was no escaping what she could no longer make herself deny. She found Aaron's presence far too threatening. He had touched a side of her she hadn't known existed, a rebellious, yearning side of her that she desperately needed to suppress. She very much feared the changes he'd caused to take place inside of her. There was no room for them in her world. The restlessness he'd awakened had to be forgotten—just as she had to forget him. He belonged to another time, another place.

Even now, a sense of unreality surrounded the memories tearing at her heart.

Pushing her hands into the pockets of her pearl-gray dress, she made a half-turn to the enormous pastel painting covering the wall. Swirls of color swept across the canvas without pattern or direction to give it order. That chaos fairly reflected how Nicole felt as Aaron stood staring at her profile.

"I wouldn't discuss something like that with him."

"Because he doesn't approve of me?"

She wasn't surprised by Aaron's conclusion. She knew her father. "My father doesn't approve of anyone who doesn't conform to his standards." She offered a shaky smile. "I guess he's a little like you in that respect."

"At least I didn't sell myself out."

Her head snapped up at the heat in his voice. "What's that supposed to mean?"

"I think he means that he turned down the job I offered him."

Nicole whirled around at the sound of her father's voice. She hadn't heard his approach and, though it obviously startled her, Aaron was only mildly annoyed by the interruption. It seemed to him that Harrington didn't like the idea of the two of them being alone together. He'd started across the room the moment he'd seen them talking. Aaron could only conclude that it must drive him nuts when he thought that they'd been alone together for over a week.

"You offered him a job?"

"In London. Plum position, too. But he didn't want it. Did you, Aaron?"

His tone was congenial, his manner friendly as he patted Aaron on the shoulder and handed his daughter his brandy snifter.

"You see, Nicole," Harrington continued, fully expecting the silence that met his question. "I wanted to repay this young man for taking care of you, but he said he didn't want any kind of a reward. I have to respect him for that. He knows his position." *And you know yours* was his unspoken conclusion as he reminded her that she'd yet to pour his cognac.

Nicole lifted the heavy crystal decanter, barely conscious of what she was doing. She had no idea how much of her conversation with Aaron her father had overheard. His manner seemed to indicate that it wasn't much, but it was difficult for her to tell. She'd lived with his faint disapproval for so long that she always saw it in his expression. She was more concerned with Aaron's reaction to her father's less-than-diplomatic explanation of his actions.

That her father was bothering to explain his actions at all was something of a rarity. His reasons for doing so, however, were clear. Aaron wasn't one of The Chosen, and he wanted to reinforce that fact. He also wanted to make sure she knew that he had turned down the opportunity to bet-

ter himself. His choice, instead, had been his precious freedom.

Knowing what she did about him, Nicole would have been
enormously disappointed in Aaron if he'd done anything
other than what he had. But any pride she felt in him for
that was circumvented by the dismissing glare he divided
between her and her father before he turned and walked
away.

"I can see where you might think you're attracted to
him," she heard her father say, his tone oddly pensive. "I
daresay half the women here are quite taken with him. But
I trust you understand that whatever happened between the
two of you has no relevance now. We'll go back to Boston
on Monday and you'll soon be back to work deciding which
hospitals and symphonies and museums get my money.
You're even going to get some help doing that." Suddenly
looking as if he might be getting ahead of himself, he cut
himself off and gave her a surprisingly sympathetic smile.
"You'll soon forget any of this ever happened."

Despite her father's assurance, Nicole seriously doubted
that. But she understood the necessity of forgetting far more
than he realized. Aaron had no use for routine and schedule and habit. Maybe someday he would, when he'd fulfilled his promise to himself. But not right now. He needed
his freedom as much as she needed roots.

Everything she'd come to depend on was here with her
father. He needed her to do so many little things for him,
and if he didn't seem overly appreciative all the time, she
knew it was only because that was the way he was. The important thing was that she *felt* needed. She was contribut-
ing and depended upon and the thought of not belonging
was too frightening to contemplate. Had she been stronger,
or braver, she might have given herself permission to try the

untested. But she needed stability and she had that in the life she'd created for herself.

Or so she'd thought.

After those first couple of hours, Nicole couldn't have imagined anything that could make the evening more strained until Kim, whom she'd first met only a few hours ago, sidled up to her. Trying to make small talk, the congressman's latest "friend" casually mentioned that Nicole must be terribly pleased about her father's engagement. Doris was, after all, a remarkable woman.

For a moment, the words didn't register. "Engaged?" she heard herself repeat.

"Well, yes. Dick said they're going to make the announcement at the party after the races. You didn't know?"

"No. No, I didn't." The moment of bewilderment was gone, replaced with the mask of reserve that served her so well. "I mean, I didn't know they were going to announce it Saturday," she lied, refusing to look like a fool. "They've known each other for quite some time." Her own father was remarrying and she hadn't known about it? Hadn't even suspected it? What had happened to Doris's ambassador? "Will you excuse me, please?"

The woman had no choice. Nicole had turned even as she'd spoken—and nearly knocked over the lady in question.

"I see I'm too late," Doris mumbled under her breath. She gave Nicole a smile that was at once apologetic and hesitant. The look she gave Kim, who didn't see it anyway because she'd headed for the cognac, would have frosted a furnace. "Your father wasn't going to tell you until tomorrow. We'd asked everyone who knew to keep it to themselves until then."

That explained why Doris had stuck so close to her side all evening, Nicole decided. To make sure no mention of the engagement would be made. Even before she could begin to wonder why they hadn't wanted her to know of it, Doris continued.

"He thought you'd had enough excitement for one day," she added, taking her by the arm to lead her away. She tossed another glare over her shoulder. "I just knew that woman wouldn't be able to keep anything to herself."

Nicole didn't ask where Doris was taking her. She was too busy telling herself that the reason for the sinking sensation she felt had nothing to do with Doris personally. Doris was nice. A remarkable woman, as Kim had said. It was only the unexpectedness of the news that had caused the sudden loss of equilibrium. That sensation was with her now, as she and Doris approached her father, the feeling that the rug had just been yanked out from under her.

She wasn't sure what Doris said as she laid her hand on Harrington's arm, but he turned to Nicole a moment later looking more self-conscious than she'd ever seen him. All he said, however, was that he'd asked Doris to marry him rather suddenly and that they would talk when they could have more privacy. He hadn't wanted to surprise her this way.

More shaky than she wanted to admit, Nicole forced herself to smile. No one would know that she was anything less than delighted for her father and the woman at his side. Since Kim had already told one of the other guests what she'd just done, everyone else now knew what the three people by the window were discussing. Their cue to come forward must have been Nicole's smile as she accepted the older woman's hug.

Nicole moved away to make room for the others. At least, that was the excuse she gave for leaving Doris beaming at her father. What she really wanted was to be away from all of this for a while.

A moment of painful honesty made her admit that what she really wanted was to feel the security of Aaron's arms. But she couldn't let herself think about that. Aaron was leaving tomorrow. She couldn't let him go without saying goodbye. And maybe telling him, too, that she'd never forget him.

He was nowhere to be seen. He wasn't outside on the veranda. Nor was he down by the fountain. When she returned to the spacious living room, he wasn't there, either. She moved toward the door, thinking to try the game room where one of the women said a couple of the men had gone to play billiards. Now that she'd made the decision to talk to him, she had to find him.

Her father's voice stopped her by the glass doors.

"Are you all right? You look a little pale."

She offered him the best smile she could muster, along with the assurance that she was fine. "I'm just a little tired. If you don't mind, I think I'll say goodnight now." She glanced around, pretending to only now notice that someone was missing. "I'd like to say good night to Aaron, too. Do you know where he went?"

Certain he had nothing to worry about, Harrington told her he thought he'd gone to the library. Aaron had mentioned wanting to make a call and was then going to retire for the evening. "You can say good bye in the morning" was her father's conclusion.

Nicole had no intention of waiting that long. The thought of possibly missing him in the morning made it all the more imperative that she see him tonight.

Aaron seemed to have become a phantom. He wasn't in the library. Nor was he in his room. A quick check of the boathouse indicated that he wasn't there, either. Having no idea where else to look for him, Nicole returned to her own room. There was nothing to do but get ready for bed and try very hard not to think.

She was still awake at midnight.

Leaning against the rail of the veranda outside her room, she turned her face to the soft breeze and let it carry the stray wisps of her hair from her face. She had braided it as she usually did before she went to bed, since it didn't tangle so much that way, and now absently ran the plaited length through her hand. The motion stopped when she caught sight of the shadow moving up the stairs.

Quietly, like the night that had folded in on the villa, she moved to the landing where her intruder would appear. Even in the pale moonlight, she knew it was Aaron. The white dinner jacket he'd worn had been abandoned, along with the tie. Now, his shirt collar lay open and he had his hands jammed into the pockets of his slacks.

Her heart felt as if it were beating in her throat when he reached the top step and looked up to see her standing there. In the moonlight, his features seemed more angular, harder. Somehow, that seemed to magnify his displeasure at finding her waiting for him.

He lowered his head, intent on going past her.

"Aaron. Please." She took a tentative step toward him, the breeze tucking the delicate batiste of her modest nightgown closer to her body. "I'd like to talk to you."

Though he said nothing, he stayed where he was. She hoped that meant he was at least willing to listen.

"I looked for you after you left," she began, feeling horribly awkward with his silence. "I don't think you wanted to be found, though."

"I didn't."

Strangers. They were acting like strangers. The thought hurt more than she thought possible. Yet, it didn't hurt nearly as much as seeing that same pain in Aaron's eyes.

It was the glimpse of that pain that made her verbalize the thought she'd been struggling with for hours. "It feels as if it were some kind of a dream, Aaron. Like it never really happened."

The admission brought him closer. "Is that why you've been acting as if it didn't? Explain this to me so I can understand it, would you please? You were fine this morning. But the minute you got here you turned into an ice princess. You wouldn't let me touch you. You barely talked to me."

"That's not true."

He said nothing. He just stared at her, letting her hear the echo of the lie in her own words. She had only one defense for herself. "It's just different here."

"*You're* different here."

"I'm the same as I always was."

"Like hell you are."

His eyes, cool and unfamiliar searched her face, as if trying to find a trace of something he'd seen there before. Not finding it, he wearily ran his fingers through his hair and turned to look across the darkened sea. The lights of Abaco Island twinkled off in the distance, mirroring the stars overhead.

He hadn't wanted to confront her. Certainly there was nothing to be gained from it. Yet, when he'd reached the top of the stairs and found her waiting for him, his defenses had kicked into overdrive.

He'd seen the stricken look on her face when she'd learned of her father's engagement. She'd recovered quickly enough, but her practiced smile hadn't fooled him. He knew the news had hit her hard and he was pretty sure he knew why. Her whole security system had been knocked out. Now that he was with her, though, now that he was faced with her restraint, he wondered why he'd worried about her at all. If she wanted to delude herself along with the rest of the world into thinking everything was just wonderful, that was her problem.

"You had something to say," he reminded her none too patiently.

All evening, she had felt torn, pulled in two diametrically opposed directions. On one hand, it was as if nothing had changed. Everything felt exactly as it had when she'd left Boston just over a week ago. On the other, it felt as if nothing would ever be the same again.

Struggling for a middle ground, hoping to diffuse the tension straining the silence between them, she did the only thing she knew how to do. Pulling her dignity around her like a protective cloak, she tried to pretend nothing had happened at all.

"Where did you go before? When I couldn't find you, I thought you might have gone for a sail. It's a lovely night for one."

Aaron wasn't buying the change-of-subject routine. He had no use for masks and she knew it. Her practiced poise hid nothing from him, anyway. All it did was annoy him.

What irritated him now was how dishonest she was being with herself. Disgust darkened his tone. "Don't waste the superficial conversation on me, Nicole. I'm not one of your crowd, remember? I'm the man who knows you."

Her response was nothing but a wary silence.

"You can hide from yourself if you want," he went on. "I think you've probably got it down to a science by now. But you can't hide from me. I've seen behind the propriety and I know the little things about you. I know how you respond when I kiss you. I remember the little sounds you make when we make love."

"Aaron!" she whispered, looking wildly around to make sure no one had overheard.

Goaded by her pretense, he grabbed her upper arms and pulled her toward him. "No one can hear me." His voice was low and angry. "No one but you. You don't want to listen, though, do you? You don't want to be reminded that you weren't daddy's perfect little girl."

"My father has nothing to do with this."

"Your father has everything to do with it. It's not your fault that your mother walked out on him, and punishing yourself by trying to please a man who barely notices you isn't going to change the fact that she did."

Nicole went stock still.

Her disbelief was evident, but Aaron couldn't imagine why she seemed so surprised by his heated observation. Granted, he'd broached the subject with an appalling lack of finesse, but her stubborn refusal to see what she'd done to herself hadn't allowed him time to consider being less than blunt.

Aaron had begun to suspect the sense of obligation she felt toward her father when she'd first mentioned that she was all he had. Bits and pieces of conversations since then— and seeing them together today—had lent a certain validity to his conclusion. But Nicole wanted no part of the idea.

She tried to pull back. The pressure of Aaron's hands only increased. "You don't know what you're talking about."

"Don't I? Look at yourself, Nicole." He drew her up short, his face mere inches from hers. "You work for him. You run his house. You entertain his friends. You're his hostess, his caretaker, the dutiful daughter who's become the lady of his manor. Hell," he muttered, "you even dress for him. But underneath, that's not what you want, is it? Underneath, you're the woman who likes the sexy lingerie, who enjoys standing naked beneath a waterfall, who even let's herself swear on occasion. When we were stuck on that island, you were happy. You laughed. You smiled. You even got down-and-dirty angry. Do you remember any of that?''

He let her go as quickly as he'd grabbed her. Stricken by the depth of his anger, and by the realization that at least part of what he'd said was painfully true, she groped for the railing.

Her eyes were haunted as she looked up at his rigid expression. She remembered, but she wasn't about to let him know that. It was hard enough to admit to herself that Aaron was far more correct in his assessment than she wanted him to be.

Part of what she'd felt tonight was a frightening sense of insecurity. Her entire existence revolved around her father and *his* life. Now, with his engagement to Doris, Nicole found her position threatened. Her father might not need her as much anymore—if he'd ever really needed her at all. Aaron was right about that, too. Her father paid scant notice to what she did; much more to what she failed to do. She'd already tried so hard to win his approval. Now, she'd have to try that much harder.

She kept her eyes on Aaron's, remembering, too, that he was leaving. Though that was exactly what she wanted him to do, that thought hurt more than anything else.

"I think we should say good night, Aaron."

He grabbed her arm as she turned away. "That's your solution for everything, isn't it. Don't discuss it. Just ignore it or deny it. It doesn't matter as long as you don't face it."

"What is it that you want from me?"

Her question was half demand, half plea and Aaron could have come up with a dozen different answers. Right now, only one mattered.

He pulled her closer, his eyes glittering hard. She could deny it all she wanted, but the connection was there. He could see it in the widening of her eyes as he raised his hand and slowly ran his knuckles down her cheek; could hear it in the quick intake of her breath when he brought his touch to the base of her throat.

"I want you to remember," he said. "I don't want you to pretend that the week we shared didn't exist. It did, Nicole. It was real. What happened between us mattered. *All* of it."

His hand slid down. A moment later, he'd grabbed her wrist and turned to the stairs.

Startled and wary, she tried to pull away. "What are you doing?"

"Keep your voice down," he snapped back, taking a perverse pleasure in the reminder. He wanted her away from here. Somewhere where she wouldn't crawl back into herself and try to hide from him again. "I'm tired of talking to Nicole. I want to talk to Nicki."

He made her sound like a schizophrenic. "Aaron, I don't—"

"Shut up, Nicole," he muttered. Scooping her into his arms when they reached the bottom of the steps, he proceeded to carry her so she couldn't keep digging in her heels.

What he'd done had a greater silencing effect than what he'd said. Concerned with maintaining her hold on his neck so he wouldn't drop her while he negotiated the remaining steps to the dock, she was hard-pressed to say anything else, anyway. She could feel the tension tightening his entire body. Another word from her and she thought he might explode.

They blended with the other night shadows as Aaron's decisive strides carried her the length of the dock. Instead of heading toward the boats, though, Aaron took the path behind the boathouse. The path lead through a tangle of boulders and trees and ended on a secluded beach beyond the villa.

Not until the villa itself was completely hidden from view did he stop to put her down.

Chapter Eleven

The moment they emerged on the beach, Nicole knew why Aaron had brought her here. Leaves rustled in the faint breeze. Pale white sand stretched into the darkness. Except for the crickets singing in the bougainvillea, no other sound competed with the crash of waves against the rocks farther down the shore. Peace surrounded this place.

As she felt Aaron's arms loosen and her feet hit the sand, she knew this is where he'd disappeared to earlier. It was just the sort of setting he'd seek if he were trying to work off agitation. Seeing the tense set of his jaw, she got the distinct impression that peace was about the last thing he felt right now.

It was certainly the furthest thought from her mind.

Taking a step back, she flipped her braid over her shoulder. Now that her initial shock at his actions had worn off and she didn't have to worry about anyone overhearing, she could let him know what she thought of his overbearing tactics.

"I don't believe you." Her tone was incredulous. "You've got the nerve to criticize my behavior, but it's okay for you to turn into a caveman? I'm surprised you didn't throw me over your shoulder to get me down here."

The thought had apparently crossed his mind. For a moment, she thought he might even admit it, but he turned confession into accusation.

"You pushed me to it."

Of course, it was her fault. For a moment, seeing his scowl, habit slipped into place. She was almost willing to shoulder that blame, to quietly accept that she was responsible for his actions so the peace could be kept. It was the kind of thing she always did. But there was no peace. There never really had been. The tranquility she'd strived to maintain in her life existed only on the surface. Now, meeting the challenge in Aaron's eyes, even that was gone.

For once she didn't want to swallow her pride.

"I pushed you to it." She repeated his conclusion calmly while years of suppressed anger at herself for accepting similar unjust accusations simmered inside. The anger struggled upward. "It's all *my* fault," she amended, her voice rising. "Just like it's my fault that I'm not behaving the way you want? Just like it's my fault that I've never been able to do anything to make my father really care about me?"

She felt herself shaking, her eyes blurring with tears as she backed away. If it hadn't been for Aaron, she could have been content with her illusion. She could have gone on pretending. But he'd seen through it and in making her see, the illusion had shattered. "I *hate* you for seeing that. I hate you for coming here and upsetting everything. You're just like him," she accused, her voice breaking as it rose. "You want me one way and he wants me another. What about me? What about what I want? Nobody's ever cared about that.''

The breeze whipped the sounds of her voice around. She couldn't believe it. She was screaming at him like a fishwife. What was worse, she didn't care. *"Nobody,"* she shouted at him.

Aaron matched her steps, seeming to stalk her as she backed blindly toward the water. He didn't appreciate her comparison. "I'm not like your father. You know that."

She refused to be reasonable. "What I know is that you want me to be something I'm not. It's the same thing."

"It's not, Nicki. He limits you. I want you to be everything that you are. There's a difference."

She couldn't see it. Not now. She felt as if a floodgate were coming open and the emotions held behind it were running over each other to escape. She didn't dare let that gate burst completely open. It was bad enough that she felt angry and hurt and lost. Heaven help her if the rest of what she could feel herself holding back should burst free, too. As it was, she didn't have a clue as to how to deal with any of it.

Like a great, dark shadow Aaron loomed closer. Already on wet sand, her next few steps took her into the surf. Water surged around her ankles. She scarcely noticed the chill.

"What is it that *you* want?" she heard him demand.

"I want you to leave me alone!"

"Not until you talk to me. Tell me what matters to you, Nicki. Tell me what you want."

She had nothing else to say to him. Nothing that would make sense anyway. On top of everything else, she felt horrible confusion. She'd been so sure of who she was. Now, she wasn't sure at all. "I don't want to talk to you anymore."

He kept coming, at the same time continuing his systematic address of each point she'd screamed at him. Over the dull roar of the waves, she heard his calm, "You don't hate me."

The water glued the hem of her nightgown to her calves, making her next backward step more difficult. She wanted to tell him that she *did* hate him. At least, she hated the way he made her feel. But the knot burning in her throat made it too difficult to speak.

He'd followed her right into the water, soaking his pants up to his knees. "You don't hate me," he said again, and reached out, taking her by the shoulders to keep her from backing deeper into the surf.

With a whimpered, "No," she tried to turn, oblivious to the low, rushing waves. "No," she repeated, her voice a strangled whisper as his gentle grip tightened.

She was shaking nearly as hard as when he'd pulled her out of the water during the storm. In its own way, what she felt now was just as frightening as that experience had been. And, like then, she felt the stabilizing effect of Aaron's embrace as he tucked her against his body and refused to let her face that struggle alone. He pulled her hard to his chest, holding her close. "It's all right," she heard him whisper against her temple. "It's going to be all right."

She wanted to pull back. Unable to believe what was happening, she wanted desperately to reassert some control. But all she seemed able to do was bury her face in his shirt and try very hard to contain the tears burning the backs of her eyes. She couldn't remember the last time she'd cried.

"It's all right," he repeated and held her a little tighter. "It's just us right now."

She barely heard his assurance. His lips grazed her temple, then moved to her eye to catch a tear. A moment later, she lifted her face to him and his mouth moved over her own.

She knew she shouldn't let him do this. But she needed him so badly that, at the moment, what was sensible and practical made no difference.

Warm. Familiar. Safe. That was how she thought of him as she clung to his back while the waves lapped at their knees. There was more, too. The heady quickening of her pulse when he angled his head to take her tongue into his mouth; the sharp stab of pleasure she felt when he groaned at her unrestrained response. But it was the comfort he offered that she needed most—and the understanding she hadn't realized he possessed.

He seemed to know that she didn't want to want him. Maybe he felt the same way about her, too.

With a soft sigh, she tightened her arms around his neck.

That was all it took for the need tearing at him to burst free. Feeling her sink against him, Aaron's more altruistic thoughts of soothing her vanished from his mind. Swinging her up into his arms, he muffled her gasp with his kiss, and carried her out of the water.

Shadows clung to the rocks beyond the shore, hiding the scrub grass until they reached it. He sat her down, remaining on his haunches while he took off his shirt and laid it over the tufts poking out of the sand.

A half-moon hung suspended in the night sky. Its light was pale, but there was enough of it for her to see the hard contours of his shoulders and chest—and the desire sharpening his features as he reached toward her.

Her breath caught at the feel of his hand brushing her breast. Instead of touching her as she ached for him to do, he picked up the end of her braid from where it rested against the gentle swell and began to undo the thick plaiting.

Concentration marked his features as he loosened her hair. Watching the dark strands fall, he spread his fingers through them and smoothed the silken tresses over her shoulders.

"It's too beautiful to bind," she heard him say, then heard nothing but the beat of her heart when his lips grazed the corner of her mouth. "It's like you, Nicki," he whispered, and curled his fingers around her nape to deepen the kiss.

She felt his chest against hers, then felt herself being pushed back to lie on the ground. Her head settled on the shirt he'd placed there and she wound her arms around him. The voice of warning sounded again. She ignored it, angling her body so he could fit her to him. She knew that she was only opening herself up to more hurt by allowing him to creep further into her heart. But in Aaron's arms, she felt safer. Not from him. From herself. As he had said, she couldn't hide from him. In his arms, she didn't want to.

"You remember, don't you?"

His words vibrated against her neck, his warm breath sending shivers through her that had nothing to do with the wet gown he'd pushed up around her waist.

She didn't have to ask what he meant. He was talking about how it was between them. How it had been since the first time they'd made love. There was no restraint. No hesitation. No holding back. Only the feeling of complete and utter rightness. When they made love nothing else existed.

"I remember," she whispered back, running her hands down his sides.

In the moonlight, with only the darkness surrounding them and the sound of water lapping at the shore, Nicole could almost believe they were back on the island; back in their own special place. But with Aaron, she was beginning to think any place could be special. "Make me remember more," she whispered.

At the raw need in her voice, Aaron raised his head. Fierce possession glinted in his eyes as they swept her face. He leaned back and began unfastening the neck of her nightgown. The almost puritanical garment parted, the tiny buttons slowing considerably the efforts of his big hands. When he finally reached the button at her waist, he gathered the wet hem and pulled the gown over her head. She'd worn only lace panties beneath it and they were stripped down her legs to be tossed atop her gown.

Sitting back on his heels, he reached for the buckle of his belt.

Had she ever thought about it, she never would have believed she would feel anything other than self-conscious lying naked before a man. The thought of embarrassment had never existed with Aaron. What she felt as his gaze moved over her was satisfaction. The smoldering look in his eyes was enough to heat her cool flesh.

"Let me." She reached for his belt and saw his nostrils flare with the ragged breath he drew. Slowly, his hands fell away.

The rasp of the zipper followed the clink of his buckle. He was on his knees. She knelt in front of him. Flattening her hands on either side of his hips, she pushed between his skin and his briefs and worked the fabric down his hips. As she did, she leaned forward and touched the tight bud of his nipple with her tongue. She smiled to herself when Aaron groaned. She hadn't known that men were sensitive there, too, until she'd discovered it this morning.

She'd discovered so many things with Aaron.

Nicole took her time ridding him of his pants. At least as long a time as he would allow before he pushed her over and began the same exquisite torture. He seemed to give no thought to hurry. He experienced no frantic need to rush to completion. He needed to explore and to hold, just as she did, and to cherish and remember. He would take his time. They had all night if they needed it.

Though neither spoke of it, each knew that the night was all they really had.

It seemed to Nicole that this knowledge made their love-making all that more compelling. And when they finally came together, she found the joy in their union easing the painful ache in her heart. Loving him healed even as it hurt.

She lay in his arms afterward, quietly stroking the sun-bleached hair on his chest. He had rolled to his back to keep from suffocating her, or so he'd said, and held her close to his side. He placed a kiss on her forehead and she smiled into the darkness.

He kissed her again and pressed her head to his shoulder. He was quiet for a long time, content it seemed to sift her hair through his fingers and watch it fall over her bare shoulders. She had no idea what he was thinking until he broke the peaceful silence with his pensive request. "Tell me what you want, Nicki. Tell me what it is you've wanted that no one's ever cared enough to hear about?"

He'd been thinking about her little tirade. It was too much to hope he'd forgotten how badly she'd acted. "I shouldn't have said all that. I was just upset."

"You were being honest," he corrected. "All the time we spent together, you never told me what you wanted for yourself. What your dreams were."

That was because, until she'd met him, she hadn't wanted to dream. She couldn't afford to let herself do that now either.

She wished she could have held reality off just a little longer. But Aaron's question had shattered the illusion.

Aaron knew the exact moment she began her mental retreat from him. Her hand went still on his chest and he felt her stiffen. Instinctively, he tightened his hold, his protective instincts alarmingly strong where this soft, guileless woman was concerned. "Someday you'll figure out that it's okay to have dreams, honey. You might even find that they're necessary."

"I don't want to need you, Aaron."

She said the words so simply. A statement of fact. They reached inside his heart, touching him at his most basic level.

Cupping her face in his hand, he looked into her eyes. Never had he seen such vulnerability. "You don't need me," he assured her. "You need only yourself. When it gets right down to it, you're the only person you're ever going to be able to rely on completely."

He kissed her then because he couldn't stand to see the helplessness that slipped into her expression. He knew that she was only now beginning to discover who she was; how very different were the sides of her he knew as Nicki and Nicole. She wasn't crazy. She was simply growing. Finally. That kind of growth wasn't easy, and she was fighting it as hard as she could. He couldn't blame her. He'd fought it, too.

Aaron knew what it was like to face yourself. He also knew that a person could only do that alone. He could stay to pursue her, or ask her to leave with him so he could push her in the direction he wanted her to go. But a change made under duress wasn't a change at all. And as unsettling as the thought was, he cared too much to exert that kind of pressure on her. He couldn't give her what she needed anyway. She needed roots and a sense of belonging. He could offer her nothing but the wind.

She ducked her head, touching her fingers to her mouth as if to seal in the warmth from his kiss. "I want to go back now."

He gave her his shirt because her nightgown was wet and full of sand, then pulled on his pants and held out his hand for her. In silence they headed back to the villa, still holding each other's hand as they climbed the stairway leading to the veranda outside her door. He left her there with the warmth of his bittersweet kiss lingering on her lips. There was nothing left to say. They had their memories, and she knew that memories were all she could let herself have of him. She tried to tell herself it didn't matter that he'd asked nothing more of her. Oddly, it wasn't quite so easy to pretend anymore.

A few hours later, shortly after the sun broke over the islands, she heard the distinctive whir of a helicopter leaving the pad beyond the garden.

"Aaron left awfully early this morning."

At Doris's observation, Nicole glanced from her to her father then back at the vichyssoise Luisa had set in front of her. The guests had all scattered earlier to swim or shop or sail and Harrington had insisted that Nicole join him and his intended for lunch.

He now intercepted the question Doris had posed. "I told him yesterday that my pilot would fly him wherever he wanted to go. He'd said last night that he wanted to leave for the airport on Abaco at five-thirty."

"Why was he in such a hurry?"

The inquiry was nothing more than curiosity. Harrington, however, didn't appear particularly willing to discuss the topic. "He didn't say."

Nicole laid her spoon down by the cold soup. She desperately wanted everything to return to normal. To her way of thinking, that could only begin to happen if everyone would stop talking about Aaron. A change of subject was definitely in order. The perplexed look on Doris's face was about to turn itself into another question.

"Is there anything special you would like for me to do for the two of you? An engagement party, perhaps?"

The lemon colored blouse Doris wore with her white slacks had a row of large, pearl buttons. Toying with the middle one, Doris smiled and graciously dropped the subject no one else wanted to talk about. "That's very sweet of you, but I think we're going to keep everything very simple. We don't want any special parties or an elaborate ceremony. Just family and a few friends. I'm going to ask my daughter to stand up with me. You remember Celia, don't you?" She tipped her head at the question, the sunlight pouring onto the patio making her hair shine like platinum. "I believe I introduced you to her at the fund-raiser for the National Museum restoration. Anyway, there will be Celia and you and Dick Holt for your father. Everyone here, of course. It would be rude not to include them since they were the first to hear of it." Folding her hand over Harrington's, her smile softened. "We're really sorry you had to learn of it as you did. I'm sure it must have come as something of a surprise."

The woman had a definite gift for understatement. Even now, Nicole could hardly believe that her father had committed himself to marriage. He'd been single for twenty years and, to her knowledge, had never expressed a scintilla of interest in the institution. Yet, there he was, looking very proud of the woman smiling at him—and a little ill-at-ease with his daughter.

It was his inexplicable disquiet with her presence that Nicole found truly perplexing. She'd never seen him anything less than completely in command of himself with anyone—especially with her.

Doris seemed aware of his odd manner, too. As she released Harrington's hand with a pat and stood up, Nicole suspected that she also knew the reason behind his behavior. She suddenly looked as if she had a thousand things to do.

"I hate to cut this short," Doris said, not appearing at all apologetic as she placed her napkin beside her plate. "But since I'm finished with my lunch, I'm going to get some sun."

"You've barely touched your lunch," Harrington said. A scowl deepened the lines in his forehead indicating his displeasure with her intention to leave.

Her shrewd hazel eyes scanned the table. A basket of rolls sat untouched by an iced bowl of butter curls. The tureen of vichyssoise remained half full, while scarcely two spoonfuls had been taken from the china bowls at each place. The only thing that had disappeared was the bud vase with the rose in it. Nicole had knocked that over when she'd reached for her iced tea and the delicate crystal had shattered to smithereens. Luisa had quickly swept the mess away. Nicole's father, to her amazement, hadn't said a word.

Heading toward the sliding glass doors, Doris gently pointed out that she wasn't the only one who hadn't finished her meal. "You've barely touched yours, either. Nicole also appears to be lacking an appetite. Talk to your daughter, Harrington. I think we'll all feel better."

With that instruction, she plucked a yellow mum from a pot by the door and disappeared inside.

The scrape of wrought iron on terra-cotta tiles pulled Nicole's attention back to her father. He had stood to move from the table. Tall and lean, his back ramrod straight, he crossed the patio. A moment later, his usual aggressive posture sagged. Propping his elbows on the railing, his hands clasped, he bent his head in thought.

Feeling very much as if she were holding her breath, Nicole rose, too. It didn't appear that circumstances were overly conducive to a return to normalcy today. Weeks could go by without she and her father discussing anything more disturbing than the weather. Yet now, scarcely twelve hours after dropping one bombshell, he seemed prepared to drop another. In between, the man who had awakened all manner of impossible dreams had walked out of her life.

Trying desperately not to think about that, she pushed her hands into the pockets of her casual dress and skirted the table. Already feeling as if she were held together by nothing other than the force of her own will, she steeled herself against whatever she was about to hear. The thought that whatever it was would further shake her already upended world was too acute a fear to dismiss.

She stood behind him, a little to one side. He must have realized she'd followed him. When she stopped she heard him say, "I don't know how to begin this."

"At the beginning?" she suggested, sounding a whole lot braver than she felt.

He gave an odd little laugh. "I think the beginning better wait until later. I want to tell you something else while you're still willing to listen."

"I've always listened to you."

"I know." A sad, self-deprecating note entered his voice. "I almost wish you hadn't.

"I don't understand."

He turned then and, to her surprise, he put his hand on her shoulder. He didn't look terribly comfortable with the gesture, but there was a determination in his weathered expression that she recognized. After giving her shoulder a little squeeze, he turned back to the railing.

She couldn't remember the last time he'd done anything like that. Even as a child, her father hadn't expressed affection the way her friends' fathers had. He'd never put his arm around her, or given her a tender pat on the cheek or touched her hair as she'd seen other men do with their daughters. His way of showing pride or approval had always been verbal. He'd never deliberately touched her.

She was wondering what had prompted him to do so now when his voice broke the awkward stillness.

"The first matter I want to talk to you about is Doris," he finally said. "It's because of you that I asked her to marry me."

"Because of me?" Clearly, she failed to understand the nature of her influence. She was a little old to be needing a mother and, short of that, Nicole couldn't imagine any reason which would have been affected by her.

"It was your disappearance, actually," Harrington clarified, then hesitantly went on to tell her that he'd never felt so helpless as he had when he'd learned that she'd been caught in the storm. The hours spent tracing her steps from Boston to Biscayne and then learning that she'd set sail with the *Valiant* had made him realize just how important she was to him—how imperative it was that he find her.

"It's not easy for me to say how I feel," he admitted in a voice that said it wasn't easy for him now, either. "I've never done that sort of thing very well. But when I called Doris to ask her to come here and wait with me, I knew that I had to tell her how I felt about her." He paused, seeming to draw in courage with the breath he drew. "There was a very real possibility that I'd never have a chance to tell you that I love you. Faced with that possibility, I realized that the Fates could take her from me at any time, too. I guess I was arrogant enough to think that she would always be there for me."

A look of self-deprecation swept the patrician lines of his face. Seeming older, frailer, he shook his head at his own foolishness. "You see, I always thought I could keep you, too."

A small, dried leaf fluttered from the tree overhanging the corner of the patio. Nicole watched it sway past the railing to disappear in the vegetation growing up the side of the hill. Oddly, she didn't know how to respond to what her father had said. There had been a time when she'd have embraced such an acknowledgement from him. But even now, he'd told her how he felt about her only in context with how that feeling related to someone else. Yet, everything *she'd* done, she'd done for him.

Her voice sounded small to her, and seemed to come from far away. "You can love someone, but not like them very much. That's how you feel about me, isn't it?"

He started to deny such a thought, but the stillness of her lovely features stopped him. There was no discourtesy or disdain. Only inquiry, then simple acceptance as she lowered her head when his silence confirmed her conclusion.

"You don't know how sorry I am, Nicole. I know I've never felt as close to you as I should, but I didn't realize how obvious that was until last night. I heard you and Aaron arguing," he said and her head snapped up. "I'd just finished a conference call to London in the library," he explained to let her know that he hadn't meant to eavesdrop. "And when I came out, I heard what he was saying about your mother, about how you've been trying to make up to me all these years for her leaving us. I don't know if that's what you've tried to do or not, Nicole. I can only tell you that he was a lot more perceptive about you than I have been."

Abandoning his post at the railing, he left her to retrieve his water from the table. For long moments he stared at the glass while Nicole felt little pieces of her world being methodically chipped away. All these years she'd struggled to please him and her efforts had been doomed from the beginning. There could be no pleasing someone already prejudiced against you.

As he set the glass back on the table, it quickly became apparent why that prejudice was there. "You were so much like your mother when you were a child. You had her spirit, her vitality. I saw it most when you were with the horses. You were like one of them, lithe and limber, with that same elegant grace Elana possessed." A pensive expression crossed his face, his voice sounding a bit more distant as he looked into the past he'd closed to himself so long ago. "Elana," he repeated. "Do you remember her?"

The recollections Nicole had of her mother were more fragments of thought than real memories. The scent of lilac in the spring would bring a quick sense of something familiar, then disappear in the time it took to blink. The sound of light, lilting laughter could sometimes do the same thing. But mostly, Nicole recalled a sense of sadness about her mother, of great, dark eyes filled with tears.

She hadn't imagined the tears. Her father, she learned when he began to speak again, had brought on many of them. He sounded reluctant enough to admit that now. Twenty years ago, his pride wouldn't have allowed it at all.

As it was, he said only that Elana had been terribly young when he had married her and that, possibly, he had treated her more as an ornament than a wife. "She'd seemed content for a while after you were born," he told Nicole as he paced between the table and the railing. "But as you grew older and went off to school, she seemed to need more from me than I had the time to give. There were rumors about an affair between her and her riding instructor, but I dismissed all that as harmless. At least, I did until the day she asked for a divorce. Her young man was returning to Europe and she wanted to marry him."

"So she left us," Nicole quietly concluded.

Drawing to a halt by the railing, he stared out at the emerald islands dotting the sea. "She left *me*, Nicole. She didn't want to leave you. I readily agreed to the divorce, but I refused to let her take you with her."

It had never occurred to Nicole that her mother hadn't simply walked out on her at the same time she'd walked out on her father. For years she'd thought in terms of the woman having abandoned them. *Both* of them. That was part of the bond between her and her father; part of why they needed each other.

The bond was shattering. "You refused to let her take me? Why?"

The focus of Harrington's mind was narrow. Even now he could only see his own purpose and not what Nicole needed to hear. He didn't say it was because he wanted his daughter, or because he cared about her and thought he could provide what her mother could not. His reasoning was more basic. She belonged to him. No other reason mattered.

"You were my daughter."

"I was her daughter, too," she said, defending the woman who'd no doubt had few defenses of her own against this formidable man.

"In those days an illicit affair was grounds for proving a mother unfit. She obviously saw the wisdom of going without a fight."

"Did she ever ask to see me after she left?"

The question made Harrington look uncomfortable. "Several times. The last was a month before her car went off a cliff outside of Vienna. I couldn't bear the thought of having her in the house and I couldn't let you go to her."

The gold signet ring he wore caught the light as he studied it, his expression hard and absorbed. He seemed to be weighing what he was about to say to see how much it would cost him.

Nicole saw him glance toward the door, the one through which Doris had disappeared. It was obvious by now that his fiancée was privy to many of his innermost thoughts and that her influence over him was considerable. Having thought of her, he apparently decided that no matter what it cost, Nicole deserved to hear the rest of what he had to say.

"You see," he began, returning his attention to his ring, "I was afraid that if I let her take you out of the house, she'd never bring you back. I loved that woman and you were all I had left of her. But when you started growing up, you became more and more like her. There were times when the resemblance was so keen that I couldn't bear to look at you." His voice became quieter. "But I couldn't stand the thought of losing you, either."

Nicole turned away, her knuckles going white as she gripped the chair back. What he had just said explained far more than he probably realized. Because of the ambivalence he felt toward her, she'd spent her life living in limbo. She'd mistaken his possessiveness for caring. Just as she'd mistaken the frequent displeasure he showed with her as the result of some shortcoming on her part. "Why have you told me all this now?"

"Because someone pointed out to me that I owed it to you."

"Doris?"

His shoes thudded softly on the tiles behind her. "She was with me last night in the library."

Which meant that she, too, had heard all that Aaron had said. It should have bothered her to know that such an intimate argument had been overheard. But she felt too numb to care at the moment. All she cared about was that for years her father had unwittingly protected himself at her expense. He'd never seen her as a person, only as someone who resembled a woman who'd hurt him. That woman had been her mother—and he'd kept Nicole from knowing her, too.

She felt her father stop behind her. No doubt after unburdening himself, he wanted to make amends. Doris had probably told him he should do that, too.

Slipping away just as he reached for her, Nicole turned to face him. Head held high, her eyes locked on his. "Is there anything else I should know?"

He didn't seem to trust the cool edge in her voice. A faint scowl touched his brow. "That's all I had to say."

"That isn't what I asked," she reminded, not caring if he thought her impertinent.

"There's nothing else."

Without saying another word, she left him standing alone.

Chapter Twelve

"You don't have to do this, Nicole."

Holding a brown dress in one hand and a beige one in the other, Nicole considered them with a frown. "Yes, I do," she told Doris and tossed both dresses onto the stack at the foot of her bed. The pile there was destined for a donation to charity. The pile on the pink chintz chair by her antique armoire was intended for her suitcase. It contained mostly the new things she and Doris had shopped for earlier in the week. Her soon-to-be stepmother was perched on the arm of that chair, obviously waiting for more of an explanation.

Nicole obliged, though most of her attention was focused on her packing. "I want everything settled in case it doesn't work out."

"But you can still keep your room here."

"Doris, I am twenty-eight years old. I'll be twenty-nine next month. No one has a room at home at my age. What I'm not taking with me, I'll have stored at the house at Marblehead."

Nicole had driven out to Marblehead the day after she'd returned to Boston from Stewart Cay. That had been two weeks ago. The house had sat empty for so long that the salt air had eaten away the paint, and cobwebs vied with sand for space. But she'd remembered the spacious rooms overlooking the ocean from its secluded rise, and had remembered, too, the many happy hours she'd spent there as a young child with her mother. She'd often thought about going back there during the past few years. Something had kept her from doing that until now. Maybe that was because, until now, she hadn't been ready.

Now, it would be her home.

"Your father wishes you'd have the place redone before you move your things in there."

"He hasn't said anything to me about that."

"He's afraid to say much of anything to you."

The idea of Harrington Stewart being afraid of anyone—most especially his own daughter—was preposterous. "I doubt it. I doubt that he cares much what I do now." Immediately conscious of her tone, she added an apologetic smile. It wasn't fair of her to take out her feelings on Doris. "After all, you'll be taking care of his house and I'm sure the Stewart Foundation will run smoother under you than it ever did under me. I never did learn how to use that computer well enough to suit him."

It hadn't been so very long ago that Nicole had been horrified by the idea of sharing, much less turning over, her responsibilities. Those responsibilities were what had tied her to her father, and what provided the sense of security she'd clung to all these years. Now, she was free of all of it. She'd resigned her position at the Foundation and turned the care of her father's home over to Doris's capable hands, where, as her father's wife, it rightfully belonged. Nicole now had no job, a home that would require weeks of work to make it livable and absolutely no idea what tomorrow was going to bring, because tomorrow she was going off to chase a dream. It was all rather frightening and exciting at the same time.

Maybe, she thought, that was what Aaron found so compelling about his freedom.

While she continued packing, Nicole was aware of Doris's quiet assessment of her. Her future stepmother was in a difficult position, caring as she did about both Nicole and her father, and Nicole was beginning to learn that she was not a person to back down. That trait could very well explain how she managed to handle Harrington Stewart.

A hint of that determination presented itself in the way Doris rose, smoothing her linen slacks as she did, and walked over to where Nicole stood frowning at a cocoa-colored jacket. She couldn't seem to decide what to do with it.

Doris ignored the dilemma. "You know I wasn't talking about the house or the office, Nicole. I'm talking about you and your father. In his own way, he cares very much about you. He just didn't know how else to cope with what he felt about Elana."

With a helpless little gesture, Nicole started to turn away. "Doris, please."

The touch of the older woman's hand on her arm was gentle, but insistent, too. "I can't blame you for feeling hurt and angry with him. His only defense is that he honestly didn't realize how much pain he caused you." Her voice became quieter, almost pleading. "I have to believe that, or I couldn't care about him as I do."

Old habits died hard. For Doris's sake, Nicole wished she could pretend that everything was as it should be. Doris wanted very much for the past to be put to rest. But there was no way Nicole's relationship with her father would ever be the same as it was, and she just wasn't as good at pretending as she once had been. Maybe, someday, she would get past the sense of betrayal she felt. Right now she needed simply to be away from him.

She also needed to make a few decisions of her own and to live with their consequences. It was entirely possible she could be quite lousy at doing that. But, at least, she'd have relied on herself instead of allowing those decisions to be made for her. She'd never really understood why Aaron had made such drastic changes in his life until she'd felt compelled to make them herself.

"Please don't worry about it anymore," she asked Doris, feeling bad enough that she worried as much as she did. "It's just going to take time." She held up the jacket. "What do you think about this? Should I wear it tomorrow?"

The change of subject was terribly obvious, but Doris knew, too, when to leave a matter to rest. Besides, Nicole had begun to exhibit a certain stubbornness of her own lately. The change wasn't overt, but those who knew her couldn't help but notice her air of quiet determination.

Taking the garment, Doris subjected it to her thorough scrutiny. "The style is good, but the shade is rather..."

"Dark?" Nicole suggested.

"'Uninspiring' was the word that actually came to mind. You can wear brown well enough. But I thought you wanted to brighten yourself up?"

Her flat, "I do," didn't sound terribly convincing. "Some, anyway. I don't want to look conspicuous."

It took time to adjust to changes and no matter how much Nicole insisted that she wanted a different "look," she wasn't the type of person to be comfortable with a drastic alteration of image. With the exception of the denim miniskirt she'd insisted on buying, her new wardrobe was still fairly conservative.

Doris reached into the closet and pulled out another jacket. "How about this navy blue one? With this?"

Among the purchases Doris had helped her make a few days ago was a stylish white jumpsuit. Adding a few newly purchased red accessories, she laid the ensemble over the bed and stepped back to see what Nicole thought of it.

She didn't look terribly pleased.

"Now that is *not* conspicuous," Doris said since it appeared that Nicole thought otherwise. "And it's very practical. You'll need the jacket on your flight because they never do get the cabin temperature adjusted correctly, and it will be warm in the Bahamas. Since the jumpsuit is sleeveless, you just take the jacket off and you'll be comfortable there, too." She smiled and immediately turned her attention to a pair of white low-heeled sandals, keeping her tone as bland as oatmeal. "Red, white and blue is also a nautical theme. That makes it quite appropriate. Don't you think?"

The hesitation on Nicole's part that had prompted Doris to justify her selection actually had little to do with the choice of clothes. The whole idea of what she was about to do suddenly scared the daylights out of her.

Turning to the antique cheval mirror in the corner, she put her hands to her face and drew a deep breath. The woman in the reflection looked different from the one she was accustomed to seeing there. Her hair swung loose and free, cut now to barely brush her shoulders. She hadn't quite mastered the knack of makeup, though. And she had felt ridiculous when she'd emerged from Doris's favorite salon wearing no less than four shades of eyeshadow. Doris had agreed that maybe she wasn't quite ready for such a sophisticated look, but had shown her how to apply color with a considerably light touch. Even still, Nicole preferred to stick to basics. She found it amazing how much difference a little mascara could make.

"What if he doesn't recognize me?"

It didn't seem to take but a moment for Doris to recognize the source of Nicole's anxiety. She set the shoes down and lowered herself back to the arm of the overloaded chair. "It's only been a couple of weeks," she gently pointed out. "I'm sure his memory is much longer than that."

The light from a nearby table lamp picked up the sheen of Nicole's hair as she shook her head. The woman didn't quite understand. "I don't think you know what it is that I want."

"I think I do." A knowing smile touched Doris's mouth. "You haven't said as much, but this trip to see Aaron isn't just a trip to visit a friend. You're in love with him. I can see that. What might not be so obvious to everyone else, though, is that I don't think you're planning on coming back. That's why you're not in any big hurry to fix up the house at Marblehead."

The woman was far more perceptive than Nicole had realized. Having put that much together, she could probably see straight through a denial. There was therefore no point in offering one.

"Whether or not I come back depends entirely on him. When he left, everything seemed pretty final." It hadn't taken long for Nicole to discover the astounding number of insecurities a woman in love could experience. Just as she would reassure herself about one aspect of her little plan, another would cause her even more doubt. But then, she supposed that chasing dreams was a dubious business at best. "It's entirely possible that he's forgotten all about me."

"I doubt Aaron could ever forget you. I heard what he said the night before he left, remember? And I know that a man doesn't sound that hurt or demand that a woman take such a close look at herself unless he feels very strongly about her."

"But what if he doesn't—"

Doris raised a perfectly manicured hand to cut her off. "No negatives. Only allow yourself to think in positive terms. You won't know anything until you sit down and talk to him, anyway. Of course," she added with a sympathetic smile, "you have to find him first."

The task of finding Aaron wasn't as easy as it sounded. The last Nicole had heard, he was headed back to the Bahamas. Specifically, Nassau. That she learned from Jake Wilton who'd tried to hustle her for a date before he'd realized that she was Nicole Stewart. Looking surprised and charmingly embarrassed, he'd turned into an absolute gentleman the moment she'd asked about Aaron, and had been most helpful in providing her with his friend's whereabouts.

Aaron had told him where he was heading. Unfortunately, he hadn't said anything about when he would arrive there or how long he would stay.

He'd thought about leaving for the past three days. On the other hand, Aaron had considered staying for another

week. The only thing he was sure of was that he was unde-
cided. That held for a couple of things.

For the third time in as many minutes, Aaron took the
envelope from the pocket of his unbuttoned, hibiscus print
shirt and toyed with the idea of mailing it. A mail sack sat
just inside the door of the bait and tackle shop. He knew it
was there because he'd already been in twice to stare at it.
The pleasant Jamaican proprietor probably thought he was
crazy. Crazy or not, all he'd have to do was walk in, drop the
envelope in the canvas bag and leave. With any luck, Nicole would have it by the end of the week.

A minute later, disgusted with his indecision, he stuffed
the letter into the back pocket of his white shorts and headed
up the pier. It was barely ten in the morning and he already
knew it was going to be one of those days.

Nassau teamed with activity. All manner of sailing vessels, from huge cruise liners to battered dingys, occupied its
docks and piers. His own sloop, *Salvation*, was tied up at a
moorage across from Paradise Island, about a half mile
from the outdoor market on Potter's Cay. That was where
he should be right now, at the market stocking up on provisions so he could get underway. That's exactly what he
would be doing, too—if he weren't so busy stalling. It was
amazing how time-consuming procrastination could be.

By rights, he should have been itching to set sail. The
Salvation was in prime condition, her brass gleamed and her
teak was as shiny as it was going to get. The weather was
perfect for a sail through the Caribbean and if he left now
he could make the Panama Canal by the end of the month.

The problem was that he couldn't seem to muster up
much enthusiasm for the journey, even with the thought of
Australia as his ultimate destination. It wasn't that he didn't

want to go. But he wondered what would he do once he got there.

He'd wondered about that ever since he'd left Nicole. In a little over one week, she changed the whole focus of his life.

It hadn't been that long ago that thoughts of a future had been less demanding than thoughts of coping with the present. But he was beyond all that now and she had made him realize that he'd never given any thought to what lay at the end of his escape. Now, the future loomed ahead of him and he saw it looking vast and empty. He'd denied that loneliness to Nicole. But that was because with her, he didn't feel it. With her, he wanted to consider the future. Not one based on what either of them had in the past, but a tomorrow built from their mutual needs.

Aaron knew what he needed. He needed Nicole.

The letter in his back pocket said a lot more than that. If he mailed it, at least she might contact him and he could see her. Just to talk.

Turning on his heel, he pulled the letter out and marched back to the bait and tackle store. Without so much as a pause, he opened the door, smiled at the perplexed owner and dropped the letter in the mailbag. Five minutes later, thinking he might as well go fishing with the bait he'd bought, his attention was drawn by the drone of a jet as it muffled the constant cry of the gulls. Shielding his eyes against the sun, he watched an airliner cut a wide arc toward the island's busy airport.

Nicole saw the sun bounce off the water, rippling curves of light along the waves. Anticipation had grown to trepidation as they circled to land. Now, in the last minutes of their approach she felt it escalate to anxiety. Most of that anxiety was due to what she could see from her window.

The view was spectacular, but it wasn't the incandescent bands of white and blue sea surrounding the lush islands that held her attention. It was the number of boats. Not just those in the water, either. There were hundreds of them lining much of the island itself. Especially to the north-east around Nassau and Paradise Island. The concentrations were heaviest, of course, at the marinas.

By the time the plane touched down and Nicole was in the terminal, she was entertaining thoughts of defeat. It would take her days to walk up and down each dock to find Aaron's sloop—if he was even here.

"I carry your bag?"

Before Nicole could think to answer, a young Jamaican boy in a Mickey Mouse T-shirt had grabbed her suitcase and treated her to a dazzling smile. Beyond him, several of his cohorts were offering their services to other passengers as well.

Adding a halfhearted smile to her distracted, "Sure," she joined the sea of people surging toward the doors. Warm, humid air rushed in to replace the more comfortable air-conditioning as those doors opened and Nicole headed toward the cabs lined bumper to bumper at the curb.

"Wait a minute." Grabbing her young porter by the arm, she pulled him out of the flow and leaned down so she could be heard over the indecipherable cacophony of people speaking in a half-dozen dialects at once. "How much do you charge for this?"

"One dollar," was his immediate reply.

"How would you like to earn five?"

"To carry bag?"

"No. To find a boat."

His dark eyes narrowed as he considered her offer. Or possibly, he was considering her. The child was only about ten or eleven, but he was street smart and remarkably shrewd. A quick glance at the quality of her clothes and he had her sized up. "That be ten dollars."

"That will be ten dollars if you *find* it," she corrected. "Five to *look* for it. Do you have any friends who want to earn five dollars, too?"

He had about twenty of them. Nicole had no idea where they all came from, but within half an hour she'd printed the word *Salvation* on the pages of an entire notepad and distributed them with twenty five-dollar bills to an assortment of pint-size detectives. The children had instructions to contact her at the patio pool of the Ocean Club if they found the boat and she would pay whoever found it the rest of his fee.

She didn't know if she should congratulate herself for being very clever or kick herself for being very stupid. As the children ran off, it occurred to her that she might have just kissed a hundred dollars goodbye.

By nine o'clock that evening Nicole had chalked her money up to tuition to the school of experience and was sitting by the hotel's swimming pool nursing some sort of fruit and rum concoction with a paper umbrella in it. She'd been there since seven o'clock as she'd told the children she would be. Having had ample time to think about it since she'd returned from her own luckless search, she decided that her idea to have them help her had been as foolish as her idea to come here. It was entirely possible that Aaron had already left the island and was on his way to Australia by now.

As logical as her thoughts were, her heart wouldn't let her admit defeat. Optimism was new to her. But she couldn't help thinking that there was still tomorrow.

With that thought in mind, she tucked the dark fall of her hair behind her ears, and reached for her drink. She'd just leaned back in her wicker chair to take the last swallow when she felt her heart slide neatly to her throat.

A man in a flower-print shirt and white shorts stood by the lobby doors leading out to the pool. Beside him, speaking rapidly as he pointed, was a young boy in a Mickey Mouse T-shirt.

A constant stream of guests flowed from the dining terrace behind her to the pool and through the many lobby doors. Nicole forgot all about them. Sounds seemed to fade; the faint clatter of dishes, the occasional splash from the pool, the muffled conversations from the people enjoying drinks in the area where she sat, all became indistinguishable from one another. Her sole focus was on the pair by the doors.

Carefully, so as not to drop it, she sat her glass beside its tiny umbrella on the table and watched the man who'd barely glanced at her.

Aaron's head was bent, his blond hair ruffled as always. Still talking with the little boy who'd accosted Nicole's bag at the airport, he reached for his wallet. A moment later, he handed the kid a couple of bills, and the grinning boy disappeared between the potted palms.

When Nicole had first met Aaron, he'd subjected her to as direct and thorough a scrutiny as she'd ever endured. As he approached now, his eyes steady on her flushed face, she suffered the same anxiety she'd experienced then. He seemed able to see right through her, to strip away her protective layers of composure and see her very soul. But his own expression told her very little. It remained remarkably bland as his glance ran from her gleaming hair and over the white jumpsuit she wore.

"I understand you're the lady who's been bribing children to find my boat."

She tried to smile, but the intent way he watched her made it too difficult. He appeared neither pleased nor concerned by what she'd done. If anything, his manner was one of indifference. And of all the ways he could have responded to her presence, that was the most difficult to take. "I wasn't bribing them. I hired them. They were supposed to tell me where you were. Not the other way around."

"I doubled your fee."

That explained it, she thought, though she said nothing as he picked up the paper umbrella she'd discarded. He twirled its bamboo stem between his fingers, watching her over the small table. He could have sat down, but he chose to stand and that made her even more apprehensive.

"You still in the neighborhood?"

By the "neighborhood" she assumed he meant the Bahamas. As the sea gull flew, Stewart Cay was about one-hundred-and-twenty-five miles away.

"I'm not still at the villa, if that's what you mean. I left there right after you did and went back to Boston. Actually," she added, because she wanted him to know this, "I'm not at my father's house anymore, either. I've moved into the house at Marblehead. The one I told you about."

She spoke with a certain casualness, but Aaron sensed the enormity of what she'd done. He remembered the house. In part because she'd described it in such detail. She'd told him how she used to remember watching the rain beat against the paned windows and how the shutters would rattle during a storm. But most of what he'd remembered when she'd talked about it was the pensive quality of her voice and the softness of her expression. That house was a place which held comfortable memories for her, a place where she could feel she belonged.

With a vague, sinking sensation, he thought that she would probably be very happy there.

"I'm not working for him anymore, either."

The umbrella went still. Nicole looked from it to Aaron's face and found that he seemed to be waiting. His quiet, "Why?" held a hint of suspicion.

Her father may have stifled her, but Aaron's insight had freed her. He'd made her realize how insecure she'd felt all those years and how she'd struggled for that security by entrenching herself in her father's life. Thanks to Aaron, she'd found the security she'd been looking for within herself. That was what had given her the courage to come after him. She hoped it would give her the courage to say what needed to be said now.

"I'm not running away from anything, if that's what you're worried about. I know what I want now, Aaron. Part of it anyway. I'm just not quite sure how to go about getting it. I guess you could say I came to you for help."

He hadn't had any idea why she'd wanted to see him. Now, he knew. It seemed that she'd finally begun to break free, which, he reminded himself, is exactly what he'd hoped she'd do. He reminded himself, too, that he'd made a point of making her understand that she didn't need him. He'd been kicking himself for a week over that one.

Feeling very much as if he were holding his breath, he calmly asked, "What is it that you want?"

Nicole glanced around, aware that Aaron had drawn the attention of the patrons at the nearby tables. She could hardly blame them for staring. He was an extremely attractive man and there was enough challenge in his stance to make their quiet conversation appear very interesting. Nicole did not care to be part of a floor show. If she was about to make a fool of herself, she preferred to do it with a more limited audience.

"Would you mind if we went someplace else to talk?"

"I think I'd prefer it."

He held out his hand.

She didn't know why the gesture made her pause. Perhaps it was because his manner was so remote. Or, maybe she didn't trust herself to touch him. Whatever the cause, she found herself looking from his hand to the stillness in his eyes. She glanced back down to his open palm, and felt her heart bump when she reached for it.

His fingers slowly closed around hers, his eyes remaining locked on her own as he pulled her to her feet. Not until she was standing could she look away. Aware of little other than the heat of his firm grip and a fluttery tightness in her chest, she let him lead her past the pool, through the garden of ferns separating the patio from the beach, and out into the night.

Neither spoke, their silence becoming more pronounced as the sounds of the hotel gave way to the lulling roar of the ocean. Farther beyond them a few couples strolled hand in hand along the edge of the surf. The night created its own intimate spaces and Nicole let Aaron lead her into the darkness.

They'd barely escaped the softly glowing lights of the hotel when he drew her around to face him. He'd held her hand. Now, he released it to brush his knuckles over her cheek. In the uncertain light she saw his glance sweep her face. Hesitating, he seemed torn between what he wanted to say and what he wanted to do.

The light of the moon disappeared as his head bent. Her breath caught. She thought she'd seen the glint of yearning in his eyes, but it could have simply been her own need she felt as his mouth came down on hers.

A ragged moan trapped itself in her throat. His mouth was hard, its pressure bruising. There was hunger and need and maybe even a touch of desperation in his kiss. It was definitely in hers. Crushed as she was to his chest, she wanted to be closer still.

Her purse fell with a soft plop to the sand. She needed to put her arms around him. Pinned as they were to her sides, she could only slide them around his waist. His hand slid over her hip and she tightened her hold, needing to feel as much of him against her as she could.

The intimate adjustment in position altered the pattern of Aaron's breathing. Within the space of two heartbeats, his fingers dove into her hair, and splayed over the back of her skull. She couldn't imagine how he could deepen the kiss, but he managed somehow. She sank against him, going weak with relief and need.

The pressure of his mouth slowly began to ease, the touch of his lips growing gentler as he carried his kiss to her cheek, her eyes, her temple. For long moments, he lingered at the corners of her mouth, as if to kiss away the bruises he might have left there, then pressed her head to his chest.

She could feel the heavy thud of his heart.

"You can't believe how badly I've needed to hold you, Nicki. Just hold you."

His words wrapped around her, drawing her in with their sweet longing. Not until that moment had she let herself admit just how big a risk she'd taken in coming after him. And not until that moment, did she begin to let herself believe that, maybe, what she remembered hadn't been a dream, after all.

She relished the feel of him; his strong arms holding her so tightly. "I've needed to hold you, too. Aaron, I've missed you so much. I was so afraid I wouldn't find you."

"I'd have found you."

She pulled back a little, just enough to see the tautness of his features. The certainty in his tone brought a question to her eyes.

"I mailed you a letter this morning," he said, watching her as he always did when he wanted to gauge her reaction. "There was something I forgot to tell you before I left. I wanted you to know in case it made any difference to you."

Anything about him mattered to her. "What did you forget to tell me?"

"That I love you."

Nicole stared up at him, hoping he wouldn't let go of her. From the way he had his hands locked behind her back and her body fitted to the cradle of his hips, it didn't seem like an immediate possibility. But she hoped anyway. Just in case.

"I believe I failed to mention something like that myself." A faint tremor took the strength from her voice. "I love you, too, you know."

His smile held relief, and maybe just a touch of possession. "I didn't know. But I'd hoped. God, how I'd hoped," he growled and pulled her back against him.

He would have kissed the soft smile from her mouth if it hadn't been for the two couples passing them just then. Though it was dark and they were beyond the main route to the shore, there was really no privacy this close to the hotel.

With the feel of her slender body causing all manner of havoc with his, privacy was exactly what he wanted.

First, he needed to know what it was that had brought her to him.

Stroking the hair back from her face, glad she hadn't cut any more of it off than she had, he felt a hint of his earlier hesitation return. It was entirely possible that whatever Nicole had discovered that she wanted for herself might be something she needed to do alone. Steeling himself for the possibility, he eased his hold on her. "You said you needed my help," he reminded and watched in fascination as she reached out to toy with the button on his shirt.

"I was just wondering," she began, "if you'd mind taking me with you." She'd never been so happy, so content within herself as she had been sailing with him; discovering with him. "You've already sailed half the world. I'd like it very much if you'd show me the other half."

She looked up at him then, her eyes luminous. He could see how vulnerable she was to him. But what he saw most clearly was that she wasn't trying to hide from him anymore. Or from herself. "I'll show you anything you want to see," he told her, "under one condition."

She looked up to see his familiar teasing smile; the one that she'd fallen in love with the day she'd met him. "What's that?"

"You have to sign on as a permanent member of my crew."

Later she would say the words. She'd be his mate. Forever and for always. Right now, all she could do was tighten her arms around his neck and answer him with a kiss. With the sound of the waves washing the shore beyond them and the moonlight wrapping them in its ethereal light, it seemed like the most appropriate thing to do.

Aaron couldn't have agreed more.

*   *   *   *   *

Back by popular demand, some of
Diana Palmer's earliest published
books are available again!

Several years ago, Diana
Palmer began her writing
career. Sweet, compelling
and totally unforgettable,
these are the love stories that
enchanted readers
everywhere.

Next month, six more of
these wonderful stories will
be available in DIANA
PALMER DUETS—Books 4,
5 and 6. Each DUET
contains two powerful stories
plus an introduction by
Diana Palmer. Don't miss:

Book Four	AFTER THE MUSIC DREAM'S END
Book Five	BOUND BY A PROMISE PASSION FLOWER
Book Six	TO HAVE AND TO HOLD THE COWBOY AND THE LADY

SILHOUETTE'S "BIG WIN"
SWEEPSTAKES RULES & REGULATIONS
NO PURCHASE NECESSARY TO ENTER OR RECEIVE A PRIZE

1. To enter and join the Reader Service, scratch off the metallic strips on all your BIG WIN tickets #1-#6. This will reveal the values for each sweepstakes entry number, the number of free book(s) you will receive, and your free bonus gift as part of our Reader Service. If you do not wish to take advantage of our Reader Service, but wish to enter the Sweepstakes only, scratch off the metallic strips on your BIG WIN tickets #1-#4. Return your entire sheet of tickets intact. Incomplete and/or inaccurate entries are ineligible for that section or sections of prizes. Not responsible for mutilated or unreadable entries or inadvertent printing errors. Mechanically reproduced entries are null and void.

2. Whether you take advantage of this offer or not, your Sweepstakes numbers will be compared against a list of winning numbers generated at random by the computer. In the event that all prizes are not claimed by March 31, 1992, a random drawing will be held from all qualified entries received from March 30, 1990 to March 31, 1992, to award all unclaimed prizes. All cash prizes (Grand to Sixth), will be mailed to the winners and are payable by cheque in U.S. funds. Seventh prize will be shipped to winners via third-class mail. These prizes are in addition to any free, surprise or mystery gifts that might be offered. Versions of this sweepstakes with different prizes of approximate equal value may appear in other mailings or at retail outlets by Torstar Corp. and its affiliates.

3. The following prizes are awarded in this sweepstakes: ★ Grand Prize (1) $1,000,000; First Prize (1) $35,000; Second Prize (1) $10,000; Third Prize (5) $5,000; Fourth Prize (10) $1,000; Fifth Prize (100) $250; Sixth Prize (2500) $10; ★ ★ Seventh Prize (6000) $12.95 ARV.

   ★ This Sweepstakes contains a Grand Prize offering of $1,000,000 annuity. Winner will receive $33,333.33 a year for 30 years without interest totalling $1,000,000.

   ★ ★ Seventh Prize: A fully illustrated hardcover book published by Torstar Corp. Approximate value of the book is $12.95.

   Entrants may cancel the Reader Service at any time without cost or obligation to buy (see details in center insert card).

4. This promotion is being conducted under the supervision of Marden-Kane, Inc., an independent judging organization. By entering this Sweepstakes, each entrant accepts and agrees to be bound by these rules and the decisions of the judges, which shall be final and binding. Odds of winning in the random drawing are dependent upon the total number of entries received. Taxes, if any, are the sole responsibility of the winners. Prizes are nontransferable. All entries must be received by no later than 12:00 NOON, on March 31, 1992. The drawing for all unclaimed sweepstakes prizes will take place May 30, 1992, at 12:00 NOON, at the offices of Marden-Kane, Inc., Lake Success, New York.

5. This offer is open to residents of the U.S., the United Kingdom, France and Canada, 18 years or older except employees and their immediate family members of Torstar Corp., its affiliates, subsidiaries, Marden-Kane, Inc., and all other agencies and persons connected with conducting this Sweepstakes. All Federal, State and local laws apply. Void wherever prohibited or restricted by law. Any litigation respecting the conduct and awarding of a prize in this publicity contest may be submitted to the Régie des loteries et courses du Québec.

6. Winners will be notified by mail and may be required to execute an affidavit of eligibility and release which must be returned within 14 days after notification or, an alternative winner will be selected. Canadian winners will be required to correctly answer an arithmetical skill-testing question administered by mail which must be returned within a limited time. Winners consent to the use of their names, photographs and/or likenesses for advertising and publicity in conjunction with this and similar promotions without additional compensation.

7. For a list of major winners, send a stamped, self-addressed envelope to: WINNERS LIST, c/o MARDEN-KANE, INC., P.O. BOX 701, SAYREVILLE, NJ 08871. Winners Lists will be fulfilled after the May 30, 1992 drawing date.

If Sweepstakes entry form is missing, please print your name and address on a 3" ×5" piece of plain paper and send to:

In the U.S.
Silhouette's "BIG WIN" Sweepstakes
901 Fuhrmann Blvd.
P.O. Box 1867
Buffalo, NY 14269-1867

In Canada
Silhouette's "BIG WIN" Sweepstakes
P.O. Box 609
Fort Erie, Ontario
L2A 5X3

Offer limited to one per household.
© 1989 Harlequin Enterprises Limited   Printed in the U.S.A.

LTY-S790RR

**Diana Palmer's fortieth story for Silhouette ... chosen
as an Award of Excellence title!**

CONNAL
Diana Palmer

Next month, Diana Palmer's bestselling LONG, TALL
TEXANS series continues with CONNAL. The skies
get cloudy on C. C. Tremayne's home on the range
when Penelope Mathews decides to protect him—by
marrying him!

One specially selected title receives the Award of
Excellence every month. Look for CONNAL in August
at your favorite retail outlet ... only from Silhouette
Romance.

CON-1